TEMPTING FATE

"It's bad luck to name a ship that," Duke said. "One company had a whole bunch of ships: *Angel's Luck*, *Luck of the Angels*, *Intervening Hand*, and the *Divine Wind*. Two were jumped and gutted by pirates. One had a reactor melt down. The fourth one jumped and was never seen again."

May was getting nervous. "That's just so much—"

"Coincidence? A decade ago, every other ship you saw was called the *Angel's Luck*, or words to that effect. Now you hardly see any."

May pushed hurriedly down the corridor toward his ship. While he waited for Duke to catch up, he leaned casually against the hull and covered the ship's name with his arm. *Angel's Luck*.

Duke drifted up to the hatch and grabbed a handle.

"After you," May said.

By Joe Clifford Faust
Published by Ballantine Books:

A DEATH OF HONOR

THE COMPANY MAN

Angel's Luck
  Book One: DESPERATE MEASURES

DESPERATE MEASURES

Book One of
Angel's Luck

Joe Clifford Faust

A Del Rey Book
BALLANTINE BOOKS · NEW YORK

A Del Rey Book
Published by Ballantine Books

Library of Congress Catalog Card Number: 89-90701

ISBN 0-345-35020-0

Printed in Canada

First Edition: July 1989

Cover Art by David B. Mattingly

For Charles T. and Jeanette

_____ ONE _____

In more polite times, Doctor Bombay's would have been called a dive. But to James Theodore May, the place looked like heaven.

The place was called Doctor Bombay's. It was crowded. The air was filled with the smoke of a half dozen types of inhaled drug. Funtime blared from an octet of Power 88 speakers, and bouncers in thick leather coversuits wandered the floor, arms crossed and eyes wandering, waiting for something to happen.

In more polite times Doctor Bombay's would have been called a dive. But to James Theodore May, the place looked like heaven.

He led his copilot through the smash of bodies and found a small table with a host of glasses littering the top. He asked a passing barmaid if it was taken.

She shook her head. The party sitting there had just been ejected.

James May sat. "I told you, Dexter. All the stars are shining to light my path. I've had Angel's Luck."

Dexter took a seat and regarded his employer. He had rarely seen May sincerely, truly happy, and it made the older man appear harmless. "There's something I'd like to talk to you about," he said, pushing the glasses to one side. The barmaid stopped to gather them onto her tray.

"No business," May told him. "We're here to celebrate. We made a killing from these hicks, so we've got the right."

Dexter slouched into his coat. "Don't talk like that," he warned.

"Nonsense," May scoffed. "Tetrans are known for being genteel."

Dexter's eyebrows knit into a hard stare. "May, we're in the one place on the planet where it's possible to get the dirt kicked out of us. Lighten up."

"Me?" May was insulted. "You want *me* to lighten up? Why can't you relax and enjoy this a little? We've waited years for this moment."

Juggling the tray full of empty glasses, the barmaid asked for their order.

"Tresell vodka," May said. "And tonic. On ice."

Dexter cleared his throat. "Water," he said.

"That's all?" May asked.

"And ice."

"No, no, no." He waved his hands to erase the last few seconds and stood. "We're here to celebrate, my friend. We are in the clear. No more being frugal." He turned to the girl. "Bring us a *bottle* of Tresell vodka and two glasses."

"*May—*"

The pilot wagged a finger. "Nonsense, Dexter. This is a time for the best."

Dexter cradled his head in his hands.

"Bring that with a bucket of ice, my dear."

She nodded and moved away.

May sat, stroking his beard. "Didn't I tell you that agricultural machinery was where the money was? Didn't I tell you?"

Dexter drummed his fingers on the tabletop. "You did."

"And didn't I tell you these people would lose their minds over a shipload of tractors and manure spreaders?"

Dexter nodded.

"Then tell me." May leaned across the table conspiratorially. "What the hell is wrong with you?"

Dexter's finger tugged at his collar. "Well, May, I can't help thinking that this really was . . . you know . . ."

May scowled. "Luck?"

The copilot nodded.

"My friend, luck had no part of this little windfall. It was *skill*."

"But you just said that—"

"I know what I said, Dexter. Our situation now was brought about by skill."

Dexter looked about nervously, not wanting to look his boss in the eye. "I suppose, then, it was your skill that caused us to lose our shirts on that industrial solvent deal at Ptolus 5."

"That was bad luck," May admitted.

"What about the computer shipment to Edas 11?"

"Bad timing."

"*Bad timing?* May, that place has deserts of blowing silicon. The last thing they wanted to see—"

The barmaid appeared and set two clean glasses before them. They were followed by a small container filled to overflowing with cubes of ice and then a bottle of crisp, clear liquid.

"Thank you," May said. "Start a tab, would you?"

"*May . . .*"

The girl nodded and disappeared.

May split the seal over the bottle top. "Dexter, I admit that I fell victim to a bad tip or two, but every trader goes through that. These guys you see with fleets of cargo ships and fighter escorts to keep the *Yueh-sheng* off of their necks, they started out just like you and me." He twisted the cap from the bottle and sniffed the contents.

"But May, I can't help thinking that they overcame their problems a little bit faster than you have."

May stared hard. "You want to go to work for Malaysia Prime? Is that what you're telling me?"

Dexter shook his head.

May picked up the tongs and started filling the glasses with ice. "Then what's your problem? What's got you down in our moment of triumph?"

Dexter picked up his glass and sucked in an ice cube.

"Come on. Out with it."

Dexter crunched the ice nervously.

"In need of a feminine caress?"

The copilot shook his head. "It's a minor thing, really. A small matter of my . . ." His eyes locked with the mouth of his glass. "Back pay."

May filled Dexter's glass with vodka. "Why didn't you say so?"

Dexter looked up in disbelief. "Well, you were getting extravagant, what with this Tresell vodka and all. I thought you might let the profit slip through your fingers like you had before."

May put the bottle down and gave his copilot a fatherly look. "I know I've been extravagant in the past, and I've been insensitive to your financial situation. The truth of the matter is, I was messed up. I was still getting over my wife's departure, and spending money made me feel better. That's all behind me now."

Dexter smiled.

May filled his own glass. "As soon as I make the next payment on the ship and get a suitable cargo to haul out of here, I'll see that you get a good lump of what I owe you."

"A good lump."

May drank and nodded.

Dexter looked solemn. "May, what the hell is 'a good lump'?"

May shrugged. "Ten percent."

"*Ten—*"

"All right. Twenty-five. And remember, I'm paying you interest on the balance."

Dexter's hands balled into fists. "Twenty-five percent?"

"I might be able to get you thirty if you want to invest in a cargo of your own. Providing, of course, we have room for it."

"May, you are way out of line."

May laughed and raised the glass to his lips. "Surely you can't want it all."

"I do," Dexter said solemnly.

May stopped in midswallow.

"I do," Dexter repeated, louder this time.

May finished his swallow. "Why?"

"Because I want to spend the money for a change."

"I give you spending—"

"I want to spend big money. I want to walk into a casino on Vegas 3 in a K'perian silk suit and a Nimrev Company coat, and I want everyone's head to turn."

"You don't have *that* much back pay," May said.

"And I want women to throw themselves at me. And I want two or three of them at once."

May opened his mouth to speak.

"And not have to pay for them."

"I could understand that—"

"I'm tired of running back and forth trying to turn a profit. I'm sick of zero gee. If I have to meet another person with another product in another dive like this—"

"This is an all right place," May said.

"I'm going to lose my mind," Dexter finished. "I want to settle down somewhere with a few women and have a good time."

May studied him. "What are you trying to tell me, Dexter?"

The copilot's face visibly changed color. He stood. *"I want out."*

May gestured for him to sit. "I understand your problem; now you have to understand mine. We have just made a sizable windfall, correct?"

"Correct."

"Now, you agree that I have to make the next payment on the ship."

"Yes."

"And I need to refuel to take us out of orbit and make jump."

"Yes."

"And I need another cargo."

"Yes."

"And I need a certified copilot to help me run it."

Dexter said nothing.

"Come on, Dexter. You know I'm right."

"You could find one here."

"Get real, pal. This is an agrarian world. These people are lucky to have airplanes."

"But you could do it."

"I could. And by the time I found one, the docking costs on the ship would run so much that—"

"Don't start," Dexter warned. "You did that to me last time, and I made the mistake of listening to you. I promised myself that I wouldn't do it again."

May put up his hands. "I merely want you to see my side of this. By the time I take care of my financial obligations, I will not be able to pay all of what I owe you."

"Then something will have to go."

"Dexter, you can't strand me here. I'll need fuel to leave and a cargo to sell at the next point."

"That's not my problem. I want my money."

"Dexter, let's be realistic. You do have a tidy sum coming, but it's hardly enough to attract one woman, let alone two or three. Now, if you were an excellent specimen of a man, things might be a little different, but let's face the facts. You and I are both sorely lacking."

"That's no problem. I can get more money."

"Then why don't you take what I can give you and be done with it?"

"Because," Dexter said calmly, "this is the first time you've had enough to pay all of what you owe me."

"Yes," May replied. "I could do that. But I won't have enough left to get a cargo unless I find something that these people are giving away."

"Manure," Dexter said bluntly.

The trader laughed bitterly. "Yeah. I can see myself taking a hundred commercial tons of the stuff across the galaxy to some rich planet so they can put it around their roses."

"You could starve."

May picked up the bottle and refilled their glasses. "All right. Do you have the venom out of your system? Are you willing to negotiate?"

Dexter sipped at the exotic drink and nodded.

"Let's get down to business, then." May raised his glass in a toast. "To free enterprise."

Their glasses clicked together.

"To women," Dexter said. "Lots of them."

They clicked together again.

"To the good times."

And again.

"To the people of Tetros 9."

Within an hour May had made enough toasts to sufficiently alter Dexter's personality. The copilot stared happily through heavy eyelids, pondering the wonders of Doctor Bombay's.

"You know, this place kind of grows on you."

"Told you." May poured what remained of the bottle into Dexter's glass.

The copilot smiled and drank it down.

"Time to get back to the ship," May said. He grabbed his copilot's shoulder, and they started for the door, making their way through the crowd. May thought the place had been crowded before, but with the business day on that part of Tetros 9 drawing to a close, people were converging on the bar. He stopped near the cashier and propped Dexter against a support pillar.

"Wait here," he told him. "I'm going to go take care of the tab."

"Get a bottle to go," Dexter said. "This is a happy time."

"Right." He slipped over to the cashier and started thumbing over a long stream of small bills. She told him to stop, but he kept forking them over, explaining that he wanted a bottle of Tresell for the road, in a plain wrapper, please.

The cashier excused herself to find a new bottle. May studied the place and smiled. He was pleased with the way he had averted the latest catastrophe. All he needed to do was take Dexter to the ship and come back down to buy a few tons of fresh-frozen food. With the profit he could turn from running it to a hydrogen tanker, he could pay off Dexter and let him go with a clear conscience. It would be much easier to find a new copilot on a tanker than on a planet like Tetros 9.

He turned to see how his charge was doing and was horrified to find him gone. He started away from the cashier.

"Here's your bottle, sir."

"Hold it."

He went back to the pillar and looked around frantically. "Dexter?"

His copilot was nowhere to be seen.

May slowly turned, looking hard, trying to spot him. He collided with someone and spun.

"Dexter!" he said with relief.

"I had to go take a leak."

"Don't move," May told him. "I'll be right back." He returned to the cashier to claim his bottle.

She handed it over in a bag, an apologetic look on her face. "I'm terribly sorry, sir. I seemed to have overcharged you for this. Let me recount your change."

May looked back at Dexter. "Hurry, please."

The cashier started to run a calculation on her machine. "The import tariff was lowered by two percent, so the Tresell people were able to lower their bottle price by three."

May's eyes narrowed. "You overcharged by three percent?"

The cash door opened. "I'll have it for you in a moment, sir."

"Oh, hell. Keep the change. I can afford—" He turned back to the pillar. Dexter was gone.

May hurried into the dark recesses of the bar. Why was it that at times like this he was sorely aware of how short he was? He went back to their table—but no Dexter. The next place he headed was the men's room.

Dexter was not there.

Exasperated, May stepped outside, hoping the humid night

Joe Clifford Faust   9

air would clear his thinking. As he looked around, he saw a familiar figure chatting with a tall blonde.

Of course, May thought. He approached the pair and grabbed Dexter's elbow. "Come on, Dex. You haven't time for that."

Dexter took the woman's arm. "She's coming with us."

"No, she's not." May nodded politely at her. "I'm sorry, miss, but he's had too much to—"

"She's never done it in zero gee," Dexter said.

May pulled him to the side. "Listen, pal, you're buying nothing but trouble. Women like this—"

"What do you mean, 'women like this'?" the blonde protested.

May turned on her. "Usually have boyfriends," he said pointedly.

"He's a hundred and three," the blonde replied. "And he's currently in a vat of rejuv soup."

"See?" May said to Dexter. "She's taken."

"But May—"

"*Not on my ship.* Now, come along."

He started to pull Dexter away from her when an imposing figure in a Tetros Security Militia uniform approached them.

"Is there some problem here?"

Dexter pointed at the woman. "He won't let me—"

May elbowed him in the stomach. "Nothing, officer," he explained. "My associate here is intoxicated, and I'm trying to get him home."

"But she—"

"*Quiet,*" May hissed. "If you would, officer, please take that woman away from here. She's got her hooks into him, and I'll be damned if I have to shell out a thousand credits for a cheap roll in zero gee."

"A cheap roll in zero gee," the officer repeated.

"I'm getting him out of here," May said. "Can't you arrest her or something? At least tell her to peddle her flesh somewhere else?"

"Somewhere else," the man echoed.

"Hello, Al," the blonde said nervously.

A lump formed in May's throat. He looked back at the officer. A platinum name tag winked under the glow of the street lamps: J. ALBERT.

"You got anything to say for yourself, spacer?"

"You don't look a hundred and three," May said.

And then the blow came, hard, to May's upper chest. He did not remember much after that except for a brief sensation of flight and the sound of breaking glass.

2

Then there were gentle violins, soft flutes, and a harp. And when May opened his eyes, everything was a mild shade of green. At the foot of where he was lying, a beautiful woman was filling out a chart and tenderly singing along with the music.

"Damn," he said.

She looked at him. "Are you in pain?"

He blinked at her. "No. I've died and gone to heaven. It's every bit as boring as I've heard."

She covered her mouth and laughed. "I'm afraid that's not the case. You're in the Nurturing Care Hospital of Callenda."

May sniffed. His nose itched. "Callenda?"

"The capital of Tetros 9," she offered.

May squinted. The memory was there. "Oh, yes." He wanted to scratch his nose, but his right arm would not move. "What's going on here?"

"You're being treated for a broken collarbone," the nurse told him. She consulted the chart. "Which you received in . . . an altercation." He could tell she had a distaste for that fact.

"If I remember correctly, I was trying to help someone," he told her. He looked at his arm and studied the way it had been immobilized. "Some thanks I get."

The nurse placed the chart on a tabletop and walked around the bed, straightening the sheets. "I'm done for now. Is there anything I can get for you?"

May looked around. "Tell them to turn off that blasted music. It's making me sick."

She laughed again. "I'll see what I can do." She placed a small box at May's side. "If you need anything, press this button."

May thanked her and lay back to stare at the green ceiling. How long would his collarbone take to heal? Three weeks with drugs? Two weeks with electrotherapy? There would be plenty of time to hunt up a cargo and make the next payment.

The door opened, and the nurse's head appeared. "Mr. May? Are you up to seeing a visitor?"

"As long as it's not the local militia," he said.

The woman's head vanished, and a man walked in. Both eyes were black, the nose was flat, and a row of black knots ran across his chin.

"Do you feel as bad as I look?" he asked.

"No," May said. "And as far as I'm concerned, you can suffer. Getting me beaten up like that."

"You?" Dexter was outraged. "You got off easy, May. That guy tried to rearrange my face."

"He did rearrange your face."

"And this is a primitive place. They don't have cartilage implants or neoskin treatments for skin damage. I'll have to go where they have real medicine to get plastic surgery. Look at this." He pointed to his chin. "Stitches. They sewed me up like some rag doll."

May smiled. "Relax. We'll get you taken care of by pros, and I'll split the cost with you. How does that sound?"

Dexter shook his head. "Money's not an issue. The militia's paying for our medical care. This guy that hit us had a reputation for his temper, and his girl thinks it's cute when it flares. This wasn't the first time he'd worked someone over, so he got his badge yanked."

"That's great. All you have to do is hang on for a couple of weeks and we'll jump somewhere where they can make you all pretty again."

"You've got a broken collarbone."

"I know. A little electrotherapy—"

Dexter's voice rose. "Haven't you been listening to me? This place is primitive. No electrotherapy. No calcium fortification drugs. This is a hang-around-until-the-body-fixes-itself hospital."

"That's still only a couple of weeks until I'm well enough—"

"Try again," Dexter said. "The militia's paying, so you have to follow their rules. They want to make sure your arm is working normally before they let you go. That's six weeks, subjective."

"*Six weeks?* We can't stay here that long!"

Dexter shook his head. "Not us, May. You. I can go because I've got to find a plastic surgeon."

May paled. "You're not going to leave me here."

"I don't have a hell of a lot of choice."

"How are you going to travel? You don't have your pilot's certification, and you certainly can't take the *Angel's Luck.*"

"I could," Dexter said.

"You won't," May said sternly. "Not without creating a legal nightmare for the both of us."

He shrugged. "I'll rent a pilot, no problem."

A groan slipped from May's lips.

"Calm down. I'll be back."

"Will you be able to find a pilot?"

"Undoubtedly. I've learned a lot from you."

May held up his left hand. The movement hurt. "Wait a minute. Let me think about this."

"I'm not leaving yet."

"Pick up a cargo of something. Vegetables, fruit, meat—"

"I'm not making a trading trip."

"Listen to me. It won't pay if you make the trip with an empty cargo hold."

"May—"

"And you can keep twenty-five percent of the net."

"Gross."

"All right, gross. Then see if you can bring something

back here to sell, same deal. Let's try to make the trip pay so we can buy more produce to take out.''

Dexter nodded. ''I'll think about it.'' He started to leave. ''I'll be in touch.''

''Right. Oh, and Dexter—''

The copilot looked at the small man in the hospital bed.

May smiled. ''Would you please send off the next payment on the ship?''

''Yeah. Right. See you in a few weeks.''

Dexter walked out, and the door slowly closed.

May let his head fall to the pillow. He felt so useless, so helpless, and worse still, he felt as if he were at Dexter's complete mercy. The copilot did not seem that bright, but if he figured for a moment that May had intentionally been pouring drinks into him at Doctor Bombay's, he might exact a terrible revenge.

When the nurse returned on her rounds, May asked her if she would call the nearest Laseron franchise and have them send over one of their couriers.

''Certainly,'' she said with a lovely smile. ''What should I tell them this is about?''

''I need to send a lase,'' May told her. ''I need to tell my creditor that the next payment on my ship might be late.''

3

Six weeks and three days later James May walked into the Callenda branch of Port Authority to press charges against Dexter. He first went to the Missing Property Bureau, but when they heard that the object in question was a stellar vehicle, they sent him to the Orbital Police. The OPs were of no help. Their jurisdiction was limited to anything within falling distance of Tetros 9, and since Dexter had clearly left orbital influence, there was nothing they could do but send May to Transgalactic Affairs.

On the T.A. floor, May went to the Vehicular Integrity department. A very nice gentleman sat him in a chair, turned on a computer terminal, and asked him what was missing from his ship.

"The whole thing," May told him.

"The entire ship?"

May nodded.

"What did this character do, cut it apart and pack it in crates?"

"No. He got in and left orbit."

The man looked dour and turned off his terminal. "I'm sorry. Vehicular Integrity is only set up to handle individual ship components that have been sold off or stolen. You want Vehicular Thefts."

"We are only set up to handle thefts from corporations," the woman at Vehicular Thefts said. "That is, a signed corporate charter and five ships or more in the fleet. Since it was your only ship that was taken, you need to report to Personal Claims."

"It sounds to me as if you were swindled," the Personal Claims clerk reported. "You need to see the people over in Fraud."

"This is strictly a legal matter," the Fraud investigator told him. "Since it involves back pay, your best recourse is to check with Legal Logistics."

The Legal Logistics clerk smiled. "The people at Fraud did the right thing, sending you here."

May sighed in relief. "Finally," he said. "Can we get on with this?"

"Certainly." With another smile, she reached under her desk and produced a large stack of forms. "If you would be so kind as to fill in these forms with complete information on your ship and components, we'll be glad to notify Port Authorities throughout the region that this vehicle has a Code Four status."

"A Code Four?"

"A Code Four is a Code Three ship with a Radical Action Suit filed against it."

"And what is a Code Three?"

She smiled. "A Code Three is a Code Two ship whose

status has fallen into litigation between two parties, one of whom is *not* one of the parties involved in the Code Two."

May was thoroughly lost. "All right. And what will that do?"

"In the case of a Code Three—"

"No," May interrupted. "A Code Four."

"Ah." She smiled again. May began to feel that the smile was rehearsed, part of the performance. "It means that you will be notified upon location of the perpetrator via a Laseron sent to your place of permanent residence."

"I'm a Free Trader," May explained. "I have no permanent residence."

The woman produced a second stack of forms. "Then you'll need to fill out these Systems Trace and Locate forms."

"And what happens when they catch Dexter?"

"Oh, they won't catch him. They'll merely notify you that he is in port, wherever he happens to dock."

"Via Laseron."

"That's correct."

"And if the lase doesn't find me?"

"It'll be forwarded." She tapped the stack of forms. "That's what these are for."

"What if he leaves the port while I'm heading for it?"

"Then you'll be notified, by lase, of his next location."

"Which means I could spend the rest of my life following this son of a bitch around."

The woman looked appalled.

"Pardon my Terran," May apologized. "Look, let's cut through all of this and suppose that the miracle does happen. Suppose I catch up with Dexter. What then?"

"You'll have to appear in court to testify on behalf of your claim to a settlement percentage." She saw the look on May's face and continued. "That's the amount of the total fines and costs levied against the defendant, less accounts outstanding—which in this case is his back pay— as extracted from funds generated by the liquidation of his immediate holdings. The amount of shares is directly proportional to the number of plaintiffs filing."

"So if he takes anyone else while I'm trying to find it, the settlement percentage will be divided between myself and whoever else files against him."

"That's correct."

"And the money I get will be cash taken from sale of his assets—"

"Yes." She smiled, happy that he was catching on.

"Which in this case is *my* freighter."

"Well, yes."

"Ma'am, are you familiar with Trader Law?"

"That's not really my department."

"Well, then, *I'll* brief *you*. What you're proposing is to give me a percentage, in cash, of my ship back. Does that mean you'd break up the ship to get that for me?"

"I suppose . . ."

"Wrong," he said loudly. "You can't break up a vehicle like that. It's illegal to sell existing components of a ship unless they're immediately replaced. That means that no matter what happens, I'm going to lose my ship."

"Not necessarily. He could always voluntarily surrender it—"

"No," he interrupted. "I somehow don't see that happening. This system makes it too lucrative for him to keep the ship for himself."

She gave the merchant a forlorn look. "Perhaps if you could tell me what you wanted, Mr. May."

He took a deep breath. "What I want." His lips turned up. "I'll tell you what I want. I want to have this man castrated."

The clerk silently produced a thick volume from the shelf beside her. She laid it on the counter and began perusing the contents. May stared in disbelief.

"Here it is," she said pleasantly. "Port Authority prescribes castration for thirteen different heinous crimes. Unfortunately, this type of situation does not fall into any of those categories. If you'd like to investigate this Mr. Dexter further, perhaps you could find evidence—"

"No," May said coldly. "I think I'll save everyone the

trouble and catch him myself. Then, if I think of other ways to torture him, I won't have to find a crime to fit the punishment.''

"I don't think that's a wise option for you, Mr. May. The legal ramifications are—''

"Stop. Not another word about the law. In my case I've lost my ship, and there's no way I'm going to get it back. What really hurts is that I'm still liable for the damn payments.''

"I could give you some forms that would—''

"Absolutely not.'' He fought to keep his voice at a social level. "It's not worth it.''

"The law has to work,'' the clerk advised. "Otherwise it wouldn't have stayed this way.''

"Works, does it? Lady, I hope this guy comes back and takes your ass. Try and get a percentage of *that* back. Then you'll see how well your law works.''

May stalked out of the office, his steps echoing on the tiled floor. He thought hard as he went, trying to make a mental list of things he needed to do. First he had to contact the Malaysia Prime Shipping Company. He had to find out if Dexter had dispatched last month's payment before taking the ship. Second, he would have to figure out how to explain the ship's loss without arousing their ire. May had been through close scrapes with them before but had always managed to get the money in on time. Rumor had it that Mr. Hiro turned into an ogre when money was late in coming.

So intent was his concentration that he hardly noticed bumping someone on the way out of the Port Authority building. He mumbled a quick apology and continued on his way, working on the wording of his story, hand patting the pocket under his coat where he kept his papers.

"Excuse me.''

The wallet was still there. He kept moving.

"*Sir,*'' the voice said urgently.

He stopped and turned around. A tall blond man in sunglasses and a suit stared at him, a sultry woman on each arm.

"I'm sorry if I bruised one of your women, mister, but it

was an accident, okay? Now, if you don't mind, I'll be on my way."

"James May."

May squinted at the trio. "Do I know you?"

"You don't recognize me," the man said.

"The voice is familiar . . ."

The man removed his sunglasses. "All I want is my back pay."

"Dexter?" May approached the three of them and studied the man's face. If he concentrated, looking past the solid, straight nose, high cheekbones, and rugged chin, he could almost see his copilot looking back at him. What threw him was the fact that the man was at least twenty-five centimeters taller than Dexter had been. "What did you do, mister?" he said, eyeing the women suspiciously. "Hire Dexter to pimp for you?"

"It's me," the man said. "I was rearranged on Vegas 3." He saw that May was still beyond belief. "You've got to watch that Tresell vodka. It'll get you beaten up every time."

May stared.

"Especially by a cop."

"It *is* you!"

Dexter shrugged the women off his arms. "They did a great job, didn't they? Everything was done organically, including the height. And you remember how I used to have to strain to open that sticky cargo access hatch? I could do it with one hand now. I'm what you call state of the art."

May felt the fabric of Dexter's suit. It was K'perian silk, he was sure. "You," he said, "are in one hell of a lot of trouble."

"I brought your ship back."

"No," May said. "With the Tetros Security Militia. You were only supposed to get your face repaired, not undergo complete body work."

"I paid for it," Dexter said proudly. "All of it except the face."

May grabbed his collar. "With what, Dexter? My money?"

Dexter brushed the pilot's hands away with a smooth gesture. "No," he said. "With the profits."

"From what?"

"From an investment." He threw a well-muscled arm around May. "Come with me, Teddy. I have business to discuss with you."

Dexter led him down the block to a small tri-wheeler that barely held the four of them. The women, who were introduced as Nona and Felice, obediently climbed in the back, and May climbed in next to the driver's seat.

"Rental?"

Dexter smiled. "Mine."

He drove across town to a restaurant where a doorman suspiciously eyed May and let him in only after Dexter assured him that things were all right. They were seated by a maître d', and Dexter tipped big. May looked around for a menu but did not see one. When the waiter came, Dexter ordered for all of them, including Nona and Felice. It occurred to May that neither woman had said a word since he had met them.

The waiter quickly returned with four glasses filled with ice and two bottles of Tresell vodka. Dexter split the seal from his and poured a glass for himself and Felice. "Do have some, James."

"I'm not thirsty," May replied sourly.

"Then be a good host and pour Nona some, would you?" He leaned across the table. "I think she likes you," he whispered.

May opened the bottle and filled Nona's glass. "How can you tell?"

Dexter laughed.

"What's the deal?" May asked. "You blowing out your back pay?"

Dexter shook his head. "Get real, Teddy. My back pay could never have gotten me this far. That motor you saw out there?" He shrugged. "My back pay wasn't enough for a down payment on that."

May shifted uncomfortably in his seat. "Would you mind telling me what's going on? Where's my ship?"

"It's fine, Teddy—"

"And what's with this Teddy business?"

Dexter smiled. "I have always wanted to call you that. Now I can afford to."

May crossed his arms. His face felt hot. "Get on with it."

Dexter sipped. "The *Angel's Luck* is back where we left it. And as a favor to you, I've had it refueled. It was the very least I could do."

May smiled sarcastically. "The least."

The newly handsome man reached inside his suit and produced a small packet. He placed it on the table and pushed it toward May. "And there's your money."

May picked up the wallet and bounced it in his hand. He looked troubled.

"Less my back pay, of course."

"Dexter, you—"

Dexter wagged a finger. "Please don't raise your voice in this place. It's a good way to get thrown out."

May gave him a killing glare and lowered his voice. "Dexter, you have some explaining to do."

"Okay." Dexter poured himself another drink. The waiter arrived with their food. "You were hospitalized, and my face had been screwed up. You were going to be laid up for a while, so it was up to me to find someone to put my face back together. Well, I asked around and discovered that the best doctors for that sort of thing are found on Vegas 3. The rich like to look perfect, and that's where the money is." He smiled.

"So?"

"So that's where I went. I found a reputable doctor whose rates would make the Tetros Militia think twice about hiring another sadistic pig like Albert. I was given the option of restoring my old face or building a new one—it cost the same either way.

"While I was thinking about it, I read this article the doctor had given me about keeping a positive mental attitude. It was called 'Making Yourself a Winner,' and it talked about what getting a new face could do for a person. That was when I decided to try it and become the person I'd always wanted to be."

May eyed Nona, who quietly sipped her vodka. "Looks like you got it."

"In spades," Dexter said. "After my new face was healed, I took my back pay and went into a casino. I plunked it down on the wheel, the double zero."

"And you won."

Dexter shook his head. "I lost. All of it. On one turn of the wheel."

May laughed long enough to realize the implications. His laughter choked off with a snort. "My money," he said. "You lost my money."

"It was *my* money," Dexter said. "And I learned my lesson. Never put anything completely into the hands of fate. That's where your money came in. I, uh, borrowed what was left of yours and went to the card tables. I figured I was still battling luck, but at least I had a little more control. And I won, May. Won like you wouldn't believe. That brochure was right. I was someone else. I was a *winner*."

"About my money . . ."

"I'm getting to that. With what I was making, I had the rest of my body worked over. The rest I put back into the cards. It was strange, May. I couldn't lose. Ultimately, I did the only thing I could do."

"You quit while you were ahead."

"Exactly. I bought some suits. I needed to look good because I had gained enough notoriety to attract—" He looked at Nona and Felice. "—attention. I decided to put the rest of my money into something tangible as an investment, a sure thing that would bring in big returns."

"I give up," May said, bored. "What did you get? Stocks? Bonds?"

Dexter chewed thoughtfully. "I bought a load of C-Plex. A hundred kilos of it, uncut, ninety-eight percent pure. Resale value is worth—"

"No!" May shouted. The restaurant went quiet for a moment, and all eyes were on him. He looked around, too angry to be embarrassed. After a moment things resumed to normal, and he finished speaking to Dexter in low tones. "Are you out of your mind, pal? Do you know how dangerous that stuff is?"

"I'm not using it," Dexter said, stabbing food with his fork. "I'm selling it."

"That's what I'm talking about. If the *Yueh-sheng* gets wind that you're dealing the stuff, you're going to end up blown out an air lock somewhere between here and Sol."

The new muscles on Dexter's face bent to give a cocky smile. "Not with my luck."

"No," May told him. "No way in hell. I worked for twelve years to stay straight and keep my business honest, and I'm not going to get involved with drug trafficking. I'm sorry, Dexter, but I refuse. You can count me out."

"You were never in," Dexter stated. "I'm doing this on my own."

May looked suspiciously at Nona and Felice. "They're androids, aren't they? That's where you've hidden the stuff, isn't it? You bastard, using my ship like that—".

"They're real," Dexter assured him. "And I didn't use your ship to bring the stuff in. I've thought this out very carefully. I brought it all in on my pleasure craft."

May looked stunned. "You own a pleasure craft?"

Dexter nodded. "I made a *lot* of money at the tables."

"And how did you get the pleasure craft here?"

He smiled. "It's in the cargo hold of the *Angel's Luck*."

"You miserable—"

"Be calm." Dexter dabbed his lips with a napkin. "According to galactic law, you're only responsible for transport of the pleasure craft itself, not its contents. If the contents are assessed to be illegal, then the consequences would fall on me."

May took a long swallow of vodka. *"But you're my damn copilot."*

Dexter shook his head. "Not anymore."

May banged the glass down. "Then why am I wasting my time here?"

"Because you need to make last month's payment on your ship."

The room started to wobble in May's vison. He felt vaguely ill. "What are you trying to do to me?"

Dexter shrugged. "Conduct a business deal."

"I'm not going to transport that ship for you, no matter how much you're paying."

"I'm not asking you to do that. All I want is for you to hear me out and answer a few questions. All right?"

May nodded.

"You said yourself that what we made on the agri machine deal wasn't enough to give me back pay, buy cargo and fuel, pay docking costs, and make a payment on the ship. Correct?"

May sighed. "Correct."

"Well, I've taken care of the fuel and docking. It's the least I could do, what with running the ship empty to Vegas 3 and all."

"You took it empty—"

"But according to my calculations, what you've got of your money still won't get you a cargo and a payment, not with the interest you'll be charged for filing late."

May looked down at the steak on his plate. He picked up the knife he had been using to cut it. "I'm just going to kill you," he told Dexter. "Straight out."

"That's where I come in, Teddy."

"Stop calling me that."

"Your old friend Dexter is going to bail you out of a bad situation."

May studied the knife edge with a certain malevolence. "Go on."

"I've been making a study of the Vacuum Atmosphere Spatial Analysis Coordinator systems, and I think I finally understand how it works. Correct me if I'm wrong—"

"Wait," May interrupted. "What has this got to do with anything else we've talked about up to this point?"

"Plenty," Dexter said. "Now, check me on this. When you buy a Vasac, you choose one based on its ship diameter rating, correct?"

May scowled and nodded.

"And the one you pick has to be rated for a sphere of detection equal to a minimum of one hundred diameters of the ship you're using."

"You're studying navigation," May said sourly. "Isn't this a step down for you?"

"Not if I'm going for my pilot's rating."

May shifted in his seat. "Dexter—"

The other man held up his hand. "One hundred ship diameters is the legal minimum," he said sternly.

"Yes," May sighed.

"And what happens if you get a Vasac rated for a larger ship?"

"Nothing. You'll have a waste of money."

"But couldn't that Vasac be tweaked to provide a better sphere of coverage, to detect at a range greater than the legal minimum?"

May shrugged helplessly. "I suppose, but I don't see—"

"Wouldn't the sphere size multiply? If I had a small ship and put in a Vasac rated to a ship, say, ten times larger, then wouldn't I have a detection sphere of a thousand ship diameters?"

"Theoretically—"

"And if I'm running that and I detect *another* ship that is ten times the size of mine, by the time we make Vasac-to-Vasac contact, I'd have ten thousand ship diameters in which to outmaneuver them."

"In three dimensions," May said. "But why the hell would you want—"

"That's it, then." Dexter looked at Nona and Felice. "If I'm going to be a smuggler . . . in fact, if I'm even going to make planetfall with that load of C-Plex, I'm going to need a better Vasac controller in my ship."

"What's wrong with the one you've got?"

"Nothing, but it's terribly conventional. It's rated for the legal minimum of one hundred ship diameters, but it measures off of the pleasure craft standard. I need something bigger."

"You want a Galactrix 9000," May told him.

"That would do it," Dexter said, "but there's one problem with that. I'd have to order one. It would be months before it got here, so that option is unacceptable. I was thinking that I would do quite well with, say, a Model 2000."

"A Model 2000 is going to be just as hard to find as a 9000 on this rock."

Dexter smiled. "I know where there's a 2000. And I know that it works."

May's expression froze. "Wait a minute."

"You help me install it, and I'll make your next payment, with interest."

May shook his head. "No, Dexter. It's illegal to sell off parts, and it's illegal as all hell to operate a ship without Vasac."

"I can't afford to wait."

"Neither can I. I've got to keep my payments going in."

"You're already behind."

"I need my Vasac."

"I need it worse."

"I can't travel without—"

"Sure you can. All you have to do is lie. Wherever you dock, just file a Condition White until you're able to buy a new one."

"This is not going to work."

"Of course it will. You need a payment. You said yourself you were going to run foodstuffs to a hydrogen tanker. You'll be able to buy a new Vasac there, and they'll have them in stock. You won't have to wait."

"Forget it, Dexter. Unless I get really lucky, I'll never be able to afford payment, Vasac, and cargo on the tanker—"

"Then you're stuck," Dexter pronounced. "You'll never get off of this planet. Hiro will put a track out on the *Angel's Luck* and find it here while you're still trying to fill your cargo hold with manure. And while you're picking up the next load, they'll take it. You'll have to roll up your pants legs and go to work."

"I filed with them," May said. "I told them that the payment would be late."

"Then lase them back. This time tell them the payment's not coming." He smiled. "Unless you want to think it over."

"Bastard," May said.

"I knew you'd see it my way." He dabbed his lips with a napkin. "I'm going to go to my hotel and put these ladies to bed. I'll meet you on *Angel's Luck* tomorrow morning, 0800 local. Bring your tools."

May sat stunned as the trio rose from the table and left, Felice in the lead, then Dexter, and two steps behind, Nona. She gave May a wistful look as they walked out the door. He swore under his breath, grabbed the nearest bottle of Tresell, and put it to his lips.

"Excuse me," the waiter said. "Management prefers it if you take your drinks out of the provided glass."

May finished his swig. "I've earned the right to drink from the bottle. Do you know what that man just did to me?"

"I certainly do." The waiter placed a coded slip of paper before the merchant. "He stuck you with the check."

4

Fifteen hours later May was back where he had started. Funtime blared from the speakers, and the world of Doctor Bombay's revolved about him. He was sullenly staring at the ice melting in the glass, pondering the mercurial nature of *Angel's Luck*. As surely as it had smiled on him earlier, it had since turned its back and was laughing. And to think that this was the kind of life I wanted, he thought. I should have taken that teaching position at the academy.

For the better part of the next two hours, May sat at the bar bemoaning his problems to anyone within earshot. Bribing them with drinks, he poured out his heart until they decided his story was not worth the reward and went elsewhere.

Soon May decided on a different tack and started listening

to others in the hopes of finding someone sympathetic to his cause. He soon learned that the populace of Tetros in general and Callenda in particular had little sympathy for an off-worlder whose personal finances were driving him to a bitter end. They had problems of their own, such as the emergence of a particularly nasty strain of locust and new competition from a nearby world whose output was cutting into their profits. There was talk of diversifying the Tetros 9 economic base, but that met with stiff resistance from those who insisted that even an orbiting shipbuilding platform would radically alter the ecology of the lush, green world.

He propped his head on his hands, staring longingly at a two-liter bottle of a potato-based hard liquor, wondering if it had proof enough to do him in.

"I'll take that," May told the barkeep. "The whole bottle."

"What, the Springs Eternal?"

May nodded.

The barkeep set the bottle before May. "You want a clean glass?"

May shook his head and studied the label. As he did, a young man plopped onto the stool next to him, a bottle of beer in each hand. "Ah, yes. The hope that springs eternal . . ."

"Springs right up your behind," May finished sourly. "What do you want?"

"I heard you're a pilot."

May looked at him and was surprised that he had been let into the bar. The newcomer was no more than a kid. He had a baby face, a light fuzz of hair on his face that might need shaving in another week, and fine sandy hair that had fallen out of a painstaking coiffure.

"My name is William," he told May uncertainly, "but you should call me Duke."

May moved his tongue across his lips. They were numb. "Why would I want to call you anything?"

"Because I heard you're looking to leave town."

"So what's it to you?" May asked.

"I need to leave town. Rather suddenly, if you could manage it."

"I'm not going anywhere without a decent cargo," May said. "And I'm short on the manpower side of things, too."

"Then I'm your man," Duke told him. "I can help."

May squinted at the kid. He did not look like any copilot May had ever seen. "You know what I'm looking for?"

"Of course. It's all over the bar." He waved a bottle for emphasis.

"You've got your certification?"

"That's why I came and sat here. I think we could benefit from this, mutually."

"Where'd you graduate from?"

Duke turned on his stool and looked May in the eye with an unsteady stare. "Are you doing this because of my looks?"

"Yup," May answered bluntly.

"Hell." Duke pouted. "That's going to bother me all of my life. I'll have you know, sir, that I am old enough to marry on this planet and, in fact, am facing impending nuptials in a double-ring ceremony."

"Then why are you so anxious to leave?"

"Because I couldn't even get along with my mother," Duke told him. "And if I can't get along with one woman, I sure won't get along with two."

"You don't have to move in with your mother," May suggested.

"Cosmos forbid," Duke said. "Three women would be too much."

"Three?" May asked. "What are you doing, marrying two?"

"That's what I said, didn't I? Double-ring ceremony." He drank from one of the bottles.

May leaned over and pumped Duke's hand. "It's nice to meet someone with worse troubles than my own."

"I hate weddings," Duke added.

"Where were you looking to go?" May asked.

Duke shrugged. "Somewhere away from people. Somewhere that I can clear my head and think about all of this."

"I can arrange that," May said.

"You can?" Duke's face lit up.

"But you have to be certified and licensed."

"I am. I swear it."

"And I'll have to see your papers."

"I don't have them with me," Duke answered, "but I can take you to my office."

May looked puzzled. "You have an office here?"

"That's the most efficient way for me to get things done."

The merchant chuckled. "That's a new one on me. Well, we can arrange a meeting or something so I can look them over."

"I understood you needed to leave right away."

"I do, but I've got an empty ship. I can't leave without a cargo. Trading pays my bills." His face wrinkled as he remembered Dexter walking off the ship, the Vasac controller perched on a dolly. "Most of the time."

Duke waved his hand. "I told you, I'm here to help with that. I can make it worth your while, if you can turn a profit on some meat."

"I might could do that," May said skeptically. "What kind and how much?"

"Beef. Fifty commercial tons."

"The price?"

"How does twenty percent strike you?"

"It doesn't." May took a swallow from the melting ice. "Standard merchant discount is thirty-three percent. You might as well let me find my own cargo, kid."

Duke looked flustered. "Well, I didn't mean a twenty percent break," he said quickly. "I meant twenty percent on the credit."

May froze. "I wish I was sober," he said. "I could have sworn you said—"

"I did," Duke interrupted. "Twenty percent on the credit."

May set his glass down with great deliberation. "You must want out of here awfully bad."

"I've got a lot on my mind," Duke admitted.

May waved the barkeep over and returned the bottle. "Are you sober enough to drive?" he asked Duke.

"Nope. Are you?"

May shook his head.

They took a taxi across town, a small tri-wheeler which rattled so loudly that sustained conversation was impossible. Finally, Duke pointed out his window. May leaned forward in his seat and saw that they were passing a complex of large, connected buildings. The driver took them to a gate bearing a freshly painted sign: ARBOR ORGANIC FOOD COMPANY. *Established 221 a.c.*

A guard sauntered around to the vehicle's side and peered in. Duke rolled down the window. "It's all right," he told the armed man. "I'm giving a customer the tour."

The man nodded and let them pass.

"Your place?" May asked.

"My uncle's. My family came over on the original colony ship." He pointed to the date on the building's inscription. "It took them a while to get their act together."

"And what would your uncle say if he heard the offer you made me in Doctor Bombay's?"

Duke thought about it. "Probably nothing."

"For fifty commercial tons of beef? If it was mine, I'd be resentful, to say the least."

"He'll consider it my share of the family fortune," Duke said, leading May into a twenty-four-hour abattoir. "Besides, the economy's bad right now. He told me to sell off the stuff any way I could."

Suddenly May felt as if he were wasting his time. If those were the circumstances, then the sight of the product was bound to disappoint.

"Come to think of it," May said, "I'm not sure if something like this will sell where I'm going. The synthetics industry is very big . . ."

"Nothing's better than fresh meat," Duke answered,

opening the door to a freezer that was roughly the size of the *Angel's Luck* cargo hold. "I'd like to see someone turn this down." He gestured at the endless rows of frozen meat.

"This is a lot of meat," May said. He felt as if the cold in the room were sobering him.

"Why don't you look around while I run up to my office? I've got something I want you to see." Duke vanished out the main door.

May wandered through, breath steaming from his nostrils. The meat was well marbled and had been frozen only the day before. The Galactic Trade Commission inspection logo was laser-etched onto every carcass he checked.

He wobbled back to the door, the siren of profit singing in his ears. Again he cursed his current mental state, unable to calculate the money involved. He went from one frozen hulk to another, checking the grades. Every one was rated the same: GTC INSPECTED CERTIFIED PRIME.

"What do you think?" Duke asked, returning with a stack of multicolored papers.

"I'll need the racks, too," May told him. "My hold's got enough floor space but nothing to hang the meat from."

"Okay," Duke said. "I'll throw in the racks if you'll add five percent."

Fifty commercial tons of prime beef at twenty-five percent on the credit. May could even afford it. His brain was spinning with possibilities: cargo, payment, Vasac . . .

"You need freezer units?"

May shook his head. "I can custom set the hold's temperature."

Duke brandished a set of papers. "I believe you wanted to see these."

May took them. They were stamped and sealed and holo-certified, and the name "William Wesley Arbor" was etched on every one.

"You're authentic," May said.

"I'd be in a fat lot of trouble if I wasn't," Duke answered.

May shook his hand. "Son," he said, "you've bought yourself a ticket out of here."

5

By midnight things were well under way. Duke made out
the sale papers, certified them, and had an incoming foreman
take charge of moving the beef up to the *Angel's Luck*. May
returned to the ship, set the hold's temperature to ten degrees
below freezing, and gathered what papers he needed to pay
the Arbor Organic Food Company.

He was headed planetside when the Arbor shuttle linked
up with the dock and asked permission to sideload the cargo.
May cleared it with the dockmaster and then continued his
trip down to Callenda. Within the hour he was back in Duke's
office, transferring the funds to pay for the cargo in full.

Duke stamped the manifest papers DELIVERED, handed
them to May, and shook his hand. "Pleasure doing business
with you," he said. He tipped up a bottle of beer and drained
it in celebration.

"Go easy on that stuff," May warned. "You've got some
work ahead of you."

Duke looked at him, confused.

"We're leaving, remember? I thought you'd want to pack."

Duke held up a finger and rolled his chair back to a large
filing cabinet. He adjusted the dial on the bottom drawer,
slid it open, and pulled out a small satchel. Smiling, he patted it. "I'm ready."

"You've got everything you need?"

He nodded. "Toothbrush, IDs, papers, money, and a
change of underwear."

"You weren't kidding about leaving fast."

Duke shut off the lights in his office and locked the door
on the way out. He took May through a side entrance to the
street, where they waited for another taxi.

"So how long have you been certified?" May asked as
the vehicle pulled up to the curb.

"Eighteen months."

"And how long have you been working for your uncle?"

"Since I got certified."

"Why so long to get out of the business?"

Duke shrugged. "I figured I owed them something. They're family." He climbed into the vehicle and leaned his head back on the seat.

The trip to the shuttleport was rocky. May swallowed a couple tabs of Leuten's Alcohol Neutralizer and spent the rest of the trip trying to get Duke to take some. The boy flatly refused, insisting that it would only make him sicker.

Things did not get any better at the shuttleport. Even at such an early hour of the morning there was still enough of a crowd to make May nervous, and the very effort of boarding one of the battered shuttlecraft caused a line of perspiration to break out across Duke's forehead.

"Told you to take some Leuten's," May said, quoting the line that had made the product famous.

"It's not that," Duke started. He looked up at May.

"Don't tell me you're afraid of flying."

Duke gestured at the *Sky Subway* logo at the head of the cabin. The paint job was faded and chipped, and what remained was mostly a stencil of the original.

"Could use a fresh coat," May commented, "but they refurbish the engines every ten thousand kilometers and the superstructure every twenty-five."

"That's not the reason. It's the slogan."

The merchant squinted toward the front of the cabin. After studying the flaking paint for a moment, he started to repeat the slogan as a question. "Flying you with—"

"Don't say it," Duke said, inhaling sharply.

"Angel's Luck?"

"Look, I told you—"

"What's your problem, son? That's the best thing you could say to someone leaving planetfall. Angel's Luck is the purest, most blessed form of—"

"It's bad luck," Duke grunted.

"You're not serious."

He nodded his head. "I am. It's not bad luck to *wish* it on somebody, but it's totally different to name a ship that."

"But these things aren't named—"

The craft hit a turbulent pocket of upper atmosphere and

rattled. A rivet from the storage compartment above popped loose and landed in the merchant's lap.

"See what I mean? Just having *that* written on it is bad enough."

May turned his head and looked out the window. Below, the port looked like a gaudy plastic toy that belched out thin columns of smoke. "Oh."

"You've heard of the Nimrev Company, haven't you? Well, they had a whole bunch of ships called that—*Angel's Luck*, *Luck of the Angels*, *Intervening Hand*, and the *Divine Wind*. Two were jumped and gutted by pirates. One had a reactor go bad and melted down. The fourth one made a jump and was never seen again."

May turned the stray rivet over in his hand. It was making him nervous. "That's just so much—"

"Coincidence? Think again. As little as a decade ago, every other ship you saw was called the *Angel's Luck*, or words to that effect. Now you hardly see any."

May cleared his throat. "I don't think I'd go—" The shuttle again trembled. Something in the back crashed to the floor, and someone cursed loudly.

"You were saying?" Duke asked somberly.

"Nothing," May responded. He was glad that Duke had not taken any Leuten's. The boy's artificially relaxed state would make it easier for him to board the trader.

The *Sky Subway* shuttle made true for the docking platform and locked onto the upper part of the outer wheel. The floor at the front of the cabin opened, and a ladder staircase rose to meet it, locking into place as the commuters rose and gathered their coats and belongings.

May waited for Duke to step into the aisle, then followed, juggling the rivet in his palm. As he passed the flight attendant, he took her hand and quietly pressed the rivet into her palm, saying, "Nice flight."

Once off the ship, May and Duke started through the battleship-gray halls of the platform, looking for the central docking core. They found a bank of elevators that led that way and stepped into the first coreward car that opened.

Putting his back against the wall, May grabbed the rail and waited as the car was slowly lifted out of gravity. His eyes settled on Duke's face. The boy was showing definite signs of stress, and his knuckles were white in their grip of the rail.

May frowned. Through his clouded thoughts, a relevant thought emerged. "Have you ever done this before?" he asked.

"Of course," Duke snapped. "Dozens of times."

"You're looking a little green."

"It doesn't mean I have to like it," he replied.

The merchant shrugged. Alcohol affected everyone in different ways.

The elevator stopped and opened its doors. The two drifted out to a thick glass wall that looked out into the central core. Across the way they could see the docking pods, whose doors opened into the core. Above was the gigantic portal through which all docking ships had to pass.

Duke stared as a pleasure craft lumbered out of a bay and twisted upward. The gate irised open and, when the vehicle had cleared, complacently twisted shut. "This is really something," he said in awe.

"I thought you said you'd been here before."

"I have. But I've never seen that thing at work before." He continued his stare, palms against the glass, fog from his breath creeping across it.

May noted the way Duke was starting to let himself drift. In his reverie, the kid had forgotten that he was in zero gee.

"Don't break the glass," May said solemnly. "It'll cause explosive decompression in this part of the tanker."

Alarmed, Duke lowered his eyes. His gaze fell a hundred meters to the very bottom of the docking bay. The sudden realization filled him with vertigo, and he slammed hard into the window.

May laughed.

"What did you do that for?" Duke demanded angrily. "What if I'd broken that window?"

"Don't you remember your training? That's not regular

glass. It's been molecularly altered. Any of the ships docked here could hit it and bounce right off.''

Duke swallowed and looked at the window. There was a smudge from his hands and face, but it was otherwise unscathed. He grabbed the rail and steadied himself. "Anything else?" he growled.

"Your catfalls need practice."

May kicked off from the window and sailed down the corridor. Duke followed suit, much less certainly, giving himself a wobbling trajectory that lacked both style and grace. By the time he neared May's ship, he was on the verge of panic.

May opened the hatch and started drifting up the ramp. He grabbed the handles on each side of the *Angel's Luck* boarding hatch and waited for Duke to appear. While he waited, his eyes came to rest on the brass plate he had fixed on the vessel's side. Looking back down to see if Duke was watching, he casually shifted into a leaning position against the ship, covering the ship's name with his left arm.

Duke drifted up to the hatch and grabbed a handle.

"After you," May said.

Duke pulled himself through the hatch with such zealousness that he flew down the corridor and hit the wall at the first intersection. "I thought you had gravity on this thing," he complained.

May grabbed him by the collar and tried to hold him steady. "I've got it shut down," he said. "Makes it easier for your people to load the cargo bay."

Duke drew a deep breath. The color had left his face. "Before I see if they're done," he said weakly, "do you suppose I could just sit *still* for a few minutes?"

"Certainly. Turn right."

May watched Duke make his way down the corridor. He had heard of those who feared zero gravity but had never seen it in someone with certification. He attributed it to the drinking they had been doing. The zero gee was making May himself feel queasy, and if he was suffering from side effects, then Duke was, too. If drinking gave the kid problems with his balance, then a lack of gravity would certainly compound things. He took Duke to the copilot's cabin and maneuvered him into the zero-gravity zipbed.

"Don't you worry," he said, drawing the zipper up to Duke's neck. "I'll handle everything."

Duke nodded and closed his eyes.

May went to the cargo hold to check on the progress of the loading. A thin layer of frost had formed on all sides of the hold, and a half dozen G-monkeys were pulling the slabs of beef out of the Arbor Company orbital transporter, tossing them into the hold, and securing them to the racks with a zero-gee clamping system. May offered to help them finish the loading, but they declined. The job was almost done.

May tipped the men with bottles from a case of rare but inexpensive liquor he had picked up in the Trireme system and went to the bridge. He rang the copilot's cabin on intership and told Duke to come forward, then activated the power plant. Checking the monitors, he saw that his cargo looked properly installed. It would probably hold, then, until they were well away from the planet's gravitational influence, when he would have time enough to double-check each rack.

Next he keyed in orders for the ship's CHARLES unit to plug into the nearest interface and prepare to assist with departure. It was going to be tricky enough working with a new copilot. Operating with no Vasac was going to make things that much harder. Having the maintenance 'bot on line for departure would make May's job a little easier.

By the time May contacted Port Authority and had departure clearance, Duke had still not appeared. May rang into his cabin again and heard nothing. Cursing, he requested a delay, unbuckled from his seat, and ran down the hall.

Duke was where he had left him, snug in the zipbed.

"C'mon, kid. Time to earn your pay."

Duke did not move.

"Duke . . ." May shook the bed. Nothing happened. He leaned forward and put his ear to the kid's chest. Duke was breathing very slowly, in long, deep cycles. May put a knuckle against his chest and rubbed his sternum. Duke frowned slightly and shifted.

May swore. He had thought things were picking up, but they seemed no better off than before. With Port Authority holding a slot for him, he was obliged to leave. There was no way he could wait until Duke slept off his binge, and he certainly would not get any of the Leuten's formula into him now. He wished he had thought to check the kid's background. The dull ache behind his eyes from his own binge served as a reminder to be more careful next time.

If there is a next time, May thought. If I don't blow myself to kingdom come on the jump.

On the way back to the bridge May convinced himself that things were indeed looking up. If Duke turned out to be a rotten copilot, he could leave him behind at the next destination to chagrin some other merchant. At a hydrogen tanker he could have his choice of copilots, and with the profit he anticipated from his load, he could hire one for a flat fee. This business of paying a percentage of the profits was for grounders.

He buckled in and hailed Port Authority. "Tetros Bay Three, this is the merchant ship *Angel's Luck*, three seven four nine one, departing for the *Saint Vrain*, cargo on board."

"Acknowledged," came a voice through his headset. "Uncoupling now."

The *Angel's Luck* shuddered.

May checked the status board at the copilot's seat. Everything was green except for one light, which winked angry red to remind him that the Vasac was gone.

"Uncoupled," May reported back. He thumbed a switch and cut the broadcast frequency. "CHARLES," he said on intership. "Energize the grid and get ready to set hull polarity on my word."

"All righty," the CHARLES said.

May cleared his throat in disgust. The CHARLES was in dire need of personality recalibration.

"*Angel's Luck*," said the voice of Tetros Bay Three. "Calibrating hull polarity as P-positive. Please acknowledge."

"Confirmed," May said, reopening the line. "Positive hull polarity."

"Charge complete in three zero seconds."

May switched lines. "CHARLES, engage positive hull polarity."

"Okeydokey," it replied.

May gritted his teeth. A line of indicators changed color.

"Right as rain," the CHARLES said.

May switched frequencies. "Hull polarity set at P-positive, Bay Three."

"Affirm," they replied. "Matching station hull polarity now."

In reflex, May reached out to activate the Vasac, but the control panel was gone. All that remained was a handful of color-coded wire leads and a few flecks of solder. He numbly looked at the console as the wall of force from the station hull hit, throwing him back into his seat.

The ship rattled as he keyed in the platform. "Thanks for the push," he said above the din. "We're on the way."

"Affirm," Port Authority replied. "Wishing you God's Speed and Angel's Luck."

May cut the frequency, thinking that he would not turn either of those away. He ran a quick calculation to determine when he would be a safe distance from the Tetros 9 sphere of influence to jump, then entered that time on the event clock. After making certain that everything in the bridge was secure and—except for the nagging light that indicated Vasac failure—in the green, he stretched in his seat, lay back against the cushions, and dozed.

When he woke, it was at the insistent nagging of the event clock. May looked around the cabin, disoriented, and panicked all over again when he saw that the Vasac was missing. Gradually he remembered all that had happened and set up his board for the jump.

May keyed into the copilot's cabin. "Wake up, William," he said. "Time to get a move on."

There was no answer.

"Duke?" May cursed under his breath and brought up the

copilot's compartment on the monitor. The zipbed was empty, the room deserted. He punched up All Call. "Duke, where the hell are you?"

No reply came.

"William Wesley Arbor," he announced. "Call in to the bridge immediately."

May waited. Still nothing. Muttering under his breath, he switched systems management over to the CHARLES, letting the monitor system scan the halls. He unbuckled and drifted to the copilot's chair to key in the destination coordinates and noticed a blinking red light. Someone was in a nearby air lock, trying to get the outer hatch open.

He kicked off from the chair and flew to the hatch, pounded a switch, and pulled himself into the hall. In a matter of minutes he had found his way down to the lock, where he was not at all surprised to find Duke between the doors, struggling with a briefcase, zero gravity, and the outer hatch access panel.

"Didn't you hear me call?"

Duke started. The sudden motion turned him end over end. "I'm really sorry," he said. "I didn't mean to sleep this long. I'll be out of your way in a minute, all right?" He grabbed the panel to slow his drift, then stabbed at the keys.

"What do you think you're doing?"

Duke gestured at the stubborn hatch. "I, uh, was trying to get this open." He grinned.

May gave him a blank stare.

"Since we're docked on the other side of Tetros, I thought I'd sort of slip planetside and quietly disappear."

"Disappear," May echoed.

"As you may have guessed, I don't really want to be found."

"Well, you won't be if you open that hatch." May extended a finger and twitched it, a signal for Duke to approach. Duke took the handholds along the wall and cautiously pulled himself out of the lock. When he was out, May slapped the switch to seal the inner hatch, then grabbed the lad by the lapels and shook him hard. "Don't you ever,

ever do something like that again. Understand? I don't care
how hung over you are. I won't stand for jacking around on
my ship.''

"I'm sorry." Duke shrugged. "I thought I'd just slip out
of your way.''

They drifted into a bulkhead. May pushed with his arms
and sent Duke sailing down the hall, then kicked and drifted
to meet him. Next he tossed him up an access tunnel, gradually maneuvering him to the bridge access.

"There's some Leuten's in the med compartment," he
said, opening the hatch. "Get in there and take some." He
threw Duke onto the bridge. Duke tumbled head over heels
and slammed into the reinforced window with a definite lack
of grace, his briefcase popping out of his hand and spinning
across the cabin.

"I really can't handle any . . ."

"Then buckle in until you're sober."

"But I am sober."

"My ass," May challenged. "If you're sober, then why
didn't you catfall into the room when I threw you?"

Duke drifted away from the window, rubbing his neck.
"Catfall?"

"Didn't they teach you catfall at the academy?"

Duke shook his head. "I never went to an academy."

May cocked his head. "Then how did you get your certification?"

"Through the University of Tetros at Callenda."

"Impossible."

Duke shrugged. "You saw my papers. You had no problem with them."

May rubbed his forehead. He vaguely remembered the
papers, remembered running his fingers over the holocerti-
fication seal, and getting nauseous when he tried to focus on
the letters to read.

"Look at them again if you don't believe me. They're—"
Duke made a sweeping gesture toward the briefcase, and the
momentum put him in a tumble.

May swore bitterly and launched himself at the briefcase.

He plucked it out of the air and did a catfall. His back hit the wall as he opened the briefcase and tossed out papers, looking for the certificate.

On the other side of the cabin Duke slammed into the bulkhead. The air left his lungs with a grunt.

May found the certificate and turned it over, the violet ink raised into an intricate pattern around the outside edge. *University of Tetros at Callenda*, read the banner. *Chartered to the Educational Wing of the Galactic Trade Commission.*

Duke slowly rotated, hands cupped over his face. His nose was bleeding.

This is to affirm that WILLIAM WESLEY ARBOR has successfully completed the required educational courses and passed due examinations, and has been LEGALLY CERTIFIED to function in sectors civil and private as a licensed—

"Commodities broker!" May shouted.

"Told you," Duke said, pulling himself into the pilot's chair.

"You son of a bitch."

"It was a legal transaction."

"That's not what I thought—"

"My uncle really did tell me to get rid of that beef any way I could."

"What about the platform? You said you'd been on the platform before."

"I always come up and make sure that the stuff I've sold gets onto the right ship."

May bounded to the copilot's console and keyed in orders. The view on the window changed. In one corner there was a bright glare of gentle blue.

"CHARLES," May said, putting on a headset. "Give me a quick estimate of fuel consumption on a return to Tetros Platform Three."

Duke shook his head. "No. You can't return me."

"And why the hell not?"

"Because I want to be dropped off on the other side of the planet. Because I have to disappear, remember?"

May listened to the figures and checked energy levels.

"Look," Duke said, staring at the blue light. "The sun is coming up on this side."

May removed the headset. "That's not Tetros," he said grimly. "That's Tetros 9."

Duke turned away from the window. "What?"

"Think about it. Tetros isn't that blue of a star. What you're seeing is a reflection of Tetros 9."

"You're going out of your way to take me a half orbit from Callenda," Duke said thinly.

"We're not in orbit." May wearily pulled himself into the copilot's position and buckled in.

"Wait a minute. I only wanted to leave Callenda, not Tetros."

"That's not what you told me. You passed yourself off as a copilot, you little bastard."

"I did no such thing. I was told you were looking for a cargo, and I offered—"

"I was also looking for a copilot. And you passed yourself off as one because you were drunk."

"I made no such representation."

"Like hell. You told me you were certified—"

"To sell commodities, May!" Duke's face was showing some color, as if the fighting spirit was reviving him. "Did it occur to you that maybe you were so drunk that you thought I was something else?"

May pursed his lips and pushed back in his seat. "There has been a terrible, terrible mistake made," he said.

"Tell you what," Duke said, trying to remain calm. "Just get me back to Platform Three and I'll catch an orbital shuttle."

May shook his head.

"Why not?" Duke's voice cracked.

"I've expended too much energy charging the jump grid. If I take you back, I won't be able to get through short space."

Duke's face lost its color. "Short space?"

"I promise that I'll put you on the first shuttle leaving the *Saint Vrain*." May started entering information on the copilot's board.

"Where's *Saint Vrain*?" Sweat was beading on Duke's forehead.

"It's a hydrogen tanker in deep space. Are you buckled in?"

"Yes, but . . ."

May watched as the board before him flickered green. "On the upper right hand side of the board in front of you, there should be three buttons glowing with an amber light. Would you push them, please?"

"Wait a minute . . ."

"Push the damn buttons, Duke."

Duke tentatively reached out and stabbed the buttons in sequence. "Give me a chance to think this out. It's probably not too late . . ."

"It is now," May said. The *Angel's Luck* began to vibrate, and a low whine filled the bridge. "That's the MiDIS."

Duke looked around the cabin, paling. "MiDIS?"

"Minimal Displacement Induction System. We're about to shift phase."

Duke's eyes grew wide. "Jump?" he said loudly. "We're going to jump?"

May nodded.

"But we can't do that. It causes the fabric of reality to become frayed. It makes people crazy."

"Folk tales," May shouted back.

"I don't like anything I don't understand."

"Nobody understands it."

Duke looked out the window. He could see the hull glowing from shift energization. "You can't take me!" he screamed above the din. "I'm not certified!"

"Don't worry," May shouted as the noise became deafening. "I'll teach you."

Duke looked around in panic, fingers twisting the lock that held him in the pilot's seat.

"Don't do it," May advised. "Sit back and enjoy the ride."

Duke looked helplessly out the window, head throbbing as if his sinuses were about to explode. The rattling slowed to a low rumble, and he studied the control panel, thinking there was perhaps something that could be of comfort. His eyes fell on an engraved platinum plate.

"Oh, no. *Oh, no. May—*"

The merchant looked at him with tired eyes.

"You've got to change the name of this ship."

Outside the bridge window, the stars vanished.

TWO

"But we haven't hit bottom," May said through the palms of his hands. "And when we do hit it, we're going to meet some bastard who will hand us each a shovel and tell us to start digging."

It took Duke about three days to accommodate himself to the ship's lack of gravity. May had turned a deaf ear to the Tetran's pleas to activate the artificial gravity, explaining that if he knew how to operate without it, he would make a better impression on future customers.

"You mean if I have a job when I get back," Duke complained.

May punched him in the shoulder. It sent them drifting in opposite directions.

"Hey," May said, twisting through a catfall and lighting with both feet against the wall. "Blood is thicker than water, right? I'm sure your uncle is going to be very forgiving when he realizes what happened."

"He's going to be mad," Duke said. "Company policy says we're not supposed to drink when we deal with merchants." He clumsily grabbed a handhold and pulled his drift to a stop.

"That's not going to endear you to any merchants, either," May explained. "Many's the deal that was made over a friendly bottle of—"

"Don't remind me," Duke said sourly. He had a white-knuckle grip on the handhold and was staring out the thick window into the blackness. "Why can't we see the stars? You'd think we'd be able to at least see *something*."

May avoided the question. Duke tended to become unnerved whenever the phase shift or a jump route was mentioned. "Tell you what," he said, drifting from the wall. "Follow me to the bridge and I'll show you how to handle the OBSYNE system."

"The obscene what?"

"The Outboard Systems Net." He started for the bridge, and Duke floated uneasily along behind. "It's a field that protects the ship during . . ." He paused to look back at Duke's progress. Which words would cause him the least discomfort? "High-velocity travel. At the speeds that stellar vehicles travel, a rock the size of a pinhead could turn them inside out."

Duke looked up at May and paled. "Really?"

May shot out his hand. "Duke, no—"

Duke slammed into the wall. May slipped over and checked him. "Are you all right?"

Duke nodded.

"Never look away from what you're doing. Let your ears listen, and always watch where you're going." He gave him a push toward the bridge hatch, then kicked off from the wall and flew past him. He slapped a switch with his hand, the hatch opened, and Duke neatly sailed through. By the time May cleared the hatch, Duke had stopped himself by grabbing the back of the copilot's seat and had buckled himself in.

"It's not that I mind learning this," he said as May took his seat, "but why do I have to?"

"Simply put, there are a number of things that need to be done on approach to a platform, especially a hydrogen tanker. The pilot's job is to cut the OBSYNE so it doesn't deflect the ship from the station or try to metabolize the station's hull."

"But *you're* the pilot."

"I am," May admitted. "But to tell you the truth, I don't think you want the copilot's job."

Duke waved his hand at the clutter of pressure pads and indicators before him. "This is very intimidating, May. What's the other job?"

"Go down to the engine compartment and clear the fuel integration system."

"Sounds easy enough. How do I do that?"

"By flooding the compartment with chlorine gas."

Duke looked back at his console. After a moment of study he said, "Which of these is the OBSYNE controller?"

May leaned over and showed Duke the components of the net system. "This is something you won't have to worry about until the tanker signals you," he explained. "You needn't worry about anything until they tell you to shut the OBSYNE down. When they do, tell them 'absolute,' then say 'executing primary net shutdown,' and flip this row of—"

"How do I tell them?" Duke asked.

"Who?"

"The tanker people. How do I tell them that I'm executing the absolute shutdown?"

"That's 'primary net shutdown,' and you'll have a head-set on. Now, you flip this row of switches into the green and—"

"Wait." Duke held up his hand. "Does it work on voice activation?"

"No," May said impatiently. "You flip this row of switches into the—"

"Not the shutdown net, the headset."

May crossed his arms. Color was rising in his face. "You're not listening. It's *primary net shutdown*. And yes, the headset is voice-activated, but you needn't worry about that because—"

"I talk to myself."

"We all do that. When you've killed the primary, then say 'executing secondary net shutdown,' pull these sliders—"

"Is there a switch where you can manually control when you broadcast?" He studied the look May was giving him. "I want to know this, May."

"It's not important."

"It is to me."

May slapped his hands down on his armrests. The motion pitched him forward against his restraints. "Dammit, do you want to learn how to shut down the net or not?"

"I do, but first I should know how the headset works."

"What's there to learn?" May's voice was rising. "You talk, and the damn thing transmits."

"But I don't want it to do that."

"But that has nothing to do with the OBSYNE."

"Then why did you even mention it?"

May said nothing. He drummed his fingers on the console.

"It's okay," Duke apologized a moment later. "Some people just weren't meant to teach."

The merchant looked at his student. And some people weren't meant to learn, my friend, he thought. He cleared his throat. "Tell you what. Let me teach you about net shutdown, then I'll teach you about the headset. All right?"

Duke nodded.

"We're getting somewhere," May announced. "When the tanker signals for you to start your procedure, tell them 'absolute,' then say 'executing primary net shutdown' and flip this row of switches into the green." He flipped one to show Duke how the indicator would change. "Just like that. Then say 'executing secondary net shutdown' and slowly pull these sliders back. Some may be at uneven levels, so try and get them all zeroed out at the same time."

Duke laid his hand on the sliders before him. "These?"

"But don't touch them now," May advised. "Next you hit this row of buttons in sequence and tell them 'net shutdown completed.' "

"That's all there is to it?"

"That's it. You don't need to touch anything else. If you do, you may blow us all to hell and gone. Think you can handle it?"

Duke nodded enthusiastically. "I'll try."

"I wish you wouldn't put it that way," May said. "Okay, let's try it."

For the better part of an hour they rehearsed the net shut-down routine. May hovered over Duke, watching him like a hawk, quick to criticize when something was done wrong.

"Not in that order," he barked, stabbing a finger against the command console. "If you do it that way, the fuel cells will dump into the reactor vents before they've been cleared, and you'll blow us all to hell and gone."

"If you do it that way," he growled a few minutes later, wheeling his arms in the air, "you'll fill the entire downside compartment with pure hydrogen. One spark and you'll blow us all to hell and gone."

"Don't do it like that," he demanded, kicking the console with his foot. "That'll expose the reactor core and—"

"I know," Duke said in disgust. "I know what it'll do to us. Heaven knows, you've shoved that part down my throat. What I want to know is if there's any way to do this routine *right*."

"Of course," May said. He bent over the console, fingers flying. "These switches, these sliders, these buttons. That's the order. Can you do that?"

Duke nodded and reached out his hand.

"That'll expose the core," May said.

Duke jerked his hand away, then uncertainly reached out for the switches again.

"All right," May said, watching. "That one . . . that one . . . that one . . ." His face twisted into agony. "*No!* Not *that* one! You've just—"

"I know!" Duke thumbed the buckle of his restraint, pushed out of the chair, and drifted to the ceiling. "I know what I just did. Did you ever hear of giving a person a chance to make a mistake?"

May watched him hover. "There is no room for error when you're doing something like this."

"Great," Duke shouted back. "Then I'll never learn it."

"You'll get the hang of it."

Duke shook his head. "I'm sorry, May. I don't work like that. I need to know if I'm doing something right."

May unbuckled and started to come out of his chair. "Do something right, then, and I'll tell you."

The broker kicked against the bulkhead and managed a smooth glide to the main hatchway. "That's all right. Forget it. I'm just not cut out to do this sort of thing. I'm really sorry, but I tried. When we get to that tanker, I'll get work of some kind and buy myself a ticket back to Tetros. You'll be rid of me then, and I can go back to work for my uncle." He sighed in resignation. "It might not be that bad being married."

May turned to face him and cleared his throat. "Listen, I'm sorry we got each other into this. I've probably not been very easy on you, but you have to understand where I'm coming from."

"I understand," Duke said, not wanting to hear the story again.

"Maybe you'll let me make it up to you, then. When we get to the *Saint Vrain*, I'll see that you get passage back to Tetros."

Duke turned to face May and bumped into the closed hatch. He drifted away, pulling himself to a stop on a nearby handhold. "That's quite all right. I'm not a charity case."

"I insist."

"No, May. I can find work. I'm a certified broker. They have product there to move, I can move it."

"I wish you'd let me do this for you."

"Why? To assuage your guilt for dragging me all the way out here?"

"Don't start with that."

"You know what I mean."

May floated up from the chair, pivoting to face Duke. "Well, I do feel guilty—"

"That's what I thought."

"But not about dragging you out here."

Duke looked outraged. *"What?"*

"I figure we share equally in the guilt over that one. After all, you're just as big a burden on me as I am to you."

"Then what are you feeling guilty about?"

"Our deal."

"Which deal was that?" He looped an arm through the handhold to steady himself.

"The meat deal."

Duke's hand went to his forehead. "Oh, no."

"You gave me such a great deal on it that I can't help feeling like I got more than my fair share out of it."

"I didn't," Duke said. The color was leaving his face.

"I was trying to think of a way to give you a little more profit on it without making it look like a kickback."

A shudder ran over Duke's features. "May," he said in almost inaudible tones. "What kind of deal did I cut you?"

May looked away. "Twenty-five percent on the credit."

"Twenty-five—" The words broke from Duke's throat in a half laugh, half cry.

"Even at full price I would have made a lot of money on the *Saint Vrain*, so I have no problem with buying you a Deluxe Class ticket home along with a few thousand to see you there."

Duke looked at him in disbelief. *"A few thousand?"*

"All right," May said quickly. "Ten thousand." He studied Duke's face. "Fifteen thousand."

"No," Duke cried. "You don't understand. I can't go home now. Chances are that my uncle has filed felony charges against me and I'll be arrested the minute I make planetfall."

"Why would he do a thing like that? You said the meat was yours to sell and that you were to dispose of it at any cost."

"*Not* at twenty-five percent on the credit, May. I wasn't doing that well to begin with, and fifty commercial tons of beef at a point two five down per wholesale credit—" There was a pause as he mentally went through the calculations. "There's a loss there, a big enough one that my uncle is going to forget what remains of our blood ties." Duke pulled his arm out of the handhold and drifted. "I should have just gotten married. With two wives I would have been motivated to do better."

May looked at him helplessly. "Duke, I'm sorry."

"Sorry? How can you be sorry? You're not the one who can never go home."

"Maybe we can work something out with the authorities. I can go to your uncle, talk to him—"

"And he'll have you arrested," Duke snapped. "You aided in the flight of a known planetary felon."

May choked. "I did *what*?"

"It's true," Duke said.

"But you weren't a felon at the time."

"Doesn't matter. Tetros has very stringent laws protecting their livelihood. You mess with their agricultural exports, and they mess with you. Badly." He pushed away from the door and stopped at the reinforced window. "I wish I could see the stars."

"I'm screwed," May lamented. "I was going to haul fuel from the *Saint Vrain* to the Jeremacis system, farm machinery from Jeremacis to Tetros, and food from Tetros to the *Saint Vrain*. It's taken me years to get into a setup like this."

"The minute you dock at a Tetros platform," Duke told him, "you're history."

May quietly settled back into his seat. "Damn."

The two of them stared out the window into the solid blackness, a shimmer coming off the charged hull. After a long silence Duke maneuvered into his seat and buckled in.

"All right," he said to May. "What is it? Buttons, sliders, switches?"

"Doesn't matter," May murmured.

"Of course it does," Duke insisted. "I don't want to blow us both up."

"You don't need to worry about it," May said dejectedly.

"Of course I do," Duke answered. "I have to. I need to learn a trade."

2

Eighteen days later the *Angel's Luck* downshifted into real space. During that time Duke had been able to learn the net shutdown procedure and had mastered a few minor opera-

tions of the copilot's board. As stars reappeared in the bridge
window, he sat down and slowly accumulated information
that May needed to calculate their distance to the *Saint Vrain*.

"You know," Duke said, shaking his head as the merchant
ran the information through his hand computer, "there's got
to be an easier way to calculate this."

"There is," May said, squinting at the hand computer's
display.

"What is it?"

"You let the Vasac do it for you."

"Sorry I asked." He sat staring out the window, marvel-
ing at the sight of the stars.

"Unless I miss my guess," May announced, entering one
last string of figures, "our time out distance from the *Saint
Vrain* is—"

A high-pitched squawk filled the cabin. Duke looked
around in alarm.

"Much closer than I've calculated," May finished. He
unsnapped the harness and floated out of his seat.

"What was that?" Duke asked, watching May drift to
another console.

"The AFA tone," May explained. "All frequency alert.
It's a general hail to all ships within the tertiary tracking
sphere of the tanker's Vasac." He made some adjustments
on the communications board. "Something's up."

The tone sounded again. Duke covered his ears.

"It's a real attention getter, isn't it?"

A voice issued from the speaker, crisp and calm. "To
the unidentified merchant class vessel approaching from the
21/88 intersect—"

May put his hand to his mouth. "Dammit. That's us."

Duke paled. "Are we going to jail?"

"You are now within Vasac range of the tanker *Saint
Vrain*," the voice continued. "Please contact us on frequency 190 as specified in section 37.91 of the Stellar Space
Lanes Code. If you are unable to make contact, please trigger
your alert beacon."

May pulled himself into the pilot's seat, put on a headset,

and plugged it into the console. "Tanker *Saint Vrain*, this is the merchant vessel three seven four nine one, *Angel's Luck*, requesting docking, servicing, and sideline permission for the next solar week."

"Absolute—" There was a long pause. "—*Angel's Luck*. We'll fit you in."

"Thank you," May replied crisply.

"*Angel's Luck*, can you give cause why we failed to make Vasac-to-Vasac contact?"

Duke looked at May, a grin forming on his lips. "You screwed up the jump, didn't you?"

"Shut up." He cleared his throat and spoke into the mouthpiece. "*Saint Vrain*, we experienced a Vasac malfunction in short space, and I had the ship's CHARLES unit pull it for repairs." He shut off the mike and turned to Duke. "That should satisfy them."

The radio crackled. "*Angel's Luck*, do you realize you've approached a Class Seven tanker without Vasac and failed to file a Condition White?"

May swore loudly. "If it's not one damn thing, it's another." He opened the mike again. "This is James May, owner-pilot of the merchant vessel *Angel's Luck*, three seven four nine one. We have a malfunction in our Vasac and would like a Condition White docking clearance."

There was a long silence.

"I'm going to go to the cargo hold," Duke said, "to hang out with the other slabs of dead meat."

"Have some faith," May snarled.

"*Angel's Luck*," the voice returned. "Under the circumstances, we are accepting your Condition White. Take into advisory, however, the fact that we are completing cleanup on one Vasac-related accident at this time, something we don't want to see repeated."

May produced a long slow sigh of relief. "Absolute," he told them.

"You lucky—" Duke started.

"Of the Angels," May replied.

"We calculate reach in about ten minutes," the tanker

advised, "so prepare to be pulled in. Remember engine shut-down and prepare for broadcast of G.T.C. regs."

"Standing by." May unbuckled and left his seat.

Another voice broke the air. It sounded muddy and worn. "Galactic Trade Commission Recording Two Sixty-Eight B. Laws of Conduct during tenure on a Hydrogen Tanker, G.T.C. ruling one one seven point three six. One. All engines and fueling systems must be purged with a prescribed clearing agent before pull is engaged. Failure to do so will result in the immediate seizure of your vehicle."

Duke frowned and looked up at the speaker. "What is this?"

"Two. Any oxidizing agents must remain on your vessels and must be at least a double seal from any section of this tanker. Failure to comply will result in the immediate seizure of your vehicle."

"The fifty-one commandments," May grumbled.

"Strict, aren't they?"

"Three. Powder combustion and beam weapons are expressly forbidden. Dart weapons may be carried only if they utilize compressed helium as propellant. Failure to comply—"

May snapped the speaker off. "Will result in the immediate seizure of your vehicle," he finished.

"Why'd you do that?" Duke asked. "I thought it was interesting."

"That's because you're hearing them for the first time."

"But I won't know how to conduct myself."

"I'll teach you when there's more time."

"But the rules . . ."

May rolled his eyes. "You want to know how to conduct yourself? First, don't go drinking with any of the tanker crew. That means techs, greasers, pullers, suiters, desk jockeys, custodians, sales personnel, or administrative types. They hate small-time merchants like us, and a drink with any of them is an open invitation to get swindled and beaten to a pulp. This goes double for the women.

"Don't go drinking with the general populace, either.

That's anyone not directly involved in the gathering and processing of the hydrogen—shopkeepers, barmen, hostel
clerks, chefs, and what have you. If you get smashed and let
slip that you're not a qualified copilot, they'll turn you in for
the reward. That goes double for the women.

"Don't go drinking with the crews from any other vehicles
that are stopped here. They'll shaft you, beat you up, *then*
turn you in for the reward. In fact, just forget about drinking.
It's too damned dangerous.

"Next, don't do any gambling. Don't even go into the
sanctioned gambling areas here because—"

"They'll beat me up, rape me, take my money, and turn
me in for the reward," Duke said sourly. "And that goes
double for the women."

"Duke, I want you to make a special effort not to have
anything to do with any of the women here. I got you away
from Tetros, but I'd never be able to pull you out of a shotgun
wedding here.

"Lastly, and most importantly, if the techs here ask any
questions, let me answer them. If we get separated and they
ask you a hard question about the ship's specs, tell them that
you don't know because you've just signed on and you haven't
had a chance to study the instruction and specifications manual because of the trouble we've had with the Vasac. If they
ask you what's wrong with it, tell them it's screwed up. If
they ask you why you don't know, tell them that you barely
passed Comprehensive Vasac.

"All in all, the best way to conduct yourself is to keep
both hands on your ass, because everyone here will be out
to get a piece of it. Understand?"

"Absolute," Duke said smartly. He turned and started to
leave the cabin.

"Where do you think you're going?"

"To the cargo hold," he answered, "to hang out with—"

"Don't get smart with me," May snapped. "And don't
leave. You've got to run the net shutdown, remember?"

"For real?" Duke asked nervously.

"Unless you want to play with the chlorine gas."

"I'll stick to what I know."

May left Duke in the bridge, hesitating at the hatch to look back at him, hunched over the console. He tried to tell himself that things could be worse, but when he could not think of how they could be, he shook his head and forced himself through into the corridor. Another moment, he knew, and he would have performed the net shutdown himself, a move that would do no good for either of them.

Slowly, he made his way down to the engine compartment and, with a great deal of trepidation, set about his work. It was not that he was afraid of the gas used in the clearing process. Rather, there was something deep inside that suggested that perhaps, if he was extra careful in his task, that care would somehow influence Duke's performance as well.

Gradually, the routine of the job overcame him, and it was not until he had finished that he realized that the ship was still in one piece. On the way back to the bridge he stopped at the secondary operations room to check Duke's work. With the exception of a purge vent that had been left open, everything had been done by the numbers. With a sigh of relief, he hurried forward.

Within two hours they were walking down one of the *Saint Vrain*'s wide corridors. Duke, May could tell, was enjoying himself immensely. Cramped as the tanker's corridors were, they were wide and spacious compared with those of the *Angel's Luck*. For someone who had spent his first weeks in space on a merchant, the tanker would seem like the great outdoors.

"Enjoying yourself?" May asked.

"I'd be enjoying it a lot more if I knew how to conduct myself," Duke complained.

May sighed. "Are you still on that?"

"Yes."

"Well, don't worry about it. None of the commandments had anything to do with you personally."

A woman in the uniform of a transgear puller passed by. May looked her in the eye and smiled, but Duke smiled, tipped three fingers to his forehead, and said, "Hello."

"Remember what I told you," May warned.

"Are you going to let me have any fun at all?"

May shook his head. "Not here. That nice-looking girl could leave you with a broken neck if you aren't careful."

"I was just saying hello."

"Remember what I told you. One wrong slip and we're caught. And if they catch us, friend, then so help me I'll hunt you down, even if I have to go all the way to Sol."

"Understood."

They came to a T intersection marked by a large window affording a view of one length of the tanker. May turned left, motioning to a sign set into the wall.

"The stores captain is the one we're going to see," he said. "Lionel Duncan. The two of us go back a long way. We were plebes together at the academy." He chuckled to himself. "There was this one senior cadet who was always giving our squadron hell because he was from Luteris 9, and Luterrans think they're the Creator's gift to the universe. He put one of our buddies in the infirmary, so Duncan and I vacuum locked him in the latrine and reversed the blowout vents. When the deck CO lined us up and asked who had done it, every guy in the squad stepped forward. The senior C never bugged us again."

He started to laugh but was disturbed by the lack of appreciation from Duke. He turned to find that he was quite alone. Duke was still at the intersection, gazing out the window.

May sighed and walked to Duke's side. "What are you doing?" he asked quietly.

"I'm trying to see something."

"Didn't you get enough of that in transit?"

Duke shook his head. "It's not what you think. I saw a body out there."

May put his hand on Duke's shoulder. "Don't worry. It's not uncommon around a tanker, although they do make an effort to recover someone if—"

"But it wasn't that kind of a body."

May stared.

"It wasn't so much a body," Duke explained, "as a . . . *carcass*."

"What," May asked, rubbing his temples, "in the known universe are you trying to tell me?"

Duke took three steps from the window, pointed back with his right hand, and spoke with dead earnestness. "I saw a cow out there."

May looked out the window. All he could see were stars and one arm of the tanker.

"If you don't believe me, bring in the dogs."

"All right," May said. "You've seen something. But I seriously doubt that it was a cow. Perhaps it was some dust or rocks that resembled a cow."

"No," Duke insisted. "It was a cow. A Terran hybrid, to be exact."

"You get lots of junk floating around these things," May explained. "And I'm sure you're homesick—"

"You're patronizing me," Duke snarled.

"No, I'm not." May continued his gaze out the window, wishing that he, too, would see such an animal and be spared the grief of challenging Duke's sighting. "I'm saying that perhaps you saw what you wanted to see, namely, the chief export of the family business."

Duke nodded contemptuously. "I get it. You think I'm too green to make a positive ID on something just because we're out in space."

"You have been in space a long time," May said in a tone reminiscent of a doctor prescribing a bottleful of placebo. "Nearly three weeks. Your mind might be . . . tired."

Duke slapped the wall. "May, I *saw* it. It came within two meters of this window. *It was a cow!*"

May turned to Duke and studied his face.

"You certainly must acknowledge the fact that I'm capable of recognizing a cow when I see it."

"I do," May said slowly. "And perhaps you did—"

Duke's face knit with frustration, but May raised his finger.

"Not here."

"May, you don't understand—"

"No," May said, voice rising. "You don't understand. I'm sure that you saw something, and heaven help me, I'm almost convinced that it was a cow. There's probably a rational explanation for whatever it was you saw, but just in case there isn't, I don't want you to mention it."

"But I can—"

"I don't care, Duke. If your sighting can't be explained, you'll be in analysis for months with tests for signs of Deep Space Stress Syndrome. Neither of us needs that."

Duke was silent.

"On the *Saint Vrain* nobody is loving or tolerant except for Duncan, and even he doesn't have much play. He might come unglued if he finds out that you're a fraud from a Class C planet."

They continued to a door at the corridor's end that read STORES CAPTAIN, *Saint Vrain*. It slid open as they approached, and they stepped through into a large, plush office. In one corner a woman sat typing information into a computer console.

May cleared his throat.

The woman looked up. After a pause for recognition, she dispensed a stern frown.

"Diedre," May said, stepping through the door. "How have you been?"

"What do you want?" she asked flatly.

"I came to see Duncan."

"He doesn't want to see you."

"He doesn't even know I'm here."

"It doesn't matter." She banged a diskfile on her desk and stood.

May looked over at Duke, who was watching the scene with great amusement. "You're not still *mad*," he said under his breath.

"*Mad*?" Diedre exclaimed. "No, not mad. *Furious*."

"Can we talk about this later? This is my new copilot—" He inched toward the stores captain's door.

"Does he know what a rat you are?" She looked at Duke with eyes like diamond drill bits.

"You knew I had to leave," May explained. "You knew that—"

"I knew," she said, closing in on May. "Five minutes before departure time." Duke watched her fingers roll into a fist. "I ought to—"

May took one step back, and the door opened into another corridor. He shot a glance at Duke, who moved around Diedre's flank to May's side.

"Explain later." He thumbed the button to close the door.

"What was that all about?" Duke whispered as the door sealed.

"None of your business," May snapped back.

"A girl in every port, May?"

"I wouldn't expect you to understand." He turned to the door at the end of the short corridor, feet shuffling on the light blue carpet that lined it.

"Of course you wouldn't," Duke said sourly. "You told me to remain celibate."

"I gave you that advice for a reason. If you get someone pregnant, you'll spend the rest of your life here pulling trans-gears."

"No way." Duke laughed. "That's not why you told me that. You said that because *you*—"

The door to Duncan's office hissed open.

"There's only one person who could put my secretary into such a foul mood."

May's face jumped from a scowl to a businesslike smile. He turned and embraced a man a full head taller than himself and, when that was done, went into an elaborate handshaking ritual.

"Duncan," he said in the traditional greeting of tanker personnel, "how the hell are you?"

Duncan slapped him on the back. "Great. How in the hell are you?"

"Wonderful. Marvelous. Has it ever been any other way?"

"Haven't changed, have you, May? When Diedre found

out we were old friends, she wouldn't talk to me for six standard months. Never could keep your piece holstered, could y—"

"Duncan!" May interrupted. "I haven't introduced you to my new copilot, have I? How rude of me! Lionel Duncan, this is my new associate, William Wesley Arbor."

Duke shook the stores captain's hand. "Call me Duke," he said, a pained expression on his face. "Please."

Duncan gave him a toothy grin. "You're rather young for a copilot, aren't you?"

"I barely passed Comprehensive Vasac," Duke volunteered, bringing a scowl from May.

"I'd love to get into biographies," Duncan told him, taking a seat at his desk, "but I'm tied up with new inventory to check in. If you could just give me the pitch . . ."

May beamed proudly. "Beef."

Duncan stared in disbelief.

"Quality beef," May continued. "Fifty commercial tons, fresh from Tetros 9. Cleaned, dressed, ready to cut, cook, and eat."

Duncan's gaze traveled the perimeter of the office, avoiding their eyes.

"I'll let you have it for a good cut under the going rate. What's the going rate, Duke?"

Duke pulled a notebook from his breast pocket and flipped the pages as May had shown him. "Going rate for beef on this tanker class is—"

"Sixty-five credits per commercial pound," Duncan said.

"I'll let you have it for forty-three."

Duncan rested his elbows on the desk and held his head in his hands. He sighed and ran some figures through a hand computer, jotting notes on a pad. Then, pursing his lips, he looked at May solemnly. "I can give you fifteen per commercial pound. I'm sorry, but that's the best I can do."

May smiled from ear to ear. "No need to apologize. I'd gladly let you have it for forty-three. Fifty is more than generous of you."

"I didn't say fifty." Duncan's voice was so calm that it

seemed to still the room. "I said fifteen. Fifteen credits per commercial pound."

May's mouth dropped open.

"That's absolutely the best offer I can make."

"Is this some kind of frigging joke? What the hell's going on here?"

Duncan leaned back in his chair. "Well, May, we've just finished cleanup on an accident—"

"So I've heard," he replied. "What's that got to do with it?"

"It was a big cargo transport en route to a new colony. It had taken on fuel and had dropped lines when it collided with a military ship. It cut a gash a kilometer long into the transport—the major control lines were severed, and what wasn't sucked out was frozen solid. No survivors.

"Well, G.T.C. claims law states that when there are no survivors on a self-contained vessel, all salvaged goods become the property of the nearest planet or starbase. That happened to be us."

"And . . ."

"It was a colony ship, May, one of the old styles. Instead of stowing everything they needed in Embryo Stasis, they were in Live Garden State. Our salvage crew went in to find beef, mutton, pork, chicken, fresh fruit, vegetables, all of it free. Every allocated food storage area is full and will be for the rest of the standard year."

"The rest of the year." May slowly walked to a chair and sat down hard.

"What's wrong with him?" Duncan asked. "He looks like he's lost his last friend."

"I think he has," Duke said.

3

Duke sat on a bar stool next to May, guzzling beer from a large frosted mug. "I told you I saw a cow," he said drunkenly. "It was out there, and I saw it with my own eyes. You didn't believe me, did you, May? I'll bet you believe me now.''

May took another gulp of his drink, which, because of the recent accident, was filled with fresh grapefruit squeezings. ''An old line transport smashed up on the front porch of the place I'm dragging food to. I was going to make a killing. Do you remember what I got that beef for?''

''I got it for you,'' Duke said, sipping.

''I could've turned enough profit to have a payment and a new Vasac controller.''

''Duncan said he'd give you the controller from the wrecked cargo ship. All you have to do is keep your mouth shut while the claim goes through.''

''Don't interrupt.'' He looked at Duke as if he was about to impart the secrets of the universe. ''Where was I?''

''Selling the meat.''

''That's right. If I sell that meat here, I'll lose my shirt. I can barely afford fuel to the next tanker.''

''You *can't* afford fuel to the next tanker,'' Duke said matter-of-factly.

''And I'm stuck with fifty commercial tons of beef that I can't give away.''

''I like beef,'' Duke offered.

''Good,'' May snapped. ''You can eat it till you choke.''

''I've got this feeling it could be worse,'' Duke said. ''I know it seems pretty bad right now, but look at it this way: We've still got our health.''

May gave him a grim look. ''Were you raised on clichés?''

''Listen to me.'' Duke tried to focus on his sullen partner. ''The ship is still ours, and they can't take that away from us, at least not yet. I'm sure we can figure out how to get fuel enough to get out of here. We'll find a place to unload the beef and pick up something else to sell.''

''I was going to buy fuel here,'' May said. ''Do you have any idea how cheap it is here?''

''As cheap as beef on Tetros?''

''Go to hell,'' May said.

"Maybe we could make enough to get to Vegas 3 and gamble what's left into some real money."

May scowled hard. "That's not funny."

"I'm serious. I think we could pull it off."

"Okay, Big Time. Let's hear your plans."

"Easy. We could eat that beef for years and not put a dent in it, and we could sleep on the ship. We could get jobs, and since we've got free bed and board, we save what we make to buy fuel. When we get to the Vegas system we could sell what beef is left, so we wouldn't be taking a loss. Then we'd have something to work with. We can do it, May."

May belched. "You're forgetting one detail. We may live on the ship for free, but we have to pay for docking. That'll run more than food and lodging for the both of us put together."

Duke sat straight in his seat, and a determined look crossed his features. It surprised May, for it suddenly looked as if the Tetran had forced himself sober.

"All right, then. We quit this stupid drinking and get out. We fuel up the ship and go straight to Vegas 3. If we only get twenty credits a commercial pound, that'll at least give us a payment. We can worry about how to live once we're there."

"The problem," May said, "is that the Vegas system is a one-way run. We take stuff in and leave empty. Their only export is people with no money."

Duke thought. "What about gambling machines?"

"Where do we sell them?"

"I don't know. How about the *Yueh-sheng*?"

"You want to deal with the *Yueh-sheng*?" May shuddered. "Forget it. I'd rather end up in jail . . . or on Sol."

"So we get something else. How many pleasure craft will the cargo bay hold?"

"Pleasure craft?"

"Repos, May. Some guy goes into a casino and drops twenty-five million. He has nothing left but his ship. What do the casino people do, strip it of twenty-five million in parts?"

May shook his head in disgust. "I taught you better than that."

"So what do they do? Impound the ship, consider the debt even, and buy him a Deluxe Class ticket home. I'd bet some of those casinos would be more than happy to sell these ships for enough to recoup their losses. We might be able to pick one up for around thirty million, then turn around and sell it for sixty or seventy."

"Marvelous." May crossed his arms and looked down his nose at Duke. "How do you plan on raising the first thirty million?"

"We don't. We work up enough for a down payment, we load up a ship, and we take off. We go somewhere else and sell it for, say, seventy million. With thirty of it we pay off the first ship. We use five for the next five payments on the *Angel's Luck*, five more for expenses, and sink the remaining thirty into down payments on more pleasure craft. We load up as many as the cargo bay will carry and go out and sell them. Once they're sold, we pay off the casino and keep the rest. We make payments, pay expenses . . ."

"And sink it into more pleasure craft." May looked up from his glass. "The *Angel's Luck* could be paid off in no time at all." He stared into his drink. "For twelve years I've been sweating out price stability and deadlines and running all over the galaxy. I've paid for half of my ship that way. Now some zero-gee-sick farm boy tells me that I've been doing it all wrong—and the hell of it is, you're right, Duke. It would work." His shoulders slumped. "Why couldn't I have thought of something like that?"

"Don't worry about it. What matters is that nobody else has thought of it, either."

May scratched his chin. "Even if someone else is doing it, it's still a wide-open field. I suggest we get on this right away." He rose from his stool, a happy look on his face. As he stood, the look went dour and he sat back down.

"I thought we were leaving," Duke said.

"Shut up and drink." May picked up his glass.

"What's wrong? Five seconds ago we were going to get filthy rich running a used-yacht business."

May looked at Duke with sad eyes. "How are we going to get the fuel for the trip?"

Duke thought about it. "From Duncan. We tell him that we're over a barrel and you need it to get out of here so you can sell the beef. Promise him that as soon as you unload it, you'll lase in the credits. Let him garnishee our account if he wants; that way he can get his money as soon as it's put in."

May studied the ice floating in his drink. "Duncan wouldn't do that," he murmured. "He trusts me."

"So are we in business?"

May slid off of the chair and pulled himself to full height. "I don't like it, Duke. It's too damned risky. We could lose everything." He drained his glass in one gulp. "But unless something better comes along, we'll have to go with it."

He decisively slapped the glass down on the bar and looked over at Duke, who was still cradling his mug.

"C'mon," he said sternly. "Let's do it."

Duke perked up at May's sudden motivation. He eased off the bar stool and followed his mentor out the door. They staggered back to the *Angel's Luck*, took small handfuls of Leuten's Alcohol Neutralizer, and crashed out in their bunks. When the CHARLES woke them three hours later, both felt fit and ready to do battle. They shaved and showered and had a breakfast of steaks from their plentiful supplies of beef.

From there they went to Duncan's office, and Duke hit him with the pitch. They had managed to find a buyer for their beef on a nearby planet and lacked only the fuel to get there. While they were broke, the profit they would realize would more than cover the cost. What they needed was for someone in a high position to spot them the fuel until they could close the deal. The proper amount of credits would then be lased back to the *Saint Vrain*, with interest where applicable. May followed with a long spiel about how each minute they tarried, they slowly died. They would have to pay the mounting docking costs, plus whatever expenses they ran up within the tanker.

Duncan listened carefully and sighed when they were finished. "This is a really tough position," he said. "I'm not supposed to do this at all. On the other hand, if you guys would default, I could fudge the spillage figures a little bit and write it off as a loss."

May shifted uncomfortably in his seat.

"Then we have James Theodore here. We go back a long way together, including the time we shitcanned a real pompous ass of a senior cadet. It wouldn't be right to let him down, in spite of the regs.

"My decision comes down to one simple thing. Diedre hasn't spoken to me since you returned, James. The sooner I get rid of you, the sooner I'll be able to work with her again. With that in mind, I'll do it."

May came out of his chair and hugged the man. Duke shook his hand vigorously. When the moment was over, Duncan called up the transfer work on the screen and put in the order for the fuel.

Within the hour they had a receipt for the fuel and were on their way to the landing director's office to make final arrangements for their departure. May was happily recounting some of his academy exploits for Duke, who was appreciatively listening until something seemed to distract him. He slowed as they approached the office, nose twitching.

"Come on," May urged. "Right through this door."

"Wait a minute," Duke said. "Something's not right."

May sighed in exasperation. "You're not going to start *that* again, are you, Duke?"

Duke looked up and down the corridor. "I mean it, May. Something's out of whack."

The merchant grabbed the broker by the collar and started to drag him down the hall. "There certainly is. It's called Deep Space Stress Syndrome, and you've got it in spades."

"Honest, May—"

"Put your hands against your temples and push, Duke. That'll keep your brains from spilling out before we leave."

Once we make planetfall in the Vegas system, everything will be fine. You'll snap right out of it." He stopped at the door marked LANDING DIRECTOR and rang the buzzer.

"You really don't want to do this," Duke said.

"Of course I do," May replied.

Pneumatics squealed, and the door opened. May put his hand on Duke's back and gently shepherded him inside.

"James May," a metallic voice said. "Greetings."

May stopped as the door closed behind him. At the desk was seated an emaciated little man with jet-black hair cut and combed straight up in the familiar blade cut. His dark eyes were partially hidden by epicanthic folds, and the smile he flashed made him look threatening.

"Mr. Hiro," May said, paling. "What a surprise."

"It's been a while," Hiro said.

"Someone I should know?" Duke asked.

May extended his hand. "Duke, this is Mr. Hiro, the man who holds the mortgage on the *Angel's Luck*. Mr. Hiro, this is my new copilot."

Hiro stood. "William Wesley Arbor. I know all about him." He nodded at Duke. Duke looked at May.

May swallowed hard and forced himself to smile. "So how in the hell are you?" he asked, trying to sound confident. He rapped his knuckles on the landing director's desk. "You've changed occupations since we last crossed paths."

"The office is on loan to me. I am here on business, James. Our business."

May sighed nervously. "You're probably here for the next payment. I can appreciate that. The problem is, they don't want what I'm selling, so I'm going to have to unload it elsewhere."

Mr. Hiro shook his head. "I came all the way out here to collect from you, and I won't let you leave until I do."

"Go to hell," May spat. "The payment isn't due for another ten days and you know it. We'll have it for you. Leave us alone and you'll get it."

"I can't leave you alone, James. I want it now."

"Forget it. I've read the contract; I know my rights. You have no authority to force a payment before it falls due."

"The contract also states that if the payee fails to make any payment on time, the holder of the mortgage has the right to demand money at any time and in any amount, as long as the demand is made in person by an authorized representative."

"That's *if*, Hiro. *If* prior arrangement has not been made for exception. *If* the payee has not filed in writing for exceptional circumstances. When I was in the hospital on Tetros I wrote a formal letter and lased it to you. I still have the receipt."

"I received your application, but I didn't accept it."

"What?"

"I don't call getting worked over in a barroom brawl adequate excuse for an extension, even if it did lead to hospitalization."

May stared in disbelief. "I don't believe this. I've been paying faithfully for twelve standard years on this, and I've been late before. You've never had any complaints with me."

"Times change, James." Hiro looked at Duke.

May turned to stare at him, too. *"You,"* he said, pointing. "What the hell did *you* do?"

Duke stepped back. "Nothing, May. I've followed all of your rules, kept my hands off of the women—"

"Not on Tetros 9," Hiro said.

Color rose in May's face. *"Who the hell were those girls, Duke?"*

"They were nobodies," Hiro answered. "They were just girls who would have made someone a mousy little wife, happy making babies and helping with the family business."

"He's telling the truth," Duke said defensively.

"Then why in the hell—"

"Imagine my surprise," Hiro said, "when a merchant ship called *Angel's Luck*, registration number three seven four nine one, turned up on the Port Authority's Watch List."

Duke paled and staggered to a chair. "What's a Watch List?" he asked weakly.

"Nothing," May said quickly. "He's bluffing."

"A listing," Hiro said, "of stellar vehicles that Port Authority is requesting be tracked because of various circumstances. A ship may be placed on a Watch List, for example, because it carries someone whose deeds are planetary but not galactic crimes."

"It could also be because the dock controller had a bad day," May said loudly.

Hiro sat and turned to a screen. "William Wesley Arbor," he read. "Age twenty-two by Terran reckoning. Licensed commodities broker. Two counts of dependent abandonment and charges pending on Class IV Embezzlement."

Duke covered his face with his hands and moaned.

"This whole thing was a misunderstanding," May said. "As soon as we unload the beef, we're heading back there—"

"No," Hiro said.

"And why the hell not?"

"Number one, you'll be operating the ship without proper ordinance. You introduced Mr. Arbor as a copilot, but I just read that his profession was in commodities. Number two, as I said, your activities have put the *Angel's Luck* on the Watch List."

"That list means nothing—"

Hiro raised a finger. "May I remind you, James, that as long as I hold a lien against the ship, the name R.K. Hiro appears on the registration forms. It just would not do to have my good name besmirched by such an unscrupulous merchant as yourself. My associates would not appreciate that."

"Your associates—" May took a long look at Hiro. "You son of a bitch," he said. "You're with the *Yueh-sheng*."

"I cannot allow any more controversy to fall on my name," Hiro explained.

"You're not even going to clear things up, are you?"

Hiro shook his head. "I'm going to repossess your ship. It's the only way to deal with this . . . situation."

"What about my cargo?" he shouted.

"I'm going to seize it when I take the ship." He paused to let it sink in. "Don't look so shocked, James. It's well within my rights to do that."

"Don't do that to us," Duke said, rising. "You can't strand us here. You've got to give me a chance to get back home so I can clear up May's name."

"Shut up," May said under his breath.

"We were on the way out now," Duke continued. "We've got a buyer for the beef. We just have to unload it before the trip back to Tetros."

Hiro put the tips of his fingers together and flexed his hands. "Unfortunately, I have a buyer for the beef, too."

"You bastard," May spat. "You accepted my application. You're using this legal noise to make off with my beef and your . . . social position as an excuse."

"I wish it was that simple," Hiro sighed. "I do admire the purity of doing something evil for evil's sake. Unfortunately, what is bad about me has spawned a great deal of good. For example, my early career enabled me to set up Malaysia Prime, which financed your vehicle.

"So I'm not doing this to you because I am, as you so eloquently put it, a son of a bitch. I take your beef because I am a businessman, and if I can sell it to the people of the *Port Elainii* for one hundred credits per commercial pound, I would be a fool not to do it. You're a bad risk, James May, and my actions are good business."

May and Duke exchanged glances.

"I wouldn't worry about making a run for the *Port Elainii*." Hiro smiled. "Your ten days would only get you a third of the way there. Besides, the landing director has orders not to let you board the *Angel's Luck*. It belongs to me now."

"We'll let the courts decide that."

Hiro gave a deep, throaty laugh. "And who are they going to believe? You can't even begin to afford a good lawyer, whereas I *own* a major galactic law firm."

May ushered Duke to the door. "We'll see about that," he said defiantly. "There's still room in the galaxy for the little guy to make a stand, and Duke and I are going to do it. We have a buyer for that beef, and nobody—not you, and certainly not your *Yueh-sheng* buddies—can stop us from delivering it.''

They walked out the door, and it sealed behind them, cutting off Hiro's derisive laughter.

4

The pneumatic door opened with a groan, and a man carrying a GasJet looked over the room's occupants.

''Which one of you is May?'' he asked.

''Depends,'' Duke answered. ''What do you want him for?''

''He's got a visitor,'' the guard announced.

''Duncan?'' Duke asked.

''I hope so,'' May said, rising from the bunk fastened to the wall. ''That'll be me.''

''This way.'' The guard motioned with the tip of his GasJet.

''Anything you want me to do?'' Duke asked.

May gave him a cold stare. ''Yeah.'' He made a sweeping gesture around the cell's interior. ''Let me know if you find any interesting graffiti.'' He turned and followed the guard out, the door hissing uncertainly behind them.

The merchant was led through grimy metal halls to a corridor lined with doors on each side. One opened, and the guard gestured with the tip of his weapon. May smiled politely and stepped in.

The room was surprisingly nice, considering the condition of the halls that serviced it. The floors were coated with a thick polyfoam, on which rested a trio of overstuffed chairs. The walls were lined with cheap salt and pepper carpeting, and in one corner rested a serviceable desk and chair. Behind the desk sat the *Saint Vrain*'s stores captain.

''Duncan,'' May said happily. ''Thanks for coming.''

''I hope I can be of some help.''

''Me, too. What were you able to find out?''

Duncan leafed through a stack of papers. ''The official

charge against you and Mr. Arbor—uh, Duke—is Conspiracy and Attempt to Steal a Commercial Vehicle. Not the best thing in the galaxy to have hanging over your head."

"Commercial vehicle?" May said, outraged. "It's not a commercial vehicle. It's a private vehicle intended for commercial use. There's a difference that—"

Duncan waved his hand to calm May. "I know that," he told him, "but Hiro had the vehicle registered under the name of Malaysia Prime Shipping."

"That scrawny little Ori bastard," May fumed.

"Calm down," Duncan said. "His race has nothing to do with it."

"In this case it does," May challenged. "Hiro's in with the *Yueh-sheng*."

"Just because he's Oriental, that doesn't mean—"

"I know, I know. But in this case, it *does* mean that. He practically confessed that fact in the landing director's office."

"Are you sure about that?" Duncan asked in low tones. "Are you sure that he wasn't speaking about something else and you misunderstood? Ryuichi Hiro is, after all—"

"I know," May barked. "A reputable businessman. Still, he had no right to put that ship under the auspices of his shipping concern. He just did that to get a stiffer sentence against us."

"I'm sure that's why he did it," Duncan said patronizingly.

May narrowed his eyes. "Will you knock it off? Here I am, your oldest friend, Duncan, and you're going to let this—this frigging gangster walk all over me. If he's got you scared, then he really has all of the angles covered."

"For the record," Duncan stated, "I'm not scared of your 'frigging gangster.' However, I do agree that he seems to have all of the angles covered."

May's eyes narrowed. "What the hell do you mean by that? Did you get to my vault and find the receipt he gave me on the application for exceptional circumstances?"

"I did."

"Then we've got a case against him! Why are you sitting there talking like a prophet of doom?"

"Because of something else I found in your vault . . . and some things I didn't find."

May sat in one of the chairs. "What are you getting at, Duncan?"

"What I found," Duncan said, "was a homemade bill of sale on a Tacoma Industries Galactrix line Model 2000 Vasac controller, sold to somebody named Dexter for the amount of—" He turned the greasy brown paper over in his hand. "—one and a quarter million credits."

May's shoulder slumped. "Oh. That."

"What I didn't find was any evidence of Duke's training or copilot certification. No certificate, no holofax of his license, no manuals or binders or microslots."

May waved his hands. "I get the idea."

"Your certs are there, no problem with that. But by law . . ."

"Yes," May said, too loudly. "I know what the law says about storage of vital documents."

"Would you like to tell me where Duke's are? I didn't even find him listed in the log, even as William Wesley Arbor."

May was silent.

"Duke's not a qualified copilot, is he, May?"

May swallowed and studied the polyfoam. "He's not even qualified to pull a transgear."

Duncan leaned back and massaged the bridge of his nose. His chair squeaked as it tilted. "May, you'd better level with me, or things are going to get rather thick for you."

The merchant sighed. "They're already thick for me."

"You haven't even started to see thick," Duncan threatened.

"All right. Ever heard of a place called Doctor Bombay's?"

After one false start and several pauses to sidetrack, May told his story to Duncan. He left nothing out, including the fact that he would not have minded meeting Dexter's friend Nona again under better circumstances. At Duncan's urging,

May moved on with the story, but he was stopped before he could chronicle the harried training sessions made on the jump to the *Saint Vrain*.

"One thing occurs to me," Duncan said, interrupting. "Why didn't you just return Duke when you found out the truth?"

May rubbed his face. "There were several reasons, primarily economic."

"You had too much fuel burn before the truth came out."

"Exactly. I did offer to send him home from here, Deluxe Class. But when he found out that he sold me fifty commercial tons of beef, racks and all, at a seventy-five percent discount, he balked. It seems his uncle is rather conservative and would have no qualms over indicting a blood relative for embezzlement."

"So you assisted in the transgalactic flight of a felon."

"No!" May howled. "He wasn't a felon when I met him. He was a scared kid on a beer drunk. I've got enough problems without having to worry about something like that."

Duncan eased back in his seat. "You certainly do."

"I don't like the sound of that."

"You shouldn't," Duncan told him. "Not in your situation."

"In my situation . . ." May's eyes darted around the room. "Wait a minute. Where's my lawyer? You said you were going to get me a lawyer."

"That's what I came here to tell you." The stores captain shrugged. "Nobody will handle your case."

"Nobody?"

"Not with the charges Hiro's filed against you. Right now you're looking at Conspiracy and Attempt to Steal a Commercial Vehicle, Operating a Stellar Vehicle without Proper Ordinance, Operating a Stellar Vehicle without Licensed or Certified Crew, Aiding or Abetting in the Flight of a Known Planetary Felon, Obtaining Goods under False Pretenses—"

"What the hell's with you?" May snapped. "Hiro send you here to get a confession?"

"No, but you see my point. Even if you had a lawyer, he

couldn't help you. The papers Hiro signed call for detention until trial. You've been labeled as high risk. No bail." He looked at May sadly. "I'm sorry. I tried."

May kicked at the polyfoam carpet and swore.

"Now, I can arrange a few little things for you. I can bring in some disks for you to read, maybe smuggle in some decent food or something strong to drink. Diedre's even offered to stop by—"

"So she can gloat, no doubt."

"But as for getting you good representation or getting you out of here, my hands are tied."

May pulled himself out of the overstuffed chair and patted Duncan on the shoulder. "Thanks," he said. "But maybe it's time that I looked to the one person who really can do something to help me."

"Who is that?" Duncan asked.

"Me," May said.

5

When the guard brought May back to the cell, Duke knew that they had problems. The merchant had been in a fighting mood beforehand, ready to strike at and fight whatever semblance of injustice might come their way. But when the door opened and May returned, Duke could tell from the slump in his shoulders that things had not gone well.

"Bad?" Duke asked thinly.

As the door sealed, May sat on his bunk and put his head in his hands. "I have seen the future," he said. "It sucks."

Duke smiled and smacked a fist into an open palm. "Well, you know what they say," he observed brightly. "When you hit bottom, the only way to go is up."

"But we haven't hit bottom," May said through the palms of his hands. "And when we do hit it, we're going to meet some bastard who will hand us each a shovel and tell us to start digging."

"Well, you know what they say," Duke advised. "Just before daylight is—"

"Shut up," May ordered. He knuckled his eyes and massaged his face. "I can't believe that this is happening to me. I absolutely cannot believe it."

"Well—" Duke started.

"No," May barked. "I don't know what they say. And I don't care what they say. Because none of what they say matters a whit to what is happening right now." He rose from his bunk. "Did you know that I was making it, Duke? I was doing all right for myself. I'd never been in any kind of trouble until I landed on your planet with Dexter."

Duke nodded. He felt it was the safest thing he could do.

"I'd been hustling for twelve years, and I'd had very few problems. For a merchant, I'd been damned lucky. In fact, I could have been considered successful. I had drinking money, I had friends, I was making payments on time. The only thing that really went wrong was that my wife left me."

"I didn't know you were married."

"Happily, or at least I thought. Met her while I was in the Merchants. We mustered out within a year of each other. I had the down payment on the ship, and she had a pilot's rating and some useful business connections. We started out, and everything was fine."

Duke was amazed. "You mean you started out as copilot?"

"Copilot-owner," May said. "And then I was copilot-coowner. And then I was the pilot-owner."

"What happened?"

May sighed. "She got tired of running all over the galaxy looking for hot deals. She said that wasn't the reason she'd spent twenty years in the Merchants. Unfortunately, that *was* the reason I'd spent twenty years in the Merchants. She left because she wanted a different kind of challenge, more mental stimulation. To tell you the truth, she deserved it. She was a hell of a pilot."

"I'm sorry," Duke said.

"Yeah." May sighed. "So am I." He paced around the outer perimeter of the cell. "I wish I had a drink right now."

"It wouldn't solve anything," Duke told him.

"You know that Duncan is on to the true nature of your copilot status?"

"I could use that drink now," Duke said.

"We've got to get our brains in gear, kid. The more they interrogate us, the more blurred the facts are going to become, especially if we don't settle on a good story about your copilot papers."

Duke shrugged. "I barely passed Comprehensive Vasac."

"That might work on some of the types around here, but you get in a courtroom with Hiro and his heap of lawyers, and you're going to be drawn and quartered."

"Then we can't let this thing go to court," Duke said.

"Great," May said, throwing his hands in the air. "Brilliant. How do you propose we do that?"

"Escape?" Duke suggested.

May snorted. "And then what? You can run on a tanker, but you can't hide."

Duke shrugged. "Why do I have to come up with all of the ideas?"

"Because," May growled darkly, "you're the one who is incurably burning with optimism's flame."

"Let me think about it."

May looked at his chronometer. "Better hurry. They'll be bringing lunch soon."

"Give me a break," Duke protested. "This is going to take some planning."

"*What* is going to take some planning? You intend to steal my ship back?"

"No . . ."

May snorted.

"Although that's not such a bad idea, now that you mention it."

The merchant slowly looked up from his hands. "What did you say?"

Duke started to pace circles around the cell. "That's not such a bad idea, May. Stealing the ship may be our answer."

"Are you out of your mind?" May rose and moved in on the young broker. "You realize we'd be stealing from the

Yueh-sheng? In case you hadn't heard, Duke, those people are mean. They are easily pissed."

"On the contrary," Duke said. "Mr. Hiro's ties with the *Yueh-sheng* are all the more reason why we should steal the *Angel's Luck* back."

May stabbed Duke in the chest with a finger. "You," he said, "have lost your mind."

Duke shook his head. "Did I ever tell you the story about how the Arbor Organic Food Company nearly went under during its early years?"

"Famine?" May asked, bored. "Earthquakes? Volcanoes? Killer asteroids?"

"Yueh-sheng," Duke explained. "In the beginning, the company operated by extending credit to the various people that were shipping product here and there, and they had a system for tracking and extracting what was due once it was sold.

"Well, one day these guys—my ancestors found out later that they were with the *Yueh-sheng*—came in with this huge order, two thousand commercial tons worth."

"That's not *that* big," May said.

"It was in the early days of Arbor Organic Food. Anyway, the company set them up and let them go with this huge debt on the credit files, and nothing ever came of it. After six months, they put out feelers, and at the end of the fiscal year, a loan had to be floated to pay taxes because value for casualty loss couldn't be determined without a sale point to determine it from.

"Well, time went on. Payments on the loan were slow, and the suppliers of product—this was back before we expanded into growing our own—were irate, too, threatening to cut us off unless we started forking over more money. Arbor was about to go under when my ancestors finally went to the authorities."

"And that's when they found out they'd been had."

"Exactly. It turned out to be a random thing, because the Tetros screening process hadn't kept these guys from coming in to disrupt the economy. With the word that the government screwed up on protecting its interests, my ancestors exerted a little pressure. In return, the government put pressure on the *Yueh-sheng* home world, and the family that had pulled the stunt came forth with a settlement.''

''That's fine, Duke, but we're talking interplanetary politics here. Those folk don't give damns for independent merchants like myself.''

''They paid us for 667 commercial tons of product.''

''You call that a settlement?''

''It wasn't much, but it managed to keep us afloat until we got on our feet again.''

''That's a really inspirational story, Duke, but I don't see how it's going to help us.''

''But it will, May. The reason that the *Yueh-sheng* was so willing to pay the company that small amount is because of some kind of code of honor they've got. It's ancient, goes back to when they were on Terra. This code says that if you've been robbed, and the person who did it pays you one-third of the value of what was taken, you have to forgive them, because you were careless enough to be victimized to begin with.''

''Yeah,'' May said sarcastically. ''I can see where that would help us a lot. All we have to do is get them to—''

''Not them,'' Duke said. ''Us. You and I. We steal the ship.''

May stared. ''What are you getting at?''

''How much did your ship cost new?''

''Duke, I really don't see—''

''Humor me, May. How much?''

''Two hundred fifty million.''

''On a twenty-five-year contract?''

May nodded. ''Payments of a million credits a month.''

''And you've been doing this twelve years, right? So the ship is half paid for, so you've got 125 million credits left on the balance.''

''It's not quite that simple,'' May said. ''There's interest—''

"No matter. One-third of that balance is what? About forty-two million?"

"I see what you're getting at," May said appreciatively. "But stealing the ship won't do us any good to reduce the debt because I don't even have forty-two million lying around."

"But you do, May. You've got the beef."

May turned away, facing the wall. "You don't understand, Duke. Even if we could get to the *Port Elainii*, that would only gross ten—"

"But we don't have to get to the *Port Elainii*. We just have to get to the Vegas system and unload it there. Remember the yacht-running business I proposed? We modify it a little. Instead of paying off what we've just sold, we continue the payments, hold back larger reserves of cash. All we'd have to do is sell two, maybe three vehicles and we'd have the cash to walk into Mr. Hiro's office and say, 'We stole your ship, we're sorry, here's our payment.' And May, he would *have* to accept it because it's part of his code of honor."

May closed his eyes. Figures were moving in and out of his head at a ferocious rate.

"Son of a bitch," he said.

"We could do it," Duke added.

"Of course we could. All we have to do is steal the *Angel's Luck* back from him."

"First things first," Duke said. "First we have to get out of here."

After a moment's thought May said, "And how do you propose we do that?"

"You're asking me?"

May nodded.

"Why do I have to come up with all of the ideas?"

"Because they seem to be better than mine."

Duke shrugged. "I can only get one good idea at a time."

The merchant turned, cracking his knuckles. "I think I can spring us, but I don't think you're going to like the way I'm going to do it."

"Why's that?"

May grabbed Duke by the throat and pulled him out of his seat. "Because I'm going to kill you."

Duke's eyes opened wide. "Me?"

May slammed him into the wall. "Yes," he hissed. "You. This whole thing is your damn fault." He shook Duke like a rag doll.

Duke tried to pry May's hands from his neck. He took a step back, and his ankle buckled, sending him to the floor. The grip was broken, but May was circling around him like a tiger about to pounce. Duke looked feverishly around the cell for something to use as a weapon, but nothing caught his eye. In desperation, he looked up at the surveillance camera and waved wildly.

May jumped. They tangled and rolled across the floor. Duke was flailing, wildly trying to land punches, but the pilot had locked onto his neck again and was pounding his head on the floor.

"You little maggot!" he shouted, slamming his head down for emphasis. "This is for Dexter! This is for Duncan! This is for the stolen Vasac! This is for setting me up with that load of rancid beef!"

"May!" Duke screamed. "Are you out of your mind?"

"This is for getting me drunk last night," May pounded.

There was a hiss from the front of the cell, and a shadow fell across the floor. "What," a voice boomed, "in the name of the Fifth Region is going on here?"

May stopped his assault and looked over his shoulder. The guard had a GasJet slung over his shoulder and was punctuating his statement with the food trays he held in each hand. May cracked his knuckles and smiled at him.

"Hello," he said coolly. "I was waiting for you."

6

Duke was ill at ease. The uniform was a terrible fit, and he was certain that the alarm was about to sound, announcing their escape. "Are you sure this is going to work?" he asked.

"Positive," May answered. He was marching ahead of

Duke with hand restraints loosely around his wrists. "Just keep pace with me and look solemn."

"Why do I have to be the guard? This uniform is more your size. I look like a fool."

"First of all, the uniform is too big for me. Second, it's more logical that Hiro would want to see the owner of the ship."

"Former owner."

"That's not the point."

"You're asking for trouble, May."

"Tell me about asking for trouble, Duke. Really. I want to know about being in trouble."

"Trouble," Duke said, "is if that guard comes to."

"Quit being so paranoid. We put enough gas in that room to make him sleep for three days."

"But do we have to board the ship this way? If they catch us, you'll never see it again."

May looked back at Duke. "That'll be definite if I let Hiro get me into a courtroom. We've got to grab the *Angel's Luck* and raise the money to buy that Ori bastard off before it's too late." He stopped and looked down the hall. "The hangar's just ahead. Remember your lines?"

"I hope so."

"Okay. Here we go."

Duke stopped May, face etched with worry. "What if they have orders to kill?"

"They don't."

"But they've got dart guns instead of GasJets."

"They have dart guns because if they get in a jam, they wouldn't have time to pull on their gas masks. The darts are probably loaded with Restcure."

"Are you willing to take that chance?"

"Shut up and act like a guard."

May began walking up the ramp as if the guards did not exist, with Duke following and trying to look as solemn as he could. One guard put the barrel of his weapon across May's chest. "Where do you think you're going?"

Duke interrupted with his lines. "I'm taking him onto this

ship under orders from Mr. Hiro.'' They started up the ramp but were again stopped.

"What for?"

May glared. "He wants the title and cargo manifests. I'm the only one with the combination to the ship's safe."

For a third time they started up the ramp. For a third time they were stopped.

"So where's your boarding pass?"

"Since when does Mr. Hiro need a pass to walk onto his own ship?" Duke said loudly.

"Well, you're sure not Mr. Hiro," the guard challenged.

"Of course I'm not Mr. Hiro," Duke snapped, "but I *am* an authorized representative of Mr. Hiro *and* Malaysia Prime Shipping. That should be boarding pass enough." He took a step forward and was blocked by the guard.

"It isn't."

May felt his stomach tighten.

Duke tapped his foot impatiently. "Mr. Hiro is meeting with his lawyers in fifteen minutes to go over the papers and manifests for this ship. If I don't get them there, he will personally have your heads."

"That's a chance we'll have to take."

"If you don't let us on this ship right now, I'm going to have to report back to Mr. Hiro empty-handed. If I have to do that, then I suggest you look into your savings accounts because your jobs aren't going to be worth a Terran dollar."

Duke stared the guard directly in the eye. The guard stared right back, immobile. They stood eye to eye. May shook his head. He looked at the other guard and shrugged. The second guard came forward and laid his hand on the shoulder of the first.

"Let 'em go. This Hiro fella is pretty hot stuff. It's better not to screw with him."

"Will you take responsibility?" the first asked.

"Hell, no. That's Hiro's problem."

May stifled a snicker.

"Besides, if this runt can jump this big guy with those hand restraints on, he deserves to get his ship back."

The first guard smiled. "G'wan. Go get your damn papers."

Duke nodded. "That's the kind of attitude I like to see."

They turned up the ramp to the *Angel's Luck*.

"I knew there was a reason I kept you around," May whispered enthusiastically. "You're an artist. Anyone ever tell you that you could sell diet pills to Biggsians? I ought to pay to send you through copilot's training."

Smiling, he turned to Duke. More accurately, he turned to where Duke should have been. He stopped cold and spun to see Duke slinking back down the ramp, GasJet poised to spray the guards.

"Duke! No!" He cursed and clapped his manacled hands over his mouth. The guards turned, and a cloud of blue gas billowed into their faces. There was a pop and the two men slumped to the floor.

"Duke! Get your ass up here!"

Duke turned and staggered up the ramp.

"Run!" May shouted. "The gas will follow us up!" He dashed to the ship's door and cranked it open. There was a strange taste in the back of his throat, and the tips of his fingers were beginning to tingle. He threw himself through the opening, with Duke wobbling in behind.

May pushed on the door. It would not move. "Help me get this thing closed," he ordered. Duke drooled out of one corner of his mouth and smiled at the red dart sticking out of his thigh. May pulled the dart out and slapped Duke's face.

"Come on," he said, throat drying. "Help me with this door."

Duke blinked, trying to get his eyes to quit burning. He put his shoulder against the door and pushed with rubbery legs. There was a budge.

"Did the door move or am I slipping?"

"You and your damned gas."

"It belonged to that guard you beat up," Duke stated.

"Push together. On three."

"Right."

Before he had a chance to brace himself, Duke was stopped

by a hand on his left shoulder. Another reached past his face and grabbed the door.

He felt ill. "May, where are you?"

"Over here." The answer came from his right. He blinked at the figure next to him, trying to get his eyes to focus, but to no avail.

The new figure pulled him from the door, and heroism sprouted in his foggy brain. He spun, throwing his entire body into a punch that would certainly make his assailant think twice about trying to rout their escape. Midway through the swing, his brain regained control of his eyes long enough for him to focus on the smiling face of the ship's android. He tried to pull the punch, but his fist sank into the side of the CHARLES's head. The synthetic flesh impacted down to the metal skeleton. A loud crack split the air, followed by a quick succession of snaps and pops. Duke watched his hand compress into the proverbial bloody pulp.

Because of the dart and the gas, Duke felt nothing. He pulled his hand out of the CHARLES's face and looked at it. He was still making a fist—a very mushy one. It looked incredibly funny to him, so he laughed.

Then he threw up and fainted dead away.

7

When Duke recovered, he found that a tube had been inserted into his nostrils and that the CHARLES was forcing liquid into his sinuses. Duke's reaction was immediate. He gagged.

May was nearby, leaning against the wall and giving himself the spray, explaining that it would counteract the effects of the Restcure gas.

With amazement, Duke felt the confusion clearing from his head. As it did, he could feel a growing ache from his right arm. He pulled his head away from the CHARLES. "No more," he said. "It's making my arm hurt."

"No, it isn't," the CHARLES told him. "It's just making you more aware of the pain. Your arm is broken."

Duke looked with alarm at the face of the CHARLES. It looked none the worse for wear. "I'm really sorry," he said.

"Don't apologize to the equipment," May grumbled.

"Oh, let him," the CHARLES complained. "Let him." He squeezed more spray up Duke's nose.

"No." Duke gagged. "No more."

May capped his bottle and set it on the counter. "Sorry, Duke, but you've got to. If we're going to make it out of here, I'm going to need all the help we can get."

"But my hand hurts," Duke complained.

"Put a Warm on it, CHARLES," May said, "and give him something to cut the pain. You can put a cast on him after we're out of here."

"Okeydokey," the CHARLES replied.

May scowled and pointed. "And when we're through with this, you're going in to have your personality recalibrated."

"As you say, sahib."

"Shut up!" May shouted, leaving the infirmary.

Duke watched as the CHARLES prepared the Warm. It was a small plastic bag that fit loosely over the injured extremity. He attached a tiny canister to a nipple on the Warm and pulled a pin out of the side of the housing. The bag inflated into a cast. A wave of pain shot through Duke's hand.

"It's going to hurt a little," the CHARLES said.

"Your timing needs adjusting," Duke complained.

"It'll also feel rather cold."

Duke turned his arm and regarded its new housing. "I thought this was called a Warm."

"It is," the CHARLES said. "It's sarcasm."

Duke thanked the CHARLES and scrambled up to the bridge, where May was making preparations for departure. He strapped himself into the copilot's seat and put on a headset.

"Switch to frequency seven nine and notify Port Authority that our intent is to depart. I've got to correlate with the CHARLES so we can steer out on our own."

"Right." Duke reached out to change frequencies and stopped.

"What's wrong?"

"Something on the board isn't right. I can feel it."

"Side effects of the Restcure."

"No, May. Something's been changed."

May stared, remembering the incident with the cow.

Duke's face lit up. "May! The hole from the Vasac is missing! Hiro replaced it!"

May jerked the straps from his chest and rolled from his seat. Where there once had been a mass of tangled wires was a cast aluminum box inscribed with the words VACUUM ATMOSPHERE SPATIAL ANALYSIS COORDINATOR.

"A Galactrix 9000," May whispered in awe. "Hiro may be a bastard, but he's a rich bastard and can afford the best." He leapt back into his seat and shouted into his headset. "CHARLES! Refit the specs for Vasac. Duke, contact Port Authority. This is going to be a cakewalk."

"What do I tell them?" Duke asked.

"Lie!" May said, rising from his chair.

"Where are you going?"

"I've got to go reprogram the central controller for Vasac."

"But I have no idea . . ." It was too late. May was out the door. Duke switched to seven nine and, after waiting for another ship to get clearance, spoke.

"*Saint Vrain* Port Authority, this is dock pod three zero R, merchant vessel *Angel's Luck* three seven four nine one, requesting departure clearance."

A moment of silence, then a tinny voice. "Absolute, *Angel's Luck*. Stand by with your manifest for clearance."

Duke put his hand over the microphone and looked around the cabin in panic. "Manifest?"

"*Angel's Luck* three seven four nine one, *Saint Vrain* Port Authority, state manifest."

In desperation, Duke said, "Absolute, *Saint Vrain*. What's this about a manifest?"

"Port Code eight six three requires a manifest check and confirmation on any craft with a zero-three status."

"Speak the language, Port Authority. I'm lost."

"Brush up on Pilot Law, *Angel's Luck*. Port Code states that a manifest check must be run on any repossessed or recently transferred vehicle when said transfer was rendered during tenure on port."

I shouldn't have asked, Duke thought. "Sorry, Port Authority. I barely passed Comprehensive Vasac."

The voice laughed. "Absolute, *Angel's Luck*. Now, would you state manifest, please?"

Duke, who had thought he had eluded the subject, cringed. For lack of anything better to say, he told them, "Meat."

"Repeat?" Port Authority asked.

"Meat," Duke said, as if it could not have been anything else. "Beef."

"Absolute, *Angel's Luck*. Do you have a copy readout number on that?"

"I'm a hanged man if I know, Port Authority. I'm just the copilot."

More tinny laughter. "We sympathize, but we need to have the number."

"Look," he said, trying to sound annoyed. "Does the name Mr. Hiro mean anything to you?"

"Repeat?"

"Mr. Hiro. Malaysia Prime Shipping. Ever heard of the guy?"

There was a long silence.

"Well?"

"Absolute, *Angel's Luck*. This is the ship carrying the beef that Hiro stole from that May character, right?"

How apropos, Duke thought. "That's an absolute, Port Authority."

"Fine, *Angel's Luck*. Just a formality that can be overlooked on this occasion. Clearance in zero five."

"Thanks," Duke said dryly.

There was a hiss, and the bridge door opened. "It was already done," May said, dusting his hands. "I hope to hell they checked for bugs." He climbed into his seat. "Did you get clearance?"

"In zero five." Duke snapped his fingers.

"Great." May stretched and wrapped his hands around the control yoke. "Shall we dance?"

"Yes," Duke said. "Let's."

Like a baby unsure of its newly discovered ability to walk, the *Angel's Luck* lifted from the floor of the pod and swayed from side to side. May cursed and told the CHARLES to stabilize magnetics until they were far enough from the tanker to use the engines. The CHARLES stated plainly that doing so would require an extra correlation with the Vasac, which was not feasible at the time. May swore and fought with the controls.

The ship wobbled out of the pod and moved into the clearance zone. The iris hatch slowly opened. The CHARLES calmly stated that owing to an imperfection in the Vasac's installation, the centrifugal gyros were about to fail.

"Stop them," May shouted.

The CHARLES replied that, given time considerations, the project was not feasible.

A shower of sparks erupted from the control console. Clouds of CO_2 streamed in from jets in the walls.

"The centrifugal gyros have failed," the CHARLES announced.

In the clearance zone the ship began to revolve like a large disk. May told Duke that they would be in for a few extra gees.

A tinny voice crackled through Duke's headset, asking if there were any problems. Duke, who felt that those few extra gees were going to mash him flat, screamed blue murder in response. In the Port Authority terminal the scream was interrupted by a recording of May's voice that calmly stated the nature of the problem and the fact that steps were being taken to correct it.

The iris hatch was fully open. *Angel's Luck* was free to leave. Magnetics coupled, and the craft began to rise unsteadily toward the gate.

May fought to keep the vessel under control. "CHARLES, is there any way you can stop this damn spin?"

"Well, *mein Führer*—"

"Dammit, CHARLES—"

"An induced failure of the secondary gyros *would* stop the spinning. Unfortunately, because it would create a brief electromagnetic disturbance within the ship, there may be—"

"Do it!" May yelled.

"—dire consequences."

"Do it!"

A metallic grind raised gooseflesh on May's arms, and a loud whine filled the air. Their spin slowed.

"We made it," Duke said to no one in particular.

"Wait for it," the CHARLES said.

Every light in the bridge went on, the lamps on the control panels glowed brightly, and four different warning alarms sounded.

"We're going to die," Duke shouted.

"Feedback," May said, shaking his head. "It'll be over in a—"

There was a loud report. A plate blew off of the lower control console and rattled across the room, accompanied by blue sparks and the smell of burning plastic. A fifth alarm sounded, and every CO_2 jet in the bridge opened, filling the compartment with thick clouds.

"CHARLES—"

"Ventilating, my liege."

The clouds began to clear. Out the window, Duke could see that they were slowly rising toward the iris.

Duke's earpiece crackled. "You're clear to exit, *Angel's Luck*. Here's your push."

"Push?" Duke asked.

"They're pushing?" May leaned toward the console and started to adjust the hull polarity.

"Have a safe trip," the voice of the *Saint Vrain* said. "Wishing you God's Speed and Angel's Luck, uh—*Angel's Luck*."

The entire ship vibrated with a low hum, and Duke felt as if he were being sucked into his seat.

"Here it is, CHARLES," May said. "Cut the artificial gravity."

"Not that, too," Duke moaned. He became buoyant as the gravity cut.

"Absolute, *Saint Vrain*," May said. "Positive magnetics contact."

Suddenly there was gravity. Duke slowly sank into his chair, and then it felt as if it were trying to suck him in. He looked out the window for relief but received none. They were racing toward the iris hatch so fast that he felt the ship was about to rip apart. Then the view went black—a solid black at first, then streaked with dots of white light.

Duke put his thumb in the center of his forehead. "Put the gun here," he said.

"Nonsense," May answered. "We're away. After the momentum from the push gets us out of the *Saint Vrain*'s safety zone, we'll kick in the engines."

The voice of the CHARLES came through the headset. "Too right."

Duke shifted in his seat, nose twitching. "Something's not right—"

"Dammit to hell," May growled. "Will you stop with that? I want you to look over at the SysOps board and give me the reading on the Vasac's function."

"It won't be much," the CHARLES advised. "I detected faulty installation before the gyro malfunction."

"No problem," May replied. "We can rewire it on the way to the Vegas system. Give me the readings, Duke."

Duke leaned forward, looking at the console that rested between the two seats.

"Over there," May said, pointing to Duke's right. "Don't you remember? The SysOps board is over there."

Duke shook his head. "I don't have to look at the SysOps board, May." He gestured at the console between them and the spill of charred wire leads that was spilling out from where the plate had blown off. May dropped his eyes to the sight, and a string of unflattering epithets spilled from his lips.

"Problems?" the CHARLES asked.

"Your dire consequences," Duke said into the headset. "We blew up the Vasac."

8

Six weeks later James May was kicking the hull of a pleasure craft called *Star of Bolivia*, demonstrating its apparent worthiness to a man called Hartung. "It's a good ship," he told his customer. "Had a friend that owned one. It's two years old and has only made three transorbital runs. You could get something like this from one of the corporations who are selling off light transport vehicles, but you're going to pay upward of a hundred million for it and still have to repaint the exterior. This little jewel was privately owned to begin with, so you don't have any of those worries. All of that for only fifty-five million."

"Repainting is nothing," Hartung said. "But what about what might be hidden in the ship by the previous owner?"

"Why would that be a worry?" May asked.

Hartung waved at the ship. "Clearly, this is a police repossession. You promised that it wasn't."

"It's not a police repossession," May reassured him.

"Then how can you give that kind of price on a two-year-old pleasure craft? You could get seventy for this, easy."

"But we're not asking seventy," Duke said.

"But why only fifty-five? With that kind of price, there must be a catch."

"It can be explained," May started.

"It had better be good, or I'll have Business Affairs on your case so fast that you won't have time to draw breath."

"It's a personal favor," Duke said quickly. May looked at him, puzzled. "We might as well level with him, May. He's got a right to know."

"Level with him?" May asked.

"Certainly," Duke answered. He turned to Hartung. "You see, this particular vehicle is one of many items that have become caught in a legal embroglio between two Sol 3 families that have been at each other's throats for centuries. Recently, arbitrators have been smoothing out the differences between them by liquidating any holdings claimed by both sides and evenly dividing the proceeds. Because time is of the essence in settling this matter, we have authorization to sell at below book value just to generate cash.''

Hartung frowned. ''I thought you said this was a personal favor.''

''But it is,'' Duke continued. ''Mister May here is longtime friends with the powers that be at Thom Arbitrage, and Mr. Thom himself asked us to personally handle this.''

''How do I know you're not lying?''

''Check the ship's title,'' Duke said. ''The bill of sale is from Thom Arbitrage and clearly states the sale was 'for consolidation of legal funds.' I can show it to you if you want.''

From behind Hartung's back, May scowled. The bill of sale was from a firm by that name and did indeed state 'for consolidation of legal funds,' but any checking beyond that would show Duke's story to be a lie.

After their escape from the *Saint Vrain*, May had set course for the Vegas system, intending to arrive before Mr. Hiro could mobilize his thugs into a search party. Within three days they were in touch with the owners of a planetwide casino chain who were more than delighted to take the beef off their hands for twenty-six credits per commercial pound.

''We should have come here first,'' Duke said to May.

The next order of business was to find a salable pleasure craft. They found one at a less-than-reputable casino on one of the less-than-reputable outer planets in the Vegas system. Using Duke's untainted credit rating and with one million credits in cash up front, May was able to get a small five-occupant craft with relatively small monthly payments.

They took the craft to the Nyad system, where they quickly sold the ship to an eighty-nine-year-old woman who was fresh from a rejuvenation session on Nyad 3. It was there she had met her fifth husband, a prodigy of twenty-four who had a flair for congress in zero gravity. Delighted with the vehicle's quality and the corresponding reasonable price, she jumped at the opportunity.

The sale did wonders for their morale. They set a return course for the Vegas star in high spirits. Upon arrival, May immediately paid the balance due on the craft they had just sold and went to a more reputable casino to look for another. With slightly bigger down payments and Duke's credit rating glowing from fast payment of the previous debt, they picked up two more vehicles, steered them into the cargo hold of the *Angel's Luck*, and headed back for Nyad.

Within a week both of those were sold, giving the two businessmen a healthy balance of over fifty million credits. Duke urged May to pay off the loans they had just taken, but the merchant refused. If they made the first payments on each and used another percentage to buy into a couple more vehicles, then after one more sale they would have enough to pay off Hiro and have product left over to continue their business.

"I don't want the money to get too strung out," May explained.

Duke protested, trying to tell May that investing in more vehicles at that point would indeed string out the money, not to mention what it might do to the good credit rating they were building. May, however, stubbornly insisted that one more sale would set them straight, and as long as they had the goodwill, they might as well pick up the extra vehicles and get things off to a good start.

Quite naturally, the management of the Redline Casino on Vegas 3 was quite happy to see the two entrepreneurs return with the intent of taking more repossessed vehicles off their hands. Within a few days they had gotten the credit extension and had bought three: the *Reconnez Cherie*, the *Insh'allah*, and the *Star of Bolivia*. The first two were steered into the cargo hold of the *Angel's Luck*, but with the third came a problem. Even with the others positioned for maximal conservation of space, the *Star of Bolivia*'s thrust port protruded from the hold enough to prevent the outer hatch from sealing.

"I don't see where it would be a problem," Duke said. "Just readjust your magnetics grid and travel with it open."

"Can't," May said. "Constantly operating the magnetics like that will screw up the Vasac—" He saw Duke's look. "—when we get it, and will put too much of a strain on the power plant. G.T.C. law states that you can't travel with an unsecured cargo."

"Then we'll have to sell the *Star* here."

"Who'll buy it when they can go to any casino and get one for themselves? We're stuck with it." He cursed a blue streak. "I wish I'd measured more carefully."

"I checked those figures," Duke said, studying the ship's frame. "It should fit." He squeezed into the hold and disappeared.

"Duke—"

"Maybe there's something we forgot."

May slumped against the open hatch, scratching his head. Perhaps he could float another small loan and install a series of tow lugs across the underbelly of the *Angel's Luck*.

Duke emerged from under the front end of the *Star of Bolivia*, face smeared with dust. "What's in the styroplast cabinet at the front of the bay?" he asked. "I don't remember that on the cargo bay layout sheet."

"That's the antipiracy system," May said. "If you don't key in the right numbers, it floods the bridge with that blue gas you like so much and correlates with the Vasac to put the ship in a holding pattern until the rightful owners can take control."

"Can it be moved?"

"Hell," May said. "It's worthless without Vasac. And since it's optional equipment, I could even take it out and sell it. Why?"

"It takes up about three cubic meters of floor space. In fact, the *Cherie*'s hull is flush against it. If we could move it out, then move the *Cherie* and the *Insh'allah*, we'd get the five centimeters we need to get the *Star* the rest of the way in."

It took May two hours to find a broker who would buy the

system. It was out by day's end, allowing them to leave for Aiaaga 12, a heavily industrialized world that was home to the headquarters of Malaysia Prime Shipping.

After docking, May went planetside in search of a customer. It was a more difficult task than on Nyad 3, but within a week May had met the man called Hartung and escorted him up to the dock to look at the merchandise.

"No," he told May. "I'm a trusting person. Besides, I have problems enough trying to read my pilot's license. I'd never be able to figure out a bill of sale."

Good thing, May thought. He watched as Hartung ran his hand over the *Star of Bolivia*'s hull, then hesitantly spoke. "I hate to be pushy, but what do you think?"

Hartung scratched his chin. "Will you accept an account plate?"

"Is it good?" May asked.

"You bet." Hartung smiled.

Elated, they took turns shaking hands, then drifted coreward to the dock's legal offices, where they filled out the bill of sale and had it notarized. A round of drinks followed, and then they headed back to the *Angel's Luck*, where Hartung boarded his new pleasure craft and began to polarize the hull. When the cargo bay doors opened, the *Star of Bolivia* drifted out, rotated, and slowly disappeared. May smiled as he watched the departure.

"Kind of gives you a good feeling, doesn't it? Look how happy that guy was."

"I'll feel a lot more benevolent when we get that account plate cashed and the money taken over to Mr. Hiro."

May sealed and repressurized the cargo bay. "This is a moment I want to savor," he said. "The beginning of a new business."

"We're going to be getting the business if we don't pay off Malaysia Prime," Duke said. "I suggest you go down to Mr. Hartung's bank and get that thing converted to cash as quickly as possible. The sooner we get this taken care of, the better."

"My," May commented. "Getting bossy in our old age, aren't we?"

Duke sighed. "It's my idea, my credit rating, and my neck I'm risking by running my name through the data networks on these constant credit checks. If the computer throws a flag on me—"

"They won't do that."

"—for extradition—"

"Not for abandonment."

"For embezzlement."

"Duke—"

"Don't 'Duke' me. This business of ours just might save my neck. After we get those *Yueh-sheng* thugs off of our back, I want to repay my uncle for that beef—"

"And give up the chance to get rich?"

"I miss Tetros," Duke said flatly.

"All right," May said. "Let's seal up the ship and do it."

They gathered up their profits and took the gravity well down to the surface of Aiaaga 12, then taxied to the main branch of the First Pan-Galactic Bank. Unlike Tetros, where the buildings were open and cavernous, Aiaagan architecture was compressed and cramped. The low ceiling and small, token waiting rooms raised the hairs on the back of Duke's neck, and the half hour it took for them to see someone about cashing Hartung's account plate was about all he could stand.

"How can people work in conditions like this?" Duke complained.

May shrugged. "I don't see anything wrong."

"Of course not. You've spent the last twelve years on a merchant ship. This seems spacious by comparison."

After another fifteen minutes of bureaucratic wrangling, May and Duke were ushered to a clerk who seemed happy to handle their account. May requested that the funds be converted to credits for immediate dissemination. With a smile, the clerk took the account plate and disappeared to take care of it.

"This is it," May said, happily patting the briefcase that

held the other credits. "We're going to have that Ori blood-sucker off of our case once and for all."

Duke just smiled.

"I'm going to prove my ex-wife wrong."

The clerk returned and slid the account plate across the counter to May. "I'm sorry, sir, but this account plate is no good."

May picked up the plate and studied it. "What the hell do you mean 'it's no good'?"

The clerk looked at him apologetically. "A Laseron check of this credit account clearly states that this account plate is a Code Three. I can show you the printout if you don't believe me."

"What's a Code Three?" Duke asked.

"A Code Three is a credit chip or account plate that is identified as stolen, embezzled, or obtained through other than realistically legal means." The clerk reached under the counter and produced a large stack of forms. "If you'd fill these out, we'll convert its status to a Code Four."

"A Code Four?" Duke asked.

"No," May said, pushing Duke back. "I've been through this before, and I'm not going to go through it again." He stuffed the account plate in his pocket.

"I want to hear this," Duke said.

"No, you don't," May said, dragging him away to the doors. "It's the same old legal bullshit that I've been putting up with ever since Dexter got me in trouble. Only this time I've had enough." The door opened, and he stepped through.

"So what are you going to do?" Duke asked, following.

"First of all, we need to get Hiro off of our backs. Once that's done, we'll have all the time we need to move those other two ships." He stepped to the curb and flagged down a passing taxi. They climbed in, giving orders to get them to Malaysia Prime Shipping before closing time.

"That's going to take some work," the driver said. "Those Oris like to close their doors—"

May stuffed a hundred credits into the driver's hand. "Get us there and you'll get another one."

The car lurched away from the curb.

"How do we go about giving Hiro his tribute?" May asked.

"I don't know."

"You said your uncle had been through this once."

"My ancestors, May. This was before I was born. Weren't you listening?"

May's shoulders slumped.

"I guess all we do is go in there and ask to speak with Mr. Hiro," Duke said.

"They won't let us in."

"We'll give them your name. He'll see us, I promise. Then we go in and say, 'Look, we lost out heads and stole our ship back from you. We feel really terrible about that so we raised this money, one-third of what we owe you, and we're giving it to you as a peace offering.' If he's working within the *Yueh-sheng* code, he'll have to accept it."

May nodded. "This had better work."

"If it doesn't, it won't matter, will it?" Duke leaned his head back and closed his eyes.

"Once Hiro is out of the way," May continued, "we'll put out a tracer on that Hartung character. And we'll sell the two ships we've got left. The problem is, Aiaaga is a bad run if we're wanting to return to the Vegas system. My best bet is to get a load of industrial solvent and run it to—"

"You guys merchants?" the driver asked. "You got a ship?"

"We're paying you to drive," May growled.

"I'm driving." He made a hard right.

"What about paying off those other ships? We're in for five of them now."

"We'll cycle payments in every month," May said. "With the *Angel's Luck* paid off, we'll have an extra million a month to play with."

"That's not going to cover five payments."

"Give me a minute," May said.

The car screeched to a stop, throwing them forward.

"Malaysia Prime corporate headquarters," the driver announced.

May thanked him and opened the door.

"My money," the driver said.

"Keep the meter running," May told him. "We won't be long."

The driver muttered as May slammed the door. Duke was right behind him, stepping up onto the gritty sidewalk.

"I expected a nicer-looking place," he said.

"Not on Aiaaga. Too much junk in the air." May tugged at the sleeves of his coat and brushed himself off. "Are you ready?"

Duke drew breath and nodded.

May smiled. "Let's give him hell."

They stepped into the metal and glass building and went straight to a dour-looking receptionist. Before she could ask what they wanted, May told her they needed to speak with Ryuichi Hiro.

"Do you have an appointment?" she asked.

"I don't need an appointment. Tell him that James May is here to see him."

She eyed his briefcase nervously. "What is your business?"

May slapped the case on her desk and tossed it open, revealing rubber-banded stacks of credit chips. "This is my business."

Inside of thirty seconds they were on the elevator to the top floor of the building, Ryuichi Hiro's suite. When the door opened, their mouths dropped. The reception area was the antithesis of Aiaagan architecture. There was a high, vaulted ceiling and a plush, thick carpet, and the room was easily one-third the size of the *Angel's Luck* cargo hold.

The door started to close. May and Duke stepped out and walked across the empty expanse of room to the desk that sat by the door.

"James May to see Mr. Hiro."

To continue the contrast, the receptionist was beautiful, an example of *Yueh-sheng* womanhood in full flower.

"He's expecting you," she said.

They started to the door, and she stood, pointing at Duke. "Young man, you are to remain here."

"No," May said. "He goes with me, or we leave."

"I cannot allow that."

"But you will," May said. He pushed the briefcase into Duke's stomach. "He's got the payroll. Besides, what does he look like to you, some thug? He's sure as hell not going to hurt anyone with that cast on his arm."

She relented, keying in the orders to open the door.

Hiro's office was twice the size of the reception area and just as bare. At the far end, against a wall of tinted windows, was a massive desk behind which sat the man himself.

"Come in," Hiro said, rising. "Do come in, James."

May looked back as the door closed behind him. "I thought I was in." He started toward the desk, Duke five steps behind him. "These are some digs."

"On Aiaaga," Hiro said, "space is at a premium."

"I wouldn't know it from looking," May said. "Ever get lost in here?"

Hiro laughed. "A rhetorical question, I'm sure."

"You know, this could be a really nice place. Some wallpaper, a few paintings, some lawn chairs—"

The *Yueh-sheng* shook his head. "All that is in my apartment." He gestured to a door across from his desk.

"Is it as big?"

"Not important," Hiro said. "What is important is why you are here." He sat down into an executive chair that was bigger than he was.

May stopped a meter from the desk and waited for Duke to arrive. They exchanged glances, and Duke cradled the briefcase uncomfortably.

"Well . . ." May cleared his throat. "As you know, Duke and I kind of lost our heads after talking to you on the *Saint Vrain*. I realize now that we probably could have negotiated something with you, but I'd had such a streak of uncertain luck that I took your news rather badly."

Hiro nodded. Was that a smile lurking just beneath his stoic look?

May cleared his throat again. "Of course, given the nature of your . . . *business*, once calm prevailed, we realized the urgency of the mistake we had made." He cast a quick glance at Duke. "We realize that we have offended your honor and have come to make amends."

Yes, that was it. A smile. The edges of Hiro's mouth were slowly being pushed up by an unseen force.

May took the briefcase from Duke and unsnapped the latches. He turned it toward Hiro and opened it, revealing the credit chips inside. Hiro licked his lips, and all vestiges of his smile vanished. He wagged a finger, and May put the case on the desk and took one step back.

Hiro picked up one of the stacks, removed the rubber band, and shuffled through the chips, making sure they were all valid. He took one at random, stuck it into a slot on his desk, and entered a code on a keypad.

"It's all legally mine," May said.

A green light flickered in testimony.

"How much is here?" Hiro asked.

"Sixty-five million."

Hiro pulled another stack of chips and repeated the test. Another green light flickered.

"I do not ordinarily do this, but I am feeling pressure from my associates to get this particular matter cleared up."

May smiled at Duke triumphantly, but Duke looked troubled.

"I accept your apology, James May."

May started to bow. "Then—"

"When can you deliver the balance?"

May straightened up fast. "What balance?"

"The other thirty-five million you still owe on your ship."

"There is no other thirty-five million," the merchant said loudly.

Duke shook his head. "May—"

"I sat down and very carefully calculated that money," he continued. "That figures in a full thirteen years' worth of payments plus the interest on the balance due, and just over a million extra for a cushion.''

"But Mr. May," Hiro said. "The ship you stole from me was valued at two hundred fifty million, and if you consider the full balance interest—"

"Like hell!" May said.

Duke tugged at the merchant's shoulder. "May, will you listen to me—"

May brushed the intruding hand away. "I consider *nothing*, Hiro. I paid off almost half of that in the normal way, and this is what falls on the balance due—"

"The ship was worth—"

"May, listen—"

"—and I even included the *interest*, you Ori bastard—"

"—and the worth on the title is listed as—"

"—do it with one more sale."

"No," May said, grabbing Duke by the lapels. "We do that and we might as well pay the rest of the frigging balance. We're through with this bloodsucker!"

"I am not an unreasonable man, James."

May shifted his grip to the back of Duke's collar and turned him toward the door. "Let's get out of here."

Duke shot a last glance at Hiro, who reached for something on his desk.

"Look out—"

May released his grip and spun. Hiro looked up in surprise, as if caught doing something he should not have done. May bolted to the desk, and the *Yueh-sheng* took a step back. The merchant hit the front of the desk in a crouch, grabbed the bottom, and lifted it up off the floor, spilling the contents Hiro's way. Hiro took another step back, tripped against one edge of his massive chair, and fell to the floor. With a final push, May upended the desk and let it drop down on the prone figure.

Duke looked at the scene with astonishment. "You've really done it now, May."

Trembling, the merchant blinked in disbelief. "What have I done?"

"Blame it on adrenaline." Duke ran to the mess on the floor and grabbed the briefcase with his good hand. Loose credit chips spilled to the floor. When he looked up, May had made it to the door and was frantically trying to get it open. "You didn't make it clear what you were paying him the one-third tribute *for*. He thought you were wanting to pay it on the original balance."

May hit his shoulder against the door, muttering racial epithets.

Duke made his way to the other door and poked at the electronics. It hissed open, revealing the living room of Hiro's apartment.

"This way," he called.

He stepped through into a small room crammed with furniture and electronic equipment. Against one wall was a host of video monitors. May's voice trailed in from behind.

"Do you know what you're doing, son?"

"There's got to be another way out of here," Duke said. "He's got to have a private entrance." He was in the kitchen. Instead of the usual food synthesizer, there were cold storage units and microwave ovens, and polished steel cutlery hung from the walls.

"This guy is some kind of freak," May said, suspiciously eyeing the utensils and appliances.

They reached the hallway. On the walls were strips of ideograms that alternated with a soft, white paper the texture of birch bark. At the end of the hall was a small table that held a videocom—and a door.

"We're saved," Duke said, opening the door. "Stairs and a private elevator."

"Still think this guy is reasonable and open to negotiation?" May asked. He had taken a box from the table and opened it to reveal an autopistol and three clips of ammunition resting on red velvet.

"Leave it."

May jammed a clip into the weapon and chambered the first round. "Not on your life." He stuffed the other clips into his pockets.

"Hit the stairs," Duke said, heading for the next door.

"Over here," May said, ringing for the elevator.

Duke turned. "Are you crazy? That's going to be the first place they look."

"No, it won't," May said. "If this is his private elevator, it'll be express, straight to the ground floor." The car opened, and May held the door with his hand. "They won't expect us to know that and will be covering the stairs."

"Don't give me that—"

"Dammit, Duke, I'm making a logical decision for once. Will you trust me?"

Duke pushed open the door to the stairwell. From below he could hear a clatter of footfalls and curses. "You're right." He ran to the car.

May stepped inside behind him and motioned to the control panel. It had one button. "See?" He smiled. "What did I tell you?" He poked it with his forefinger.

The door slammed shut, and the floor vanished from under their feet. As one, they screamed.

9

It was closing time for Eltex. From one corner of the city to another, Aiaagans were abandoning their posts and heading for their vehicles, getting ready to engage in the planetary pastime of forgetting.

But some employees of the Malaysia Prime Shipping Company, on their way out of the building that evening, saw something they were not soon to forget. At one corner of the building a soft chime sounded, announcing that the rarely used elevator was about to discharge its passenger. A few people stopped, knowing full well that it might be a rare opportunity to see the boss outside the work environment.

Unfortunately, they did not see a small figure emerge with a great air of dignity. Rather, when the door opened, two rather clumsy figures appeared. One was waving a pistol and staggered across the small plaza until he was able to catch himself on a small light post. The taller one took three steps out, dropped a briefcase, fell to his knees, and sprayed the sidewalk with vomit.

Before anyone could react, a battered taxi jumped the curb and raced across the brown lawn, scattering employees and divots. It stopped a meter from the kneeling figure, and the driver jumped out and dragged him into the backseat. The armed man saw what was going on and made for the vehicle in an ill stagger. The taxi started to move, and he jumped blindly at the front passenger door. The window had been left open, and his upper torso neatly popped through, legs flailing and kicking against the outside.

Tires spun on the sidewalk, and the taxi reversed, plowing out onto the main thoroughfare and sending the rush-hour traffic in all directions. There was another prolonged screech, and the vehicle changed directions, mixing in with the flow of the other commuters.

It was a very strange sight indeed, and it would make sense only when some of the employees later reported seeing the boss making his rounds in a grav chair, both legs bound in casts.

10

"Angel's Luck!" Duke gagged. "I don't believe it! I've had Angel's Luck!"

May pulled his legs into the car and looked up at the driver. "You, sir, deserve a raise."

The driver's head bobbed loosely. "It looked to me like things had gone to hell for you."

"Oh, yeah . . ." May said.

"That usually happens when people deal with those *Yueh-sheng* bastards."

May squirmed into a sitting position. "You know that Malaysia Prime is connected with the *Yueh-sheng*?"

"Oh, hell." The driver laughed. "Everyone around here knows that."

"I wish I'd known that twelve years ago." May spoke in almost a pout.

From the backseat, Duke gagged and cleared his throat.

"Listen," the driver said, quickly maneuvering through the thick traffic. "You said something about owning a merchant ship—"

"That's right," May interrupted. "You've got to get us to the shuttleport right a—"

The driver knuckled the wheel into a hard left, throwing May against the door and rolling Duke across the backseat. "I should've figured that," he explained.

"Where else would we go?" May complained.

"Not that. We're being followed."

May looked out the rear window. All he could see was a tangle of cars.

"Look for two little black tri-wheelers."

May studied the traffic. "I don't see—"

The driver made a hard right. Duke slid across the seat and hit his head on the driver's side door.

"Let's keep them off balance, then."

"I hope this is a shortcut," May said. "If those are Hiro's boys, they're going to be heading straight for the shuttleport."

"It is, of sorts." The driver glanced up at the rearview mirror. "Damn." He threw the wheel left, taking them across a line of oncoming vehicles. "I thought you were watching."

May looked back out the rear window. "I didn't see them."

"The drivers of those things have no scruples. They're driving worse than I am."

Duke slowly pulled himself up into a sitting position, blocking the view. May pushed him back down.

"You had said something about owning a merchant vessel," the driver said tentatively.

"That's right," May answered. A small black pod appeared from around a corner and slid in behind them. "And we're going to lose it unless you break this tail and get us to the shuttleport."

"Hang on."

He kicked the brake. The pod sailed straight for them,

wobbled, and slammed into the rear of the taxi, tossing Duke
to the floor. Chunks of black fiberglass sprayed the street and
rained across the rear window.

"We're going to die," Duke whined.

"Scratch one," the driver said. He floored the gas and
sped off, leaving the decimated tri-wheeler behind.

"You are one crazy son of a bitch," May complained as
they made a left. "This is getting serious."

"Hold your water. I'll get you there." Again he checked
the rearview mirror. "Dammit, you're supposed to be
watching our rear."

May turned back to his surveillance. The second tri-
wheeler had appeared and was running right behind them.

"I can't pull the same gig on this one," the driver said.
"He'll be expecting it."

"Just get us to the shuttleport."

"Not with him on our ass like that." The driver pointed
at the glove compartment. "There's a pouch in there. Get
it."

May opened the compartment. Toll receipts and kwikfood
wrappers tumbled to the floor.

"It's under the vehicle registration."

He plucked up the registration and studied the name.
"You're Maurice Vonn?"

"Forgive me for not shaking," Vonn said. "Will you get
the damn pouch?"

May tossed aside the embossed registration card and
picked up a rectangular leatherlike pouch.

"Unzip it and put it in my lap."

He did so.

"Where's our friend?" Vonn rolled down the window,
and the cold Aiaagan night air blasted in.

The merchant looked over his shoulder. "Same place."

"All right. Grab your ass."

May clutched the handle on the door. The driver hit the
brake with both feet and spun the wheel left. The taxi went
into a sideways skid, scattering traffic on all sides like billiard

balls. The tri-wheeler saw the move, braked, and spun completely around, stopping some five meters from the taxi.

Vonn drew a pistol out of the pouch.

"Oh, *no*—" May started.

The tri-wheeler's door flew straight up, and its driver
started to rise, bringing with him a long metal tube. Vonn
pulled back the hammer of the weapon, stuck it out the
window, and fired. The tri-wheeler's driver sat back in the
vehicle's seat and did not move. Vonn hit the gas.

"They'll think twice about messing with us now."

"Bring in the dogs," Duke groaned. "I confess."

"You're dealing with *Yueh-sheng*," Vonn said. "Remember that."

"Don't remind me," May said.

"I hope you've got a clear shot to your ship," Vonn said.
"I should be at the port in—" He squinted out the windshield. "Oh, damn."

A black tri-wheeler had wandered out of the opposite lane
of traffic and was heading straight for them.

Vonn laughed. "Crazy bastard thinks I'm going to stop."

May looked back at Duke. "Hang on," he squeaked.

Vonn moved the wheel—very slightly—to the right.

The taxi shuddered under the impact. Its metal frame
sheared away the entire right side of the fiberglass opponent,
and black chips rained down on the street. Something large
bumped under the vehicle's wheels, and their speed picked
up. They careened wildly down the street, blew through a
traffic-control device, and went into a long skid, stopping in
front of a familiar building. The inside of the vehicle filled
with the aroma of scorched rubber.

May shook his head to regain his senses. "Thanks," he
said, cranking open the door and rolling out.

Duke staggered out right behind him, and they ran for the
shuttleport doors.

"Aren't you forgetting something?" Duke asked.

"Let's get the hell out of here," May said.

Vonn's voice came to them as they went through the door.
"You cheap bastard!"

"You just made a big mistake," Duke told him.

"Move," May ordered. He grabbed Duke's good arm and pushed it up between his shoulder blades, guiding him through the crowds in the shuttleport.

"You can't just forget Vonn!"

"He can take care of himself. We've got to get to our ship."

"But you promised him—"

"I'll take care of it later."

"How will you do that?"

May pushed Duke in the direction of an escalator, and they started up to the departure level. "I don't know. I'll think of something. Our first order of business is to get off of Aiaaga before Hiro nails us."

Duke protested. "Why don't we just give him one of the yachts?"

"If we do that, we'll be strapped for cash." They stepped from the escalator and started to weave through the crowds. "Besides, I don't feel like going up to him and giving him the title."

"We could do it through Vonn."

"Don't you understand?" He pulled up on Duke's arm for emphasis. "I'm not giving any more money to that leech Hiro."

"You've got to do something to appease him."

"I'll turn renegade first. I'm not going to strap myself just to—"

"But we'll have one other yacht to sell."

"What if we run into another Hartung?"

"What are the odds that we will?" Duke stepped sideways, and May broke his grip. "We'd be fools not to buy Hiro off while we've still got the chance. It can't get any worse than it already has."

May shook his head. "You're young. You've only heard stories about the *Yueh-sheng* and the way they operate."

"I seem to know more than you."

"But you can't possibly imagine how nasty they really are. You just can't imagine it."

Duke took three steps forward. "You're right, May, I can't imagine it. And do you know why? *Because you won't tell me!* Every time I want to know something, like the Fifty-one Commandments—"

"You're not going to bring that up again, are you?"

"—or when I wanted to learn about the headsets, or even with Vonn. Did you notice he kept asking if we had a merchant ship? I'll bet he knew of a cargo to run!"

"That's not important right—"

"And that's another thing. Whenever I want to know something, you tell me it's not important and that you can teach me what I really need to know later. I feel like you're keeping me in the dark about things because you don't think I have anything worthwhile to contribute."

May gave Duke a patronizing pat on the shoulder. "Believe me, kid, this is one time you'll be glad you left your dark glasses on and trusted your old guide dog." He shoved. "Now, let's leave."

Duke stumbled but quickly regained his balance. He stopped cold, then backed up and raised himself to his full height. For the first time May realized how much the kid towered over him.

"I'm not going anywhere until you tell me where we're going."

"Tell you what. Let's run now and I'll tell you on the way."

Duke stared blankly.

"Be reasonable, Duke."

"No, *you* be reasonable. If you want to run, I have a right to know where."

May said, "It's my ship."

"But it's my life. I'll bet you don't even know where you're going, do you?" He gave May a piercing stare. May looked at the floor. "You don't, do you? You have no more idea where you're going than I do. You're going to run out into space and hope you get lucky. Just remember you owe Hiro, you owe the Redline Casino, and you owe Duncan, Vonn, and *me*. You might as well head for Sol. You're going to end up there, anyway."

May went red. "Are you coming?"

"No," Duke said fiercely.

"Why not?"

"Why should I? I'm tired of running. I've been doing little else since I got mixed up with you—running to trade and running to make deadlines and running from Hiro. Since it's only a matter of time until we have to stop and fight, I'm going to stay here and get it over with."

May looked eye to eye with Duke. He had to stretch up on his toes to do it, but he felt it was worth the effort. "And just what in the hell do you think you're going to do on Aiaaga 12, farm boy?"

"Maintain some dignity." Duke sneered.

May spun on the balls of his feet and stalked to the ticket gate doors. Halfway there, he turned and glanced back, expecting Duke to be tagging along like a forlorn puppy. Instead, he saw him holding his ground, smiling contentedly. Seeing that May was looking back, he waved as if seeing relatives off on a cruise.

"Write when you get to Sol!"

May bolted out the door.

Duke breathed a sigh of relief, then started to wander the upper lobby in a daze. Now that he had won his independence, he had to figure out what to do with it. In that respect, May had been right. What in the universe would a broker of agricultural commodities do on a heavily industrialized world? With the cast on his arm, he was not even qualified for grunt labor. He had no more idea of what he was going to do than May did with his plans of running away.

He looked around the shuttleport. He was beginning to get stares from security guards and assorted passersby. While only Hiro could connect him with May, he was still nervous about being in such a large place. If he roused too much suspicion and was questioned, the fact might surface that he was a wanted man on Tetros. That information would not be welcome news to the Aiaagan natives, especially if someone tied him to the incident at Malaysia Prime Shipping.

With a sigh, Duke started down the escalator. The late evening crowd was starting to thin, and as the shakes from confronting May died down, it became easier for him to think. He slouched into his coat, moving slowly, trying to think of where he could go from there.

Someone grabbed his shoulder.

He raised his casted arm and spun.

"It'll hurt you more than it hurts me," a voice said.

Duke stopped: "Vonn—"

"Where's your partner?"

Duke shrugged. "I kissed him off. Listen, about the money—"

"Not now. It's more important that we get to him before he leaves. I've got someone who needs his ship."

Duke shook his head. "He's not interested. He's on the chicken run, and he's trying to get his finances—"

"That's exactly why he should hear what I've got to say. He'll have a chance to make a bundle of money by driving a red-hot poker up the *Yueh-sheng*'s ass." He studied the look on Duke's face. "More specifically, the owner of Malaysia Prime Shipping."

Duke raised his casted arm. A finger pointed toward the escalator. "This way."

They rode up to the departure level and headed straight for the ticket gate. Before they arrived there was a commotion at the doors, and two security guards appeared to clear commuters out of the way.

Vonn quickly turned his back on the scene. "Let's wait."

"No," Duke said. He took Vonn by the shoulder and turned him around.

The guards were holding the pneumatic doors open for an unlikely-looking trio that was the source of the disturbance. Two of the men wore the uniform of Malaysia Prime Shipping Security Transport. Manacled between them was a small, struggling man.

It was May.

11

"I'm telling you," May tried to explain, "you're making a huge mistake."

"Hiro will be the judge of that," one of the uniforms said.

"Who is this Hiro you keep referring to? What does he want with me?"

The other uniform smiled. "You'll find out soon enough."

"You can't do this to me!" May shouted. "I'm due to meet my mother on Mattoid 6!"

"If you've never heard of Hiro," the first uniform said, "then why don't you want to meet him?"

"It's not that I don't want to meet him. You're making me miss my flight, and my mother hates for me to be late. She hasn't long to go, is pushing a hundred and thirty. If I don't show up, she'll have a relapse."

"A relapse of what?"

Before May could invent the new information, a young man burst from the men's room, bumping into one of the uniforms. The uniform muscled him into the wall with a free hand, sneering. "Watch it."

The young man threw his arms, cast and all, around the guard. "Help me," he gasped. "You've got to—"

The bathroom door opened again, and a bearded man with a wild look in his eye studied the scene.

"It's him!" The young man locked his arms around the guard.

"Don't get in our way," the wild man warned. He grabbed his target by the waist and started to drag him back into the men's room. "You little bastard, I'll teach you to put my profits up your nose."

The first uniform struggled to get free but could not. The second uniform barked a warning, and May stumbled along behind, working his wrists inside the manacles.

When the first uniform was halfway through the door, the kid broke his grip, spun, and punched the emergency door seal. The door slammed shut and pinned the uniform's arm midway between elbow and manacled wrist.

"Take him, Vonn."

The wild man stepped up and rammed his fist into the uniform's solar plexus—once, twice, three times. Arm still trapped, the uniform slid to the floor, fighting hard to recapture his breath.

The moment he saw the bathroom door close, May jumped on the second uniform's back and shoved him into the wall. The uniform shook off the blow and looked menacingly at his prisoner.

"Duke!" May shouted. "Hurry it up!"

The second uniform started to pull away from the wall, but the door opened, and he fell backward. The chain jerked tight, and May came tumbling after, landing on top with a loud grunt. Duke and Vonn pulled them into the men's room and resealed the door. The second uniform tried to struggle to his feet but became tangled in the chains. Vonn kicked him in the back of the head, and he went down.

Duke rifled the guard's pockets, found a ring of keys, and removed the manacles from May's hands. Then he wrapped the chain around the two unconscious uniforms and locked them up. Meanwhile, Vonn grabbed May by the collar and pinned him to the wall.

"You cheap son of a bitch. Where's my money?"

"I forgot," May stammered. "I honestly, truly—"

Vonn shook him. "You know what my kind likes to do to your kind?" He produced a pistol from his waistband and poked the barrel up May's nose.

"Duke," May said. "Help me."

Duke shrugged. "I told you not to stiff him."

"*Duke—*"

"The man's a psychopath. I can't be responsible for his actions."

Vonn shook him again.

"It's in my briefcase," May said.

"You weren't carrying one," Vonn said through clenched teeth.

"That's because it's probably on the ship by now. The

Malaysia Prime security people took it up when I was arrested.''

Vonn let him go. "Damn."

"It was only a hundred credits. I can probably get it for you."

"Not that," Vonn said. "Your ship."

"It's Hiro's ship now."

"That's the problem," Duke said. "We need the ship, May."

May gave both of them a troubled look. "Wait a minute. You guys need my ship?"

"He's got a job for us," Duke said.

"A pickup and delivery," Vonn explained. "I'm working for someone who needs some merchandise, shall we say, reappropriated.''

May dusted himself off and stared hard at Vonn. "What line of work are you in?"

"Let's just say that I'm fond of trouble."

Duke groaned. "Not a detective."

"A mercenary," Vonn corrected. "An associate and I are in the process of going on a little rescue mission. By virtue of owning a merchant-class stellar vehicle, you're more than welcome to come along."

"What does it involve?" May asked suspiciously.

"Getting back at Hiro," Duke said.

"How?" May demanded.

"You'll get your ship back," Vonn said. "And there's reward money involved. A *lot* of reward money."

"How do we get the ship back?"

Vonn chambered a round in the pistol. "We go up there and take it. Right now."

"Sounds good," May said. "And where do we take it?"

Vonn gestured with his thumb. "Rentor. It's a city half an orbit from here."

"We stay on Aiaaga?" May was outraged.

"That's where our sponsor is."

"Look," May said, closing on the mercenary. "I don't know if you understand this, but we have to leave this planet.

It's going to be crawling with Ryuichi Hiro's *Yueh-sheng* buddies looking for me and my ship.''

''Which is exactly why we have to stay here. When your ship leaves the dock, Hiro's people are all going to go out-system looking for you, and he'll be monitoring the ship regs from surrounding planets. He won't expect you to be on the other side of the planet.''

May, confused, glanced at Duke.

Duke returned a modest look. ''Can I help it if it was a good idea?''

''By the time we're ready to leave, Hiro will have his people scattered all over. We're going to be jumping around so much over the next couple of weeks that they'll never be able to catch up to us. Not until it's too late.''

''Duke—''

''It's our best shot, May. I say we go with it.''

May scratched at the floor with his foot. ''You were right, Duke. It's time we stopped running and started to fight. Count us in.''

''Great,'' the mercenary said. ''Now, in the interest of establishing a good business relationship, why don't you tell me what to call you? Any name will do.''

''I'm Duke. My apologies for not shaking.''

''James May.'' They shook.

''Nice to meet you. My name is Vonn. I hope we live long enough to become friends.''

12

Getting on the *Angel's Luck* proved to be no problem. With the word out that May had been captured, the powers that be at Malaysia Prime sent their security officers back to their normal duties, leaving a pair of second-line guards in charge of the ship.

With that in mind, May tried to board the ship by walking right past them. The older guard was lethargic, but the face of the younger one lit up right away. ''It's you!'' he stammered in disbelief. ''How did you get away?''

May swore and turned to run away but fell in order to allow the guards to catch him. They yanked him off the floor with enthusiastic abandon.

"You boys are just too clever for me," May told them.

The older one shook his head somberly. "You couldn't have gotten into your ship, anyway. They changed the code on the pod bay lock."

May sighed. "I suppose you're going to take me to Mr. Hiro."

The young guard laughed. "I don't know how you got away from two of our best men, but you can bet your life on one thing—we're not going to make that same mistake." He removed a plastic card from his breast pocket and slid it into the lock. "We're going to keep you on the ship until someone can bring a restraint chair."

"That's exactly what I wanted to hear." May tore his arms from their grip and bolted through the door. The guards drew their weapons and gave chase, oblivious to the clatter from behind.

Vonn hit the older one running and knocked him out, sending his weapon spinning down the hall. The younger one saw what was coming and brought his knee up to connect with Duke's stomach. Duke fell with a gasp, and a stray shot from the young guard's weapon blackened the ceiling.

Vonn rolled off the older guard and crouched to pounce on the younger, only to find a weapon pointed at his face.

"Freeze, or I'll burn you down." The young guard had put his back to the wall, putting Duke and Vonn in his line of fire. "You're messing with trained security people here," he taunted.

"Worked the last time," Vonn said sadly.

"Worked this time, too," May said.

The guard turned and saw blue smoke spinning into his face. He wheeled to fire but never got the chance. Vonn's foot connected with his wrist, cracking bones and snapping the weapon in May's direction. The guard gasped, took in a lungful of blue smoke, and settled peacefully to the floor.

Vonn grabbed Duke and pulled him into the ship as May shut off the GasJet and sealed the hatch.

"I have this strange feeling," Duke said. "Hasn't this happened to me before?"

May slapped the kid's face. "You're mixed up. It's the effects of the gas."

"Speak for yourself." Duke held up his right arm. The cast crumbled off.

They pulled him to his feet and headed for the bridge.

"This is where I get sent to the CHARLES for medical attention, right?"

"First we have to get out of here. We'll give you something to hold you over."

Duke managed a weak smile. "Oh, boy. More drugs."

"Wait a minute," Vonn said, looking around the ship. "I'm certified for assists on anything up to a Class L." He looked over at Duke. "I don't mean to steal your thunder, but it's going to be hard for you to work with a broken arm."

May smiled. It was the happiest Duke had seen him in a long time. "He's got a point. Go ahead and have the CHARLES repair your arm."

"You're sure?" Duke asked uncertainly.

"Positive," May urged. "No sense in your making things worse than they already are, right?"

"Right." Vonn nodded in agreement. "See you in a short."

They went to the access shaft and started up the tunnel. Duke gave a painful shrug and wandered to the medical section. The CHARLES was nowhere to be seen, so Duke hit the SUMMON button on the communications pad and waited.

The android soon appeared, shaking his head at Duke's story. He laid him on the medicouch and scanned his arm, clucking his rubber synthate tongue against his anodized aluminum hard palate as he inspected the damage.

"I'm afraid you've jarred the bone out of place," he told Duke. "I'm going to have to reset it and put on a new cast."

"Just put a Warm on it," Duke snapped, the taste of panic rising in his throat. "I'm needed in the bridge."

"You're going to be worthless," the CHARLES told him. "The Warm will hurt until it numbs your arm, and you're going to develop a fever within the hour. Stick around."

"Give me the damn Warm, CHARLES."

The android looked at him blankly. "All right, but you'll be back." He slipped the Warm over Duke's arm and jerked the pin out of the canister.

Duke cursed as the soft vinyl enveloped his arm. The color drained from his face, and he broke out in a sweat. Yellow splotches began to grow from the center of his vision and spread outward until he could see only out of the corners of his eyes.

His consciousness vanished, and he pitched forward. The CHARLES calmly grabbed him by the shoulders and laid him down.

Head clearing, Duke gradually became aware of his change in position. His injured arm was in flames. He leaned up on his good arm and looked over at the CHARLES.

"Told you so," the android said.

Duke cursed. May was right; the CHARLES was in dire need of personality recalibration. The "told you so" was bad enough, but the smile was more than he could handle.

He sat up. "I'm going to the bridge."

"Whatever you think."

Duke hopped off the table, holding himself up with one arm. "CHARLES, do me a favor and turn off that stupid grin." He wiped sweat from his forehead with the back of his hand. "You're making me sick."

The CHARLES's face went alarmingly blank. "You'd better get going if you're going to be of help."

Duke headed straight for the access shaft. He looked up the ladder and leaned against the wall, panting. He fought his throbbing arm and spinning head until a shudder ran through the ship.

"May needs me," he said thinly.

He wavered on the tips of his toes, grabbed the highest rung he could reach, and began to pull up, fitting his trembling legs into one of the lower rungs. He braced himself, gave a weak shove, and rose. He leaned into the ladder, shot out his good arm, and grabbed another rung.

Breathing hard, he lifted one leg, found a rung, and planted a foot on it. Pushing, he boosted up, his other leg searching for somewhere to rest. He put it down on what he thought was a rung and shifted his weight to it. The foot slipped off, and suddenly Duke was falling, his weight jerking hard on the one hand holding him up.

He screamed.

When the echo stopped, he realized that he was still on the ladder, legs dangling off the side. Painfully, he slipped each through a rung, then hung in the shaft, eyes slowly closing.

When he came out of his doze, he felt a prickly sensation as if his entire body had gone to sleep. Duke cursed, wondering what he had done to himself. He put his good arm out and stretched—

He shouted and flailed for the rungs. Then he stopped, realizing that he was not falling headfirst down the tunnel. He was leisurely leaning back, legs still tucked in the rungs of the ladder.

The gravity was off.

Duke relaxed and drifted serenely into the tunnel. The zero gee felt good, and he wondered if it was therapeutic.

Then he rolled, grabbed a rung, and pulled. He smoothly glided up the shaft and into the compartment it serviced, moving slowly enough to stop by bumping gently against the ceiling.

Allowing his feet to drift toward the wall that was now behind him, he kicked, drifting toward the bridge door. He stopped to catch his breath, waiting an extra minute to rest his injured arm. Then he thumbed the access button and entered the bridge.

May and Vonn were hunched over the control console. They were having a terse conversation in a technical language that Duke had yet to understand.

"I can't imagine how you got by," Vonn said between snippets of jargon, "without a copilot and Vasac."

"I managed," May replied.

"Here I am," Duke said, trying to sound enthusiastic.

May and Vonn swiveled in their chairs to look at him.

"What are you doing up here?" May asked sourly.

"I came to help."

"Don't be stupid. Get your arm in a cast."

"I came to help you run the console until you break Vasac with the docking station."

"We broke fifteen minutes ago."

"I can help with the Nav."

May sighed. "Listen, Duke. Vonn is certified. In fact, he could fly this thing alone if he had to. I don't need you." He paused. "I don't need you up here, that is. Now, go back down to medical and have the CHARLES put your arm in a cast."

"Okay," Duke said numbly. He pushed off from the wall and floated to the hatch in one smooth motion.

Later, as the CHARLES built a new shell around his broken arm, he wondered about May's remark. The merchant had been right. Duke was worthless. He had been a burden ever since leaving Tetros, taking a small share of the funds and doing nothing in return. Now that Vonn was on board, he might as well jettison himself.

It was amazing, he thought, how May seemed different all of a sudden. It all seemed tied to the fact that Vonn was a qualified copilot. Was that the way he treated everyone when things were going well? Was that the real reason his wife had left him? Or was he faithful to his crew, as well, looking with disdain upon everyone who hindered or did nothing to help himself and his ship?

May had changed, all right. And Duke was not sure he liked it.

13

Nor did May like it when they arrived at the home of their sponsor in the city of Rentor. Vonn rapped smartly at the door of the StresPlas home, and after a moment a balding man with a thin mustache answered.

"Mr. Vonn," he said, delighted. "So happy to see you."

May stared hard at the mercenary. "You bastard. You've put us right into the fire."

"Don't jump to conclusions, May."

May stabbed his finger at the bald man. "I'm not working for some Ori bastard because—"

"You think I work for the *Yueh-sheng*," the man said.

May looked at him, surprised.

"I feel it only fair to warn you. I *do* in fact work for the *Yueh-sheng*."

The merchant looked at Duke. "Before I say we're leaving—"

"Let's put our prejudices aside," Duke finished. "Let's hear him out."

May nodded and sighed. "Apologies," he said, offering his hand. "I'm James May. You can call my associate Duke."

"Myron Li," the bald man answered, shaking his hand with a powerful grip. "Mr. Vonn, I believe you know."

May nodded politely. "Should we make a scene here, or may we come in?"

Li scratched behind his ear. "Oh, yes. Please, do come in." He led them to the living room, bade them sit, and took their orders for drinks. Once everyone had been served, Li sat with a drink of his own, sipping carefully as he addressed the mercenary.

"So who have you brought to me, Mr. Vonn?"

Vonn drummed his fingers on his glass. "Mr. May and his assistant were having some difficulties with Malaysia Prime Shipping. Something to do with, I believe, a merchant vessel."

Li smiled in interest.

Vonn motioned at May. "Do you want to continue?"

May shrugged. "What's there to tell? I busted my ass for twelve years paying off half of the mortgage on my merchant ship, and Hiro decided to foreclose after I'd had some bad luck. He claimed I made him look bad to his *Yueh-sheng* buddies.''

''Sounds reasonable enough,'' Li said. ''For Ryuichi Hiro.''

''We tried to pay him off, but that fell through. Now we're at the point where we've stolen the ship from him twice and have no real recourse against him.''

''You have stolen the same ship twice from Ryuichi Hiro, Mr. May?'' Li turned and looked at Vonn, very pleased. ''You know how to choose them.''

''Vonn said you had need of a merchant-sized vessel. Something about a pickup and delivery.''

Li took a long swallow of his drink. ''I suppose it really is more of a rescue mission. He scratched at his ear and studied their faces. ''I suppose I should start at the beginning. Have any of you ever heard of the Loevell process?''

There was no response.

''Back to the *very* beginning,'' he sighed. ''Any of you ever hear of the concept of Shared Knowledge?''

Duke perked up. ''Isn't that where you can supposedly learn something that someone else already knew by eating part of their brain?''

Li looked repulsed. ''That's it in a very crude sense. It started several centuries ago on Sol 3. Some scientists experimenting with a small worm called *planaria* discovered that if you taught them to run a simple maze, then fed them to other *planaria*, the second group knew how to run this maze that they'd never seen. This made the scientists think that information was stored in the brain in some biochemical manner.

''They took the idea to rats. They taught some to run a complex maze, to push a certain switch for food, and so on. Then they fed their brains to a second group of rats, and damned if this second group didn't somehow have that knowledge the first time they were exposed to the stimulus.

''This theory was played with for about a century, and by the time they worked up to human beings, using injection instead of ingestion, they hit a snag. The problem was that the learner had to have the same tissue cross match as the donor in order for the information to be successfully transferred. If this wasn't done, the body's defenses would treat the injected information as an intruder and would produce antibodies that would destroy it. It seems that the information took on the form of a complex protein chain that closely resembled the tissue type of the originator. Hence, when you injected the information from a person with one tissue type into the body of someone with another, it had roughly the same effect as injecting type B blood into someone with type A.

"This had everyone stumped until a guy named Loevell came along. He got the idea that if the protein chains were disguised, the body might absorb them. He began to work with enzymes and came up with one he called *Pseudoase*. This stuff clustered around these protein chains and appeared to be ingesting it. Once inside the body, they appeared to be useful in making neurotransmitters, so they ended up in the brain. The enzymes were absorbed by the surrounding tissue with no ill effects, and along with them went the chains of information."

"A sugar coating," Duke said.

"Exactly. About this time, Loevell died. His brain was processed, and the information was injected into one of his colleagues—the acid test, if you will. It wasn't perfect, because the *Pseudoase* tended to digest randomized bits of information. However, the colleague was able to get enough out of the Shared Knowledge to work out the bugs."

"That's a nice story," May said, "but how does all this fit in with the festivities you have planned?"

"Loevell's colleagues have been very busy since then," Li explained. "They've been busy making brain extract, only they prefer to call the finished product 'Essence.' They set up the Essence Corporation and began to ask great thinkers for the rights to their brains—when they were through with them, that is. In the century since the process was perfected, all they've done is process the minds of the great to pass on to the future."

"After all that time they must have quite a collection," Duke said.

Li nodded. "Two hundred phials. Two hundred of the most important minds in recent history, and they're all gone."

Duke sat up. "Gone?"

"Gone. You see, after accumulating all that great brain-power, the Essence Corporation realized that they had a problem. They had no policy to decide if someone should be immediately recycled or saved for later. And if someone was recycled, who should be the recipient? Who should the recipient work for? How should that person use the shared information? Would there be an obligation to the estate of the donor? The Essence Corporation? It became a legal nightmare, so they decided to turn the phials over to a security house for safekeeping until things cooled off. They decided to ship the goods to Council 5 but had the bad judgment of choosing Malaysia Prime to ship it there."

"So it never arrived," May said.

"But not in the way you'd expect. It had all the outward appearances of an act of piracy. Malaysia Prime put the phials onto a freight bus bound for the Council system. It was found drifting in deep space, gutted, about a year later. Essence received a nice insurance settlement, but by that time they realized they had underestimated the value of their product."

"Where are the phials now?" Duke asked.

"In the hands of the *Yueh-sheng*. I imagine the criminal investigators in the lot will go down the nearest drain, and the rest will be held for their own purposes."

May emptied his glass and set it on the table. "So how do we fit into all of this?"

"Let's say that the Essence Corporation wants the phials back very, very badly. All of them—not just selected cuts."

"Reward money," Vonn said. "Not enough to meet the *Yueh-sheng*'s ransom demands, but sufficient to motivate a rescue attempt."

"We won't live long enough to spend it," May said.

"You'll have a virtual guarantee that the *Yueh-sheng* will

not be looking for you in the aftermath,'' Li said. ''First of all, we will be heroes to the rest of the galaxy, and no one, not even the *Yueh-sheng*, would dare murder a hero.''

''Care to put money on that?'' May asked.

''Second, if there is any heat to come from this, it will certainly be directed upon myself. The *Yueh-sheng* rarely messes with outsiders, but they always go after traitors. In fact, they have a rather uncanny knack for tracking us down.''

''That doesn't make me feel any better,'' Duke said.

''As far as monetary compensation, my rough estimate indicates that the share going to you will come to around seventy-five million credits.''

Duke choked on his drink. ''Seventy-five? May, that's enough to—''

''I know,'' May said, not wishing to discuss his financial difficulties. ''It sounds good, Li, but why should I believe you? How do you know where the phials are?''

''You want to know where the stuff is hidden?'' Li asked. ''Cosen 3. They're sitting in a big warehouse. My superiors, it seems, are also having problems deciding what to do with the phials.''

''You're crazy,'' May said. ''Cosen 3 is the *Yueh-sheng* home world. It's a fool's errand.''

''It's the easiest job you'll ever pull in your life. After news of the reward came out, the *Yueh-sheng* started to get nervous about keeping the stuff in a warehouse. They're going to transfer it to a maximum-security life science lab 217 kilometers away.''

''Maximum security, huh?'' May stood and started to pace. ''Well, what does that make the rest of the planet? Some kind of self-service bank?''

''Vonn is to pull a plug to black out radar coverage in a given sector,'' Li said. ''You and Duke land your ship unnoticed and open up the cargo bay. I drive the armored car carrying the phials inside, we gas the guards in the back, take the phials, and get the hell out. That's all there is to it.''

''You're a lunatic, you know that? What makes you think

that you're going to be able to drive an armored car into my ship with no problems?''

"You weren't listening," Li said. "I said I was the driver of the armored car."

May studied Li's face. "*The* driver?"

"Now you know what I do with the *Yueh-sheng.*"

There was stunned silence. Finally, May laughed. "That certainly changes my perspective on this. How did you get into such an enviable position?"

"Like anyone else, I started out in the company and worked my way into a position of trust."

"Why are you all of a sudden wanting to stab them in the back?"

Li looked May in the eye. "What would you believe? Revenge? Passed over for promotion? Moral outrage?" He shook his head. "There's only one truth here, and that is greed. The price is right. There's enough money in this for me to buy a new face, a new identity, a new home. I can disappear and retire."

"What if I don't buy it?"

"There's the door," Li said. "But remember that you have everything to lose."

May and Duke exchanged glances.

"Do I count you in?"

"Tell me about it," Duke said. "One more time. In detail."

"What's there to tell? The phials are currently at Jaxx, a center for processing and cataloging what the *Yueh-sheng* has acquired through one means or another. Since the disposition of the Essence product is up in the air, they have decided to send it to a maximum-security bio lab in case somebody starts getting ideas.

"As driver, my responsibility will be to pull the trigger on the man riding shotgun. May and Duke, your job will be to land your ship in a meadow I have picked out that's about halfway between Jaxx and the center. You'll land undetected because Vonn is going to pull the plug on the radar substation before you land and will leave a bomb that will take it out as we're leaving.

"In the meantime, you'll have the cargo bay standing open. I drive the armored car in, and we flood it with Restcure to take care of the guards inside. We dump them in the meadow, lift off, and hop over to some decent, law-abiding planet and hand over the two hundred Essence phials."

May looked at his young partner. "Duke? Opinion?"

"How badly do you want to get back at Mr. Hiro?" he asked.

"What do *you* think, Duke?"

"This is your fight," Duke said. "I'll respect your opinion, whatever you decide."

"You have a good man there, Mr. May," Myron Li said.

"All right, then," May said firmly. "Let's take him."

"Very good." Li began to gather empty glasses from the table. "Your first order of business is to take Vonn to Cypress 13 and pick up the gentlemen who will be helping us. Duke, you may wish to stay here, in order to rest your arm."

"What friends do you have on Cy 13?" May asked.

Vonn propped his feet up on the table. "The ones who'll be handling the escort."

"Escort," May said suspiciously. "What escort?"

"Standard operating procedure," Li answered. "The *Yueh-sheng* will be giving the armored car a security escort due to the nature of its contents."

"How much of a security escort?" May demanded.

"Two tanks and a helicopter."

"You didn't tell us anything about that," May said angrily.

"It doesn't concern you."

"It sure as hell does if I'm taking my ship down in the middle of a firefight."

"You won't be taking your ship into a firefight," Li reassured him. "It'll be over by the time you get there."

"It had damn well better be."

"Give me a laser carbine," Vonn said, "and I promise you won't have a lick of trouble."

"And what about fuel? I can't get my ship there on good-will."

"I'll foot that part of the bill," Li said. "As of now, you are on my payroll. Just don't get sloppy. I've saved enough to pull this off, but we'll have to be frugal until we can collect the reward."

"And then," Vonn said, "big casino." He took out a large knife and began to clean his fingernails.

May smiled at Duke. "No problem. We know all about frugal, don't we?"

Duke did not answer. He was watching Vonn work the blade across the tips of his fingers, wondering with a certain unease exactly what he had gotten himself into.

14

"Are you sure he's going to show up?" May asked.

"I'm sure. I've never known him to pass up the chance to make money," Vonn replied.

"We don't have much time."

"Quit worrying about it. He's my brother."

May and Vonn sat in the dim light of a run-down bar on Cypress 13, slowly guzzling drinks and waiting on the arrival of a man named Anders.

Before leaving Aiaaga they sent a lase to the Cypress system, an ambiguously worded message that read ANDERS—FOUND A JOB MONEY TO SEND HOME MEET ME AT THE SAME OLD TIME THE SAME OLD PLACE CY 13—VONN. They left minutes after sending it, while Duke remained on Aiaaga to help Li with the administrative end of things and give his arm a chance to heal.

While en route to Cypress, they docked at a colonial trading post to buy weapons with an account plate that Li had given them. Vonn ordered a case of Danteum Gel and picked up four antitank rifles, two cases of shells, assorted camouflage clothing, face black, and a dozen jackets of body armor.

"There are only four men going after the escort," May said. "Why get a dozen?"

"Several reasons," Vonn said. "One, Li's buying. Two, in situations like this, one tends to go through body armor rather quickly. Third, when you're in this business, you always expect to have more people along than you need."

May held up one of the body armor jackets. The material was thick and slippery and would cover a man from neck to crotch. "Why?"

"When you want someone in particular for a job, he's usually in the company of others. For example, I want Anders in on this, but it happens that he's been working with a guy named Alan Jents. So Jents will probably be along for a piece of the action. If someone saves your ass in a firefight, you always try to repay them."

"Interesting."

"Besides," Vonn said coldly, "in this business people tend to get killed."

May shivered and tried to distract himself by looking around the store. It did not help. There were machine guns. Knives. Parachutes. Pistols and revolvers. Flare guns. Ammunition canisters. Hand grenades. Suddenly the whole plan had lost its carnival game aura and was looking grimly real.

With a sigh, he decided to be practical. The sooner they got out of there, the better. "I don't see any laser carbines," he told Vonn.

Vonn put a finger to his lips. "They're under the counter," he whispered, "providing they have one in stock."

They conducted a muted conversation at the checkout counter that resulted in their being given a crate marked WINCHESTER POLYTECHNICS GSXA-12 LASER CARBINE WITH BATTERY PACK. To that they added a case of grenades, paid for their order, and left. They carted it all in a rented truck, unloaded it into the cargo bay, and stashed it in the halls of the *Insh'allah*. Returning the truck, they paid the parking fee at the airfield office and departed once more for Cypress 13.

Arrival found them an hour past their rendezvous time, which grew into two and a half hours by the time they docked and caught a taxi to their meeting place. They flashed their IDs, checked their weapons at the door, and made a slow walk-through to see if Anders had arrived.

"We probably missed him. I'll bet he's already left," May said sourly.

"If he beat us here, he'll still be waiting."

"How do you know?"

"Anders and I go back a long way. He's my—"

"Brother," May said. "I've heard."

"Besides, I know for a fact that the only thing he's ever on time for is a firefight."

When the walk-through produced no results, they took a table and placed orders. After several rounds of watered-down drinks, May was showing more signs of discouragement. "I think your friend must have found a better deal elsewhere."

"Calm yourself. We don't have to be back for eight days."

"I'm not sitting here that long," May complained.

"Have a little faith," Vonn said wearily.

"I don't see why we need all of these other people along to begin with. If Li's driving the armored car, why can't he just drive it away from the escort?"

"The way Li has this set up," Vonn said, "it's going to look like he was a victim along with the other people in the escort. That should alleviate some of the suspicion."

"So your people have to put their necks on the line to take them out."

"The deck is stacked," Vonn continued. "According to Li, the route to the bio center passes through a planetary forest reserve and past a landmark called the Great Cliffs. As the convoy moves around these cliffs, each vehicle will be out of sight of the other for approximately twenty-five seconds."

"That's not much time," May said.

"It's enough. The plan is to put antitank rifles at each end of the curve and a laser in the middle to take out the helicopter. Between Anders and the guy that Li wants to bring in, we should have it covered."

"The more men, the greater the odds of somebody talking," May said.

"The more men the *Yueh-sheng* has to look for, the smaller their odds of finding you," Vonn answered.

"I still don't like it," May grumbled.

"What's wrong?" Vonn taunted. "Afraid of getting your hands dirty?"

"I don't want to spend the rest of my life looking over my shoulder. Anyone who thinks it's worth the money is crazy."

"Watch what you say about my brothers," Vonn snapped.

"The lion sleeps tonight," a voice said from behind.

Vonn smiled. "And hunts in the cool of the morning."

He and May turned to face two lanky figures with drinks in their hands. One sported thick black hair and a scar that ran from ear to chin. The other was a gaunt man with an almost adolescent face. Vonn stood and embraced the man with the scar.

"Anders! Glad you could make it!" He broke with one arm to pump the hand of the other man. "Jents, you old cur. How long has it been?"

Jents flashed his teeth. "Not long enough."

The three of them laughed.

"May, I'd like you to meet a couple of guys I've been in more fights with—on and off the battlefield—than I care to remember. Loren Anders and Alan Jents."

May stood and shook with them. "James May. Nice to meet you." Jents grabbed May's hand as Anders released it.

"Are you going to offer us a seat?" Anders asked.

"Shut up and sit," Vonn urged. "The drinks are on us."

They arranged themselves around the table. "I got a note that said you need the help of some battle-scarred professionals," Anders continued. "What have you got?"

"A hit and run," Vonn said. "Some bad boys stole something that didn't belong to them, and we're going to go take it back."

"Who are the bad boys?" Jents asked, sipping his drink.

"The *Yueh-sheng*."

Anders shivered. "When you said you were going to find something big, you meant it."

"The money had better be worth our while," Jents said. "What about heat distribution?"

"It's an inside job," Vonn explained. "That'll take the pressure off of us."

"But not all of it. What are the details?"

"Some time ago, the *Yueh-sheng* lifted some merchandise that didn't belong to them. What they got was very near and dear to those who owned it and has a great significance to the rest of the galaxy."

"Not the Essence phials," Jents said, clapping his hands. "We're going to be bloody heroes."

"In more ways than one if we're not careful," Anders said. He looked at Vonn. "Is he right?"

"On the nose."

"How's the lift going to work?"

"In a nutshell, our sponsor is going to be driving the armored car that will be carrying the phials when we make our move."

Jents was rubbing his hands. "An inside job. Cakewalk. I love it."

Anders looked piqued at Jents's behavior. "What do we need to take them?"

"I've already got it. Our sponsor's buying the heavy equipment, so all you need are your personal weapons."

"Got them along," Jents said. "Locked and loaded."

"How about manpower?"

"The sponsor says we can do it with three on the ground, but we're shorthanded as far as I'm concerned. I'd like to have at least six men down. May here will be running the ship, and the sponsor will be in the armored car, leaving the three of us to do the work. Ideally I'd like to have three three-man fire teams. Did you bring any stringers?"

"We got stringers." Jents chuckled. "A really winning pair."

"Will you knock it off," Anders snapped. "They pulled us out of a bind, didn't they?"

"Barely." Jents laughed.

Anders sighed. "They got into the business because nobody else would have them. But they're good."

Jents spat. "They're competent at best."

"They're good," Anders insisted. "It's a George and Lenny pair. A small guy does all the thinking and can handle any weapon you put in his hands. The big one can't think to save his life but will give until it hurts. He's stronger than hell."

"They're idiots."

"Let me be the judge of that," Vonn said shortly. "Did you bring them?"

"They're next door grabbing a sandwich. I'll send for them, if you're ready."

Jents snickered.

Anders slapped him on the shoulder. "Since you're so fond of them, go get them."

Jents sobered and headed for the door.

"He's turned into such a jackass," Anders said.

"What's gotten into him?" Vonn asked.

"Ego. He's starting to think that he's the galaxy's gift to combat."

"Same thing happened to Belmont."

"Let's hope he doesn't turn out the same way."

"What happened to Belmont?" May asked.

"He's dead," Vonn said coldly.

15

"Don't take this wrong, but this stuff smells terrible," Duke said.

Li nodded. "I know it does, but you should still try it. It's called the hero's drink. Brewed right here on Aiaaga."

Duke took a sip. He immediately gagged.

"I'm proud of you. You didn't spit it out," Li said.

"What is this stuff supposed to be?" Duke glared at the glass.

"It's supposed to be gin."

"This tastes like somebody drowned a fish in it." Duke shivered. "What's all this business about it being a hero's drink?"

"It was very popular during the Arcolian War," Li explained, "especially with the frontline vacuum fighter pilots. They were supposed to have the best of everything, you see, but by the time the supplies got to their post, all the good stuff had been dickered away by company clerks or appropriated by generals. All that was left was this Arcolian gin, which people thought tasted like shit."

"I won't argue with that."

"Well, the pilots were under such stress that they'd drink about anything, and a whole bunch of them, including Denis Weir, Eric Dickson, and the lovely Leigh Brand, got rather attached to the stuff. It became a symbol of courage then. You weren't really a true vac fighter until you could drink the stuff."

Duke raised the glass to his lips, studied it for a second, then set it down. "Sorry, Li. I'm not that brave."

"It's an acquired taste." Li took a swallow and cringed.

There came a steady knock from the front door of Li's house. "There's our man."

Duke put his glass on a table and opened the door. He was surprised to find himself face to face with a gaudily dressed woman.

She held out her hand for him to shake. "Myron Li?" she asked. "My name is Dawn."

Duke looked back at Li. "I think we've got a problem here."

Li came to the door and smiled. "There's no problem here." He shook the woman's hand. "Myron Li. My young friend is named Duke."

Duke looked back. The woman had been joined by a broad-shouldered, muscular figure of a man.

"Duke, this gentleman is Parnell Sullivan. Par's an old . . . acquaintance."

Duke shook the man's hand. The grip was powerful. "Nice to meet you."

"Duke what?" Sullivan demanded.

Duke glared. "Duke *sir* to you."

Li cringed. Sullivan raised his finger as if in warning, but Dawn reached over to calm him.

"You had it coming, Par. Besides, you have to admire this kid's guts."

Guts indeed, Li thought. Duke was tall, but Sullivan was enormous. The distance from the tip of his shoulder to his spine was the entire width of Duke. He had a hardened face, carried a battle knife on his left hip, and had a shotgun slung across his back. He was not the type of person to antagonize.

"Yeah, he's got guts," he told Dawn. He turned to Duke. "How'd you like to see them, kid?"

Duke looked at Sullivan, his spine tingling. There was something about him that he did not like. "I don't care if you could spit a hole in my chest," he said calmly. "I took a vow that I was going to get respect from the people who work for me."

"And when did you take this vow, little man?"

Duke looked at his watch. "About twenty seconds ago."

"Let's sit down, shall we?" Li said quickly. He led the party into the living room.

"Another thing," Sullivan warned. "We're not working for you. We're working *with* you."

Duke looked at Li. "Do I have to put up with this? Why do you need him?"

Li returned a stern look. "I owe him."

"Really?" Duke said, turning to Dawn. "And what do *you* do?"

Sullivan removed his shotgun and leaned it against the wall. "I ought to take you apart."

"I'll wait for you in hell."

"Duke's had a few too many," Li said. "This gin goes straight to a person's head. Sit down, Duke."

Duke extended his hand to a vacant chair, staring Sullivan down. "Ladies first."

Sullivan absorbed that for a moment. A large smile crept

across his face, and he slapped Duke on the back, nearly pitching him across the room.

"I think I like you," he said. "You have guts, and you know how to use them." He sat and waited for Duke to follow. Duke slowly lowered himself into a chair.

Li looked at Dawn and smiled politely. "If you'll excuse us, we've got business to tend to."

"She's with me," Sullivan said.

"That's obvious," Duke said.

Sullivan started to rise, pointing a finger. "Listen, you . . ."

Dawn put her hand on his shoulder and tried to get him to sit. "Calm down."

"Look, Par," Li said. "What we're walking into won't be easy. I'm not going to jeopardize things by dragging a woman into it."

"I can hold my own," Dawn snapped. "Anytime, anywhere."

"I'm sure you can," Duke smirked, standing.

Sullivan was on his feet. "You little bastard—"

"Duke!" Li said loudly, pushing him toward the kitchen. "Why don't you get us all something to drink?"

"I'm not thirsty."

"Do it."

"Take his advice," Sullivan ordered.

"I'll have a whiskey sour," Dawn said.

Duke quietly surveyed the room. His hand found the back of his neck and brushed across hairs that were standing straight up. "All right," he said.

He turned and hurried into the kitchen, banging glasses on the countertop and slapping ice inside them, spilling liquid as he mixed and stirred.

What was it about that man? Certainly not the size. Duke had learned from countless encounters with classroom bullies not to let a person's size intimidate him, so Sullivan's mass was not a factor.

Wish I could put my finger on it, he thought.

He wiped up the spillage with a rag, then his hand again found the back of his neck. His hairs were still bristled and would not stay down.

16

Inside of a standard week there were ten of them sitting in the house on Aiaaga 12. In spite of Duke's objections, Li had officially recruited Sullivan and Dawn. May and Vonn had returned from the Cypress system with Anders, Jents, and the two stringers who had become known as Winters and Bear.

On seeing them for the first time, May had wondered if Jents's assessment had been right. Bear was short, oily, and no more than a kid—twenty at the oldest. He had a pimply face and tangled hair. He bit his nails constantly, and when he was excited, his speech disintegrated into a soup of random syllables interspersed with exasperated gulps of air.

Winters was a tall, skinny man with an oversized jaw and hydrocephalic skull. His black hair and dark eyes were a contrast against his pale skin, and his nose was large and bent. He was much older than Bear and looked worn. He was given to uneven bursts of emotion and became unruly on occasion, but he would always listen to Bear, provided that Bear could get the words out of his mouth.

"You must owe these guys one hell of a favor," Vonn had said to Anders.

"Looks can be deceiving," he had answered. "They do good work, and I'd trust either one of them in a tight spot."

"How much?"

"More than Jents."

"As long as he trusts them," May had told Vonn, "that's good enough for me."

Facing a crude map that Anders had drawn on a large sheet of cardboard, Li stood with his hands in his pockets.

"Once more," he said, "for luck. It is now 0800 hours

in the city of Jaxx on Cosen 3. The convoy is pulling out of the parking lot. May, where are you?''

"In the *Angel's Luck*, approaching Cosen 3. Everybody is making final checks on the equipment.''

"Sullivan and I are already there,'' Dawn said. "Doing the same thing.''

"0815 hours.''

"Dawn and I leave for the Great Golden Forest,'' Sullivan said.

"I get the *Angel's Luck* ready for geosynchronous orbit over the Great Golden District.''

"0930 hours.''

"We stop at the picnic area and watch the convoy roll by,'' Dawn said. "After it's gone, we jump in the car and head for the Jaxx radar substation. I create a diversion and shut it down for ten minutes.''

"I plant a bomb in the main power line and activate the receiver,'' Sullivan said.

"When I hear the radar beacon stop,'' May said, "I tune into the frequency of the portable beacon that Li's planted in the meadow. Then I've got ten minutes to land the ship.''

"At the end of ten minutes,'' Dawn said, "we put the radar back up and head for the Great Cliffs on a secondary road. We stop at the lake, roll the car in, and carry our weapons two kilometers to our point on the line.''

"Upon landing,'' May said, "I stay with the ship while the others find the van hidden in the meadow and load up. They leave for their points on the curve.''

"If all is on schedule, what time is it?''

"Ten hundred hours,'' Duke said.

Li pointed to the map. "What does this X signify?''

"The sweet spot,'' Anders said. "At the convoy's rate of speed, each vehicle will be out of sight of the other for about thirty seconds. You'll pull out your trusty revolver and put away the guy riding shotgun, then stop the vehicle.''

"I take the laser carbine and take out the helicopter,'' Vonn said.

"We take the front tank," Bear said quietly.

"Sullivan catches his breath and hits the rear tank," Dawn said.

"We plug the Restcure canister into the air circulator on the top of the armored car and gas the guys in back," Vonn said. "We talk like both drivers are dead, and Li stays out of the way. We drag them into the forest, help ourselves to their uniforms, and handcuff them to a tree."

"Why can't we just wait and gas them in the cargo bay?" Alan Jents protested.

"I don't want them coming to and shooting up my ship," May said. "This way we can plant some false leads that they'll take back to their superiors. Besides, I haven't had any Restcure tanks since my last visit to the Vegas system."

"You're begging to be pirated," Jents said.

"What next?" Li interrupted.

"We grab the phials," Vonn said.

"Everyone meets at the armored car when the tank is dead," Winters said.

"Everyone piles in," Sullivan said.

"You drive to the ship," May said. "I have the cargo bay doors open and the engines running."

"I join Mr. May in the bridge," Vonn said. "We turn on our special little transmitter, click the button twice, and the radar station blows up."

"I get to press the button," Winters announced.

"We leave Cosen 3," May said.

"Home free," Duke added.

"Not quite," Li said. "There's still the matter of getting to Council 5, turning the phials over to the Essence Corporation, and collecting the reward."

"Anonymously," Anders said. "Let's not forget that important detail."

"Speak for yourself," Li said. "Me, I want the protection that comes with being a hero." He studied his watch and stretched. "Enough of this. You've all learned your parts well. All that remains is to put them to use in real time. If you'll excuse me now, I must turn in. I'm leaving early in the morning for the Cosen system.''

Winters giggled. ''Just think. This time next month, we'll all be rich.''

''Or dead,'' Alan Jents said.

THREE

"I thought we were supposed to give the Yueh-sheng *a bloody nose."*
"We did," Vonn said. *"And in return they broke both of our legs."*

Li took a long look in the mirror. He had been wearing the uniform for years, but never before had he realized that it did not look right hanging on his small frame. The color made his face pale and his hair too dark. The cap threw a shadow over his eyes, making his mustache look funny, and it rested on his ears, making them stick out.

There were other problems, too. Had he gained weight, or had the shirt shrunk? The collar was too tight. His leathers fit loosely, and it felt as if they were about to pull his trousers down to his ankles. Those same trousers were tight in the crotch in a way he had never noticed before. The socks made his calves itch and sagged around his ankles, and the shoes pinched his toes together.

He held his hands up and watched them tremble. He slapped them together. Leaning into the mirror, he watched beads of perspiration form on his forehead. He dabbed them off with his sleeve and loosened his tie.

"Nervous?"

Li felt his stomach plunge. He steadied himself against the counter.

"Hey, I didn't mean to startle you," the voice said. It was

Carlin, a lumpy-looking kid with bad teeth. "What's wrong with you? You look terrible."

Li shook his head. "I overdid it last night. I was at a party for some guy who was being transferred to Gallegos. We had about a hundred damn farewell toasts."

Carlin adjusted his tie. "I think there's some Leuten's in my locker."

"No, thanks. I'll get sicker if I take something now."

Carlin put his hand on Li's shoulder. The movement made him jump. "If you're feeling sick, I can drive. You can take shotgun and sleep."

Li refused. "Admin'll get upset if we change the schedule."

Carlin agreed. "Pro'bly right." He stretched and checked his watch. "Ten minutes till. Better get going. Don't want to be late, do we?"

Li shook his head. "No. We wouldn't want to do that."

2

Anders finished pulling the oily rag through the metal barrel. "Come in," he said. The door rose, and Duke looked at him from the hatchway. The mercenary held the barrel up to the light and peered inside. "Hello, kid."

"You wanted to see me?" Duke asked.

Anders polished the outside of the barrel with the cloth. "I hear that you're from Tetros 9. Is that true?"

Duke shoved his hands in his pockets. "Yes."

Anders weighed the barrel in his hand. "I don't want to sound superstitious, but I'd like you to be on my fire team. I'm sure May won't mind. It won't take both of you to watch the ship while we're doing our business."

"Superstitious?"

"I just like to have the odds stacked in my favor."

Duke tapped his right arm. "What about this cast? You're sure you want a cripple tagging along?"

Anders scowled. "You're not a cripple. I've finished battles in worse shape than you are now. Besides, we'll give you light duty—driving or carrying equipment.''

Duke shrugged. "Sure. Why not?''

Anders playfully punched Duke in his good arm. "We'll make a merc out of you yet.'' He peered in the barrel again. "Squeaky clean. Nothing looks better than the inside of a gun barrel when it's freshly cleaned. You can see every little detail.'' He laid the barrel on his lap. "How are we doing on time?''

"We're six minutes ahead of schedule.''

"I can tell this is someone else's planning. I never run less than fifteen minutes late.'' He began to click parts together until they resembled a machine gun.

"So I've heard,'' Duke said weakly.

Anders shoved a clip into the weapon, then ejected it. "What's wrong, kid?''

"I'm afraid that I'll be in the way, that I won't be serving any real purpose. I may get killed. It's scary.''

Anders put the weapon down. "It's damn scary. I never get used to it.''

"You? The professional? You're kidding.''

"Happens to the best of us.'' Anders shrugged. "Listen, Duke, nothing's going to take out that feeling you get in your gut when you get ready to pull something. All you can do is find some way to deal with it until the shooting's over. When it is, the high you get makes it all worth it.''

Duke thought it over. "How do you deal with it?''

"Me? I remind myself of why things are going to go right. For example, nothing is going to happen to me as long as you're on my fire team.''

"Why do you keep saying that?''

"You honestly don't know?''

Duke shook his head.

"According to what I've heard, Tetrans are special. See, colonization not only causes the planet to change, it causes the people to change, too.''

"That's grade school biology,'' Duke said. "How does it relate to me?''

"Correct me if I'm wrong, but Tetros 9 was unstable during the colonization years. A lot of sudden volcanic activity, earthquakes, stuff like that. Your ancestors kept getting wiped out by assorted turmoils, but they learned to sense when they were coming. Generations of this bred in an increased awareness of one's environment. If something is wrong, a Tetran is going to notice it before anyone else. The rest of the galaxy passes it off as luck."

"That's it? That's your big superstition?"

"That's it. I'm surprised you haven't noticed it by now. Of course, since you grew up on Tetros, I'm sure you never noticed."

Duke sighed. "That does explain a lot of things that have happened since I've been away." He frowned. "Is that the only reason you want me along?"

"Of course not. Vonn and I need you to carry the tank of Restcure up to the armored car. Vonn's got the laser to deal with, Jents will have the blower unit, and I'll be covering the three of you."

Duke looked around Anders's cabin. When their eyes met again, he said, "Why not? Count me in."

"Welcome aboard," Anders said, shaking Duke's left hand.

3

"What the hell are you doing here?"

Duke picked up the wrench that Jents had dropped. "I'm sorry. Anders wanted me to see if the Restcure canister was ready."

"Next time knock, okay?" He shoved a brass coupler in his pocket. "If I'd dropped the can, we'd all be dead right now."

"It's only Restcure."

Jents sighed and handed the canister to Duke. "It's only Restcure, but it's under a lot of pressure. There'd be shrapnel if it ruptured."

"This thing? Rupture?" Duke batted the release valve with his finger.

Jents leapt to his feet and grabbed the canister. "Are you trying to kill us?"

"But it's only Restcure," Duke protested. "Are you always this nervous before a hit?"

Jents exhaled and handed the canister back. "Have you ever worked with Restcure?"

Duke thought of the GasJet. "Not really."

"All right, then. If I say it's dangerous, then damn it, it's dangerous."

"If it's so dangerous, then how did you get it into the canister without killing yourself?"

Jents glared. "I went into the engine room and bled it off of the master tank. Okay?"

Duke shivered. "Okay. I was just curious."

"Get all the questions out of your system before the hit. I won't stop to tell you what caliber of bullets are being fired at us." He slapped Duke's arm. "And be careful with that canister."

Duke cradled it like a baby. "Trust me," he said, and walked out of Jents's room.

As the door slid shut, Jents said, "No way. No way in hell."

4

Li checked his watch. It was a quarter to nine. They were right on schedule. He gripped the wheel of the armored car a little tighter and watched a road sign crawl by. They were very near the Great Golden Forest. Everything should work out about right.

He felt as if he were being watched and stared at his partner out of the corner of his eye. Carlin leaned against the door, shotgun in his arms, eyes shut. What's the bastard up to? Li thought.

Carlin stirred and put the shotgun down. He looked at Li through gluey eyes and blinked. Li stared back.

"Watch it!" Carlin shouted.

Li looked out the windshield. He yanked the wheel and twisted. The armored car veered to the left, then lurched back into place.

The intercom from the rear compartment crackled. "Watch it, willya? We got hot coffee all over th' damn place!"

Li bit his lip. He had never before known the feelings he had been experiencing since waking that morning. Here he was, a big hero, getting ready to stab his employer in the back, and he was choking.

You'd choke, too, he thought, if you had to wear this shirt. And if you had some mediocre fat bastard staring at you like some damn dead fish.

Li looked at Carlin. Carlin smiled back.

That was it.

Carlin knew. He had to. He was probably an agent from Internal Security who was waiting for the right moment to blow the whistle.

Suddenly Li did not want to be there. He wanted to be anywhere, anywhere else in the galaxy. If he wished hard enough, perhaps his molecules would separate, pass through to another plane, and reassemble somewhere else, somewhere comfortable. It did not happen. He could not concentrate on it. He dripped sweat and felt his hands rattle against the steering wheel.

They snailed past the sign heralding the Great Golden Forest. The picnic grounds were around the next curve, and the first tank was already there. Once Dawn and Sullivan saw the armored car, the wheels would be set in motion, and there would be no turning back. All he had to do was hang on. The rest would work itself out. He wiped the sweat from his face and forehead with his sleeve.

Carlin was staring at him again. Out of the corner of his eye, Li could see him doing it. There was no curiosity, no wonder in the man's face. It was a blank, businesslike stare.

Not yet, Li wished. Hang on . . .

The armored car was on the curve. The picnic area was less than a minute away.

"Li . . ." Carlin said.

Li jumped and gripped the wheel.

"Li?"

"Not yet."

"What?"

"I said not yet! It's not time yet!" Li looked at him, wild-eyed, sweat running from his face. Carlin turned away, shifting his attention to a paper bag at his feet. To Li's horror, he opened it and reached inside.

Damn it, I said not yet!

Carlin looked at him numbly and drew his hand from the sack. A cry broke from Li's throat, and he tore the revolver from its holster and gave a sloppy jerk to the trigger. A vacuum bottle shattered and sprayed hot coffee across the cab, filling the air with a warm, sweet scent. Carlin looked blankly at where the bottle had been. His jaw dropped in shock when he saw that his hand was gone, too.

That jaw went next, going out in a bright red smear. Carlin's head snapped back against the window, making a spider web of cracks. There was a noise that sent a spike of pain into Li's right ear, making him wince. In rage, he fired again. There was another spike of pain, and Carlin slammed into the passenger door, then slumped down.

Suddenly it was quiet. Li's left ear was ringing madly. His right ear ached and was strangely silent. There was an oozing red mass across the cabin from him. The window was intact, holding his first two bullets in a maze of cracked safety glass. The air was heavy with nitrates and hot coffee and blood.

Li stopped the vehicle, jerked the door wide open, and jumped out. He managed three steps before his legs buckled and he fell to his knees.

Then he threw up.

5

Duke stared at his watch.

"What time?" Vonn asked.

"Nine twenty-three."

"They should be hitting the forest soon."

Duke leaned forward in his seat and stared out the window. "I wonder what Li's thinking about right now."

"Probably counting the ways to spend his money," May said.

They laughed.

6

Sullivan was lying flat out across a large boulder. Dawn was standing behind it, hidden from the view of the Jaxx highway.

"Can you still see the convoy?" Dawn asked.

Sullivan looked up from his optoculars. "Yeah," he said flatly. "They've stopped."

"Stopped?" Dawn looked up at her partner. "What happened?"

"I don't know. The armored car skidded to a stop, and Li staggered out and collapsed."

"Is he all right?"

"I don't know." He put the lens back up to his eyes. "He's getting back up now. It looks like the whole damn convoy has stopped. Some men from each tank are going over to the truck."

"And what's Li doing?"

Sullivan did not answer. He watched as Li waved his arms at the tank man and pointed at the vehicle. Then he leaned over, braced his hands against his knees, and thick fluid shot out of his mouth.

"Par, what's going on?"

"He's puking," Sullivan told her. "And he's covering his ear with his hand."

"He's always doing that," Dawn growled. "I mean, what

is everyone else doing? We don't want things to get screwed up this late in the game."

Sullivan grumbled. Through the eyepiece, he saw the tank crews inspecting the cab of the armored car.

"*Par*," Dawn insisted. "What's happening?"

"The tank crew," Sullivan said, shifting on the rock, "has taken a tarpaulin off of the back of the lead tank. They're unfolding it and taking it to the passenger side of the car." The uniformed men crowded around the cab of the vehicle, and he watched them pushing and pulling and crawling inside. "I can't tell what they're doing. I wish to hell I knew what was going on."

"What's Li doing?"

He trained the field of view on the small man. Li was leaning against the lead tank while a man covered his ear with a bandage. Sullivan described the scene.

"Something went wrong," Dawn said. She looked at her watch and shivered. "I wish I knew what that tarp was for."

"It's the man riding shotgun," Sullivan said calmly. "It's got to be." He propped himself on one elbow and looked down at Dawn. "Li's the only one out there in an armored car uniform. The tank crew took something heavy out of the passenger side of the car, wrapped it in the tarp, and tied it to the back of the lead tank. Another crew showed up with a big can of something, and they're wiping out the inside of the car."

Dawn cursed. "He pulled the trigger," she said in disgust. "Why the hell did he do it now?" She stared at Sullivan. "Don't just sit there. Tell me what's going on."

He turned and scanned the situation. "Everyone's going back to their vehicles now. Li's getting back in the armored car."

"I hate this," Dawn said. "I hate not knowing."

Sullivan sat up on the rock and packed the optoculars back into their charging pouch. "They're going," he told Dawn. "Let's get out of here."

She watched as he jumped down from his vantage point. "I don't like this," she told him.

"Nobody said you had to like it," he replied.

Dawn scowled as her partner started down the path to their vehicle. How could he be so nonchalant about what was happening? Didn't it bother him that something was amiss?

"Are you coming or not?" He was smiling, holding his hand out to her. She joined him but kept her arms folded. "What's wrong with you?" he asked.

"I want to know what that old bastard's up to."

"Don't worry about it." Sullivan laughed. "Just some hair-trigger trouble."

"I still don't like it," she insisted.

7

Li sighed in relief. His face cracked and revealed a sly grin. Within seconds he was laughing and pounding on the steering wheel.

"They believed me," he cackled, very much amused. "Those stupid bastards bought it."

8

"Geosynchronous orbit established, Great Golden District," May said.

"How soon do we land?" Duke asked.

May checked the clock on the console. "Could be any time now. All we have to do is wait for the signal."

9

At first Harbeson thought the tapping was the effect of the ozone and the hot smell of the electronic equipment on his brain. He ignored the sound and continued perusing the holodisk of Laragian nudes.

But the sound came again. He looked up from the screen and scanned the room. It was coming in above the humming of the equipment. He checked the alarm net and made other checks, but to no avail. He noted the noise in his log and went back to his three-dimensional entertainment.

There came another sound, a pounding. Harbeson looked around nervously and drew his gun. "Gunther?" he asked in a thin voice.

He cracked the door and looked into the lobby. His partner was nowhere in sight, but on the other side of the main door a woman was peering wistfully through the reinforced window. Scowling in disgust, he holstered his weapon and walked over.

"What do you want?" he demanded.

"In." Her voice sounded metallic through the speaker.

"Sorry. Can't do it."

"Please. I have to use your telecom."

"There's an aid station about five kilometers from here. They have one you can use."

"I can't go that far. I'm on foot."

"I'm sorry. Absolutely no unauthorized personnel are allowed inside."

"My ex is after me, and when he catches me he'll kill me. You've got to let me in."

He sighed. "Sorry. No can do." He turned to leave, and the woman opened her blouse. He stared uncertainly. In his current state, it looked better than anything he had seen on his new holodisk.

"I'll do anything to get to a telecom," she said enticingly. *"Anything."*

Harbeson reached for the code release.

10

Listening to the information coming in over the headset, Vonn cocked his head. "That's it," he said. "The beacon's down."

"Great." May buckled into his seat. "Let's do it."

11

Sullivan placed the bomb on a conduit that ran from the generator to the power supply. Once it blew, the power to the substation would be cut for at least a week. All they needed was ten minutes.

He checked his watch. Dawn had been inside for fifteen minutes. How long was she going to take? She had managed to shut the system down right away, but she was taking her time getting out. The *Angel's Luck* would be down by now. Any longer and he would have to go in and drag her out.

Walking around to the front of the substation, Sullivan looked through the lobby windows. The first guard was leaning against the entrance to the electronics room, listening to the noises coming from the other side of the door. Occasionally he would laugh.

Sullivan could feel his face burn with rage. His initial impulse was to burst in, weapon blazing, and pull Dawn out. He quickly thought better of it. Perhaps the bomb would take care of things. Perhaps it would cause the entire substation to explode, and those miserable guards would die.

That was something to think about.

12

The *Angel's Luck* shuddered. May leaned back in his chair and unbuckled. "We're down," he announced. "A little sloppy, but we're there."

"It's not the smoothest landing I've ever assisted," Vonn said. He tapped one of the gauges and frowned. "Rough on the ship, too. We've lost some clearing agent."

"As long as it hasn't filled the cargo bay," Duke said, leaving the bridge.

"Li didn't pick the best landing sight on the planet," May said. "I'll speak to him before we do this again."

May and Vonn made their way to the cargo hold. The others had already arrived and were going about their business. Anders was going from one crate to another, removing parts, polishing them with a rag, and assembling them. Jents was laying out ammunition belts according to caliber and attaching four grenades to each. Bear was assembling anti-tank rifles and tuning the lase-assist sights with a small screwdriver. Winters happily toted crates from the *Insh'allah* and laid them open on the deck floor.

"Where's Duke?" May asked.

"Sent him looking for the van," Anders replied.

May shook his head. "And who will you send to find Duke?"

"He'll do just fine," Anders snapped. "Give him a chance."

They finished unloading as the van pulled up to the cargo bay doors. All save May changed into camouflage clothing and grip boots. Over those went the body armor, helmets, and Jents's prepared ammo belts. Duke asked why he had to carry a belt and was told that *everyone* carried ammunition. He was also given a pistol and shoulder holster, which made him uneasy.

"I never did like guns," he said, holding the weapon with two fingers.

"Nobody's perfect," Vonn said.

"Look at it this way," Anders suggested. "If you get into a tight spot, somebody is going to think twice about running you in."

Duke gingerly holstered the gun. "I hope it doesn't come to that."

"Don't sweat it," Alan Jents said. "Everything is going to go real smooth. The guards won't give us a bit of trouble."

He winked.

13

Sullivan drove too fast. He could not dodge the potholes and craters on the decaying road, and each time their vehicle hit one, it shuddered.

"What's wrong?" Dawn asked.

"We're behind. Did you have to take both of them?"

"I had no choice. I was with the first one when his partner showed up and wanted a share."

He stared blankly at the road and knuckled the wheel.

"You're jealous, aren't you?"

Sullivan did not answer.

"I told you it was part of this job."

He remained silent.

She stared at him, openmouthed. "You're in love with me, aren't you?"

He winced as the vehicle hit another crater.

"Oh," she said. "I am so sorry."

14

Anders took two pistols in shoulder holsters, a knife in a leg scabbard, and a machine pistol.

Bear took an antitank rifle and lugged a case of ammunition for the same. He shouldered a machine pistol and wore a blade against his leg.

Winters took a machine pistol and wore two belts of grenades across his chest. He held one grenade in his hand and looked at it lovingly.

Jents took a pistol, a knife, and a machine pistol. In one hand he carried the case that held the gas blower.

Duke found a knife and scabbard that attached to his hip. He felt better about it than about the pistol in his armpit. He held Jents's prepared canister and the keys to the van.

Vonn cradled the laser carbine in his arms. He checked the charge on the battery pack, then hoisted it onto his shoulders. Around his waist was his lucky holster and revolver. He plugged the carbine into the backpack and polished the stock with the end of his sleeve.

They had each collected a gas mask and were piling into the van when May called Duke aside and offered him his hand.

"Come back, dammit," he said.

Duke nodded. "I will."

May turned to the van and pointed. "And *you*, Mr. Vonn, get your ass back here in one piece so we can fly out of here."

Vonn gave a mock salute.

Duke kicked the floor of the cargo bay and watched the others pile into the van. Vonn was waving him over, telling him to hurry.

All right, so May doesn't need me, Duke thought. He's baby-sitting the kid. Beyond driving and toting, I'm dead weight. Why should he want me to come back? He started walking to the van. But then, who says I have to come back?

15

"We passed the lake."

Sullivan had not said a word in the last dozen kilometers.

"I said we passed the lake. Aren't you going to stop? We were supposed to ditch the car!"

"Haven't got time," he growled. "It's cold out, and I'm not going to lug a heavy weapon and drag you along in whatever time we have left. If you want to ditch this thing, you can while I'm shooting."

"You're going to risk screwing things up this late in the game?"

He gave her a burning stare. "Whose fault is it that we're behind? Tell me that, Dawn."

That was all he needed to say.

16

Duke took the van out of gear. He looked up at the huge cliffs and the way the road stretched around them and disappeared.

"Here's your stop, Bear."

Bear nodded, and Winters began to babble about blowing things up.

"When you're done," Vonn said, "hurry on over. The quicker we get this over with, the better."

Bear and Winters jumped out of the van and scrambled across the asphalt.

Anders looked at Duke. "Ready?"

"Ready," Duke said weakly.

"Relax, kid. You'll be fine."

There's that word again, Duke thought.

Vonn looked up into the sky, listening. Duke listened, too, and soon he heard what the mercenary's trained ears had already detected. In the distance, he could hear the beating of a helicopter.

17

The car skidded in the dirt and raised a cloud of dust. The door flew open, and Sullivan jumped out, keys in hand. He looked down the road to the intersection with the main highway and saw a tank roll past. He stuck the key in a slot and popped the trunk open.

"That had better be the first tank." He pulled out the ATR and a crate of ammunition and ran toward the intersection.

Dawn slipped out of the car and glanced down the road. The armored car slid into view behind the tank. She sighed in relief and ran after Sullivan.

18

Li felt good, better than he had in weeks. He took deep breaths of air and exhaled very slowly. Be calm, he told himself.

He watched the lead tank start on the curve. It disappeared from view. Then, off to his left, he noticed a cloud of dust hanging in the air. He followed the cloud down to a car. Overhead, the helicopter had slowed and was scrutinizing the situation.

He slapped the steering wheel and cursed.

19

"There they are!" The words slipped from Duke's lips and were almost drowned out by the rumble of the tank as it lumbered by. He looked at his hands. They were shaking.

Jents was giggling. Anders jammed a clip into his weapon and pulled back the bolt. Vonn wiped off the scope on the laser carbine with a cloth.

"Time to earn our keep, boys."

He crawled to the edge of the road as the first tank took the corner. Rolling on his side, Vonn aimed up and watched for the helicopter. His finger trembled on the trigger.

"Where in hell are they?" Jents asked.

"Wait."

There was a roar, and the helicopter barreled around the corner of the cliff much lower than Vonn had anticipated. It swooped within a meter of the road and rose to graze the treetops, blowing dust and leaves into a small storm. Vonn's finger jumped on the trigger, and a beam of light lanced out, striking the cliffs with a sizzle and throwing sparks into the air. The helicopter twisted to face him, and the weapons mounted on the landing rails began to cackle.

"Son of a bitch! They know we're here!"

Vonn got up and ran. A rain of fire followed him into the woods, shattering rocks, spitting up dust, and splintering trees. He leapt behind a boulder and checked the laser's charge as bullets chewed the rock and created a hail of stone chips. From another part of the woods was more gunfire.

"Take the damn thing!" someone shouted. The voice was cut short as the helicopter turned to face the new source of aggression and fired.

He looked up. It was directly above him, hovering and returning fire. He slapped the carbine to speed the charging time. The green light flickered. He adjusted the shot duration down to half a second.

Aiming for the fuel tanks, he squeezed the trigger. A beam of light pierced the undercarriage and sent the helicopter spinning. He cursed and tried to take aim at the wobbling target but could not get a bead on it. In anger he clicked off two more shots. They were both clean misses.

The helicopter stabilized, and a body plunged to the ground. Vonn ducked and cuddled the weapon. The helicopter veered to the right and fired. There were shots from the ground, and more sparks spit from the craft. It wobbled, spun, and charged Vonn again. He jammed the duration back up to five seconds, knowing he would never get it all. He aimed into the front of the cockpit, snapped the trigger, and used the light to draw a line from one side of the vehicle to the other. Through the scope he saw glass melt and the pilot jerk back, taking the severed stick with him. The helicopter began to climb, slipped sideways, then vanished in a ball of flame.

Vonn stood, watching debris fall into the woods. Then he was seized by panic and ran blindly through the trees, screaming for the others. He slammed into Duke.

"Is everyone okay?" Vonn babbled.

"We're fine," Duke assured him. "They got a little closer than I'd have liked, but we're fine."

Jents appeared, screaming and trembling. "You took your sweet fuckin' time about it, didn't you? What the hell were you trying to prove, Vonn?"

Duke pushed him away. "Stop it. We're all alive, aren't we?"

"Maybe," Anders said, appearing from a clump of trees.

"What do you mean by that?"

"Look for yourself." Anders pointed to the highway. "You need to watch those stray shots, Vonn."

Vonn saw the problem immediately. His first shot had undercut a large section of rocks, loosening them and sending them to the pavement.

And in hitting the pavement, they had crushed the front end of the armored car.

20

Bear drew a bead on the tank as it rolled around the curve. He led his target and in doing so found a seam in its armor. Cheap Scalarian tanks, he thought with a smile.

There was a loud thump, and Winters reported a ball of flame rising into the sky. Bear filled his lungs with air, then let half out and held the rest. He lined the cross hairs up with the seam and fluidly squeezed the trigger. The launcher hissed and kicked against his shoulder, and a trail of smoke snaked out and connected with the side of the tank, followed by a metallic bang. Winters shouted with glee.

The sound of grating metal and shouting men flew from the assaulted vehicle, and it wobbled to a halt. Smoke gushed from a newly formed hole in its side. Bear reached down and calmly grabbed a second round. He was lining up the cross hairs again when the top hatch opened and a man tried to climb out, accompanied by great volumes of blue smoke. Winters fired his weapon. An arm lanced out, took the coughing man by the gun belt, and dragged him back in. The hatch slammed shut.

"Good job," Bear shouted.

He returned the cross hairs to the hole in the tank. A face peered through the hole. He smiled and fired.

There was a roar. Flame spat from the hole, and the top hatch popped off and spun into the air like a flipped coin. There was another concussion from the tank.

Bear grabbed his machine pistol and crawled to the road's edge, keeping an eye on where the top hatch had been. Winters scooted up to the edge of the tank and scrambled around the side opposite Bear. He emerged near the back and found the fuel tank. He pointed at the fuel cap and looked at Bear. Bear nodded.

Winters wiggled with excitement as he twisted off the cap and tossed it over his shoulder. It hit the pavement with a clang, and Bear winced. Then he watched as Winters removed his favorite grenade from the belt. Winters stared at it for a moment, kissed it softly, pulled the pin, and dropped it into the tank. He did not move. He put his ear to the opening to hear the splash.

Bear leapt to his feet and screamed. Winters looked over at him, suddenly looked shocked, and then ran, trying to count at the same time.

"One! Two!" he said loudly.

Then he stopped to pick up the fuel cap. Bear screamed again.

"Three!"

He turned to face the tank as it exploded. The turret separated from the body, the carriage collapsed, and all was ablaze. Winters was knocked back four meters and spun to the ground.

Bear was on his feet, screaming and yelling. He ran to Winters and fell to his knees. Winters's face was red with smears of black soot. His eyebrows were singed off, and his clothes were smoldering. Tears dropped from Bear's eyes as he shook him. Winters's face popped into an animated grin. Bear jumped back, heart in his throat.

"Did you see it, John?" Winters exclaimed. "It blowed up just like you said! Wasn't it great? Fire and stuff *everywhere*!"

Bear screamed and shook him again, hands around the big man's throat.

21

Sullivan threw the ammunition canister on a picnic table. The end tank had taken note of the dust raised by the car and had stopped. The hatch had opened, and a man was looking in their direction through optoculars. Sullivan, off to the right of the car, loaded the ATR and took aim.

"He'll see you," Dawn said.

"He's looking at the car, not me."

Through the scope, he saw the man converse with those inside the tank. The man took off the optoculars, shook his head, and went back inside, closing the hatch.

"He's getting away!" Dawn shouted. "Get him!" She

pounded Sullivan's shoulder. He jerked the trigger and sent a charge into the treads of the tank. There was a burst, the treads snapped, and the tank spun helplessly to the left. It stopped, almost facing the car.

Sullivan backhanded Dawn, and she fell away. He snatched up another round and tried to jam it into the weapon. It would not go. He swore and forced it.

The turret of the tank calmly rotated until the main armament faced the car. It slammed out a round that went long and to the left of its target.

Sullivan clicked off the forced charge. Smoke darted out and pointed to a hit above the fuel tank. The charge slammed into the metal and held fast.

"Bear told you not to force the charges," Dawn said bitterly, wiping blood from her lip.

There was a hiss and a roar. They looked back to see the flaming carcass of their automobile fall to the ground. The turret searched for the picnic table.

The next charge slid smoothly into the gun. Sullivan fired. It went in a straight line, intersecting where the turret fit onto the body of the tank. There were reports from inside, and the main armament wilted. The tank bled black smoke. Sullivan threw down the ATR and plucked a grenade from his belt, weaving between trees and rocks. He thought he heard Dawn shout, but there was no time to listen. He jumped down into a ravine and followed it until it came to a culvert that went under the highway. He went up the embankment and out onto the asphalt.

A man was on top of the tank, struggling to get out of the hatch. Sullivan jerked the pin from the grenade and moved to throw. The man, black with soot, spun. Something struck Sullivan's shoulder, and he fell back. The grenade missed badly, striking the pavement and defacing it with a roar. The man in the tank ducked falling asphalt pellets and shot Sullivan again. He took aim for a third shot, but before he could take it, a hole was punched in his chest and he fell back. The pistol fell harmlessly to the ground.

Then the tank exploded.

Dawn returned her weapon to her shoulder bag and ran to Sullivan. By the time she got to him, he was sitting up, right arm against his stomach, blood leaking from his mouth.

"Call a taxi," he said.

"Why don't you ever listen to me?" She pulled a scarf from her bag and wrapped his shoulder. "You're hurt." She burst into tears.

"As long as you're going to cry, I've got one here, too." He moved his right hand to reveal a sticky puncture. "I suppose I should thank you. They say the third time is a charm."

"If I helped you, do you think you could walk?"

"Oh, yes," he said. "And dance, too." He closed his eyes, and his head fell to his chest.

22

Jents led the charge.

He was through the woods and onto the road before the others could stop him. They followed, shouting in protest.

At the edge of the pavement, Duke froze. He stared at the armored car for a split second, then threw himself down, sending the canister spinning.

"Duck!"

Anders went down next, and then Vonn. Jents heard the canister hit the road and turned around, swearing loudly.

"I told you to be careful with—"

Slots on the side of the armored car flipped open, and gun barrels appeared. Bullets raked a path to Jents and danced up his back. He jerked and staggered forward, collapsing face down on the road. Anders returned fire. Duke crawled to Jents and turned him over. A beam of light sank into the car.

"Hold the laser," Anders shouted. "You might get the merchandise."

Vonn shouted at Duke. "How is he?"

"Dead," Duke said, choking.

"Use him for cover," Anders yelled. "We'll retreat."

Duke pulled the machine pistol from Jents's hands and

tried to fire at the armored car. The weapon bucked and wobbled in his hand. Bullets ricocheted from car, cliff, and pavement. Vonn turned and ran for the woods. Shots spat from the slots, the battery pack exploded on his back, and he went down in the trees.

Anders fired. Duke grabbed the blower and canister, then doubled back to where Vonn had fallen. The mercenary was up and had ditched the laser and backpack. His body armor had been burned off, but he seemed none the worse for wear.

"Give me your gun. We've got to bring in Anders." He took the weapon from Duke and laid down suppressing fire from the edge of the woods. Anders came back, alert but bleeding.

"You okay?"

Anders was clutching his right arm. "More or less. I'm glad I'm a southpaw." He stared at the armored car. "I believe we've reached an impasse."

"I don't suppose they'd give us the phials because we're such wonderful people," Vonn said.

"We can't wait all day. Somebody's going to come along and find our little mess, and the last thing they'll think of will be a picnic."

"We've got to keep the guards pinned in the vehicle so we can gas them."

"Great. And how do we deliver it?"

"Bear and Winters," Duke said. He pointed to two figures who had rounded the curve and were casually approaching the stopped vehicle.

"They're walking right into the line of fire," Anders said.

"Give me five minutes," Duke said. "I'll take the gas and go around from the back of the car. All you have to do is keep them from leaving the vehicle."

"I think we can do that," Vonn said.

"Beats trying to be polite about it," Anders said.

Duke set off at a dead run through the woods, stumbling over small stones, bumping into saplings, tree branches tearing at his face and clothes. When he reached the edge of the road, he was driven back by gunfire.

"Don't shoot!" he shouted frantically. "It's Duke!"

"Duke?" Bear asked.

"What's the password?" Winters shouted.

"Password? There is no password!"

"Come on out, Duke," Bear answered. "It's clear."

Duke scrambled out of the woods to meet them.

"Haven't you gotten the phials yet?" Bear asked.

"We hit some snags. Li's dead; so's Jents. The laser's ruined, and Sullivan hasn't shown yet. For all we know, the rear tank could arrive at any second."

"Hell," Bear spat. "I ditched my ATR."

"Let's not worry about that," Duke said. "Let's crack the armored car."

Moving against the cliffs, they made their way to the front end of the vehicle. The boulders had completely flattened the engine housing and the passenger side of the cab. Duke went around the far side and waved his scarf at Vonn and Anders, then turned back to the vehicle.

He looked right into Li's face. The dead man's head was cradled inside a bubble of cracked glass. Duke shook, thinking he had heard Li whisper, but the sound was coming from the top of the rock. Bear was ready to jump down on top of the car's vault.

"Hand me the pumper."

Duke stepped onto the twisted running board and handed him the case. Bear opened it and tossed one end of a hose down to him.

"Got the canister ready?"

"Yeah."

"Great." He tossed down a Krilian wrench. "Get your mask on, then plug the hose into the canister and use this to loosen the safety bolt. Give it about three turns."

"What about the other part?"

"What other part?"

"Isn't there a brass coupler that goes on the top of the canister?"

Bear shook his head. "I don't know what you're talking about. The can and the pumper are all we need."

"But Jents had—"

"Get your gas mask on." Bear turned and repeated the order to Winters, who was on the other side of the rock watching for the second tank.

But Jents had a brass coupler, and he put it in his jacket pocket, Duke thought, putting his mask on.

He fumbled with the hose until it clicked neatly onto the canister. He tugged, and the connection came loose, smacking the faceplate of his mask and startling him. Be careful with that canister, he told himself. Jents said it was dangerous.

He looked into the connector and noticed a small chunk of dirt. He tapped it against the side of the rock. When he looked again, it was gone. This time the connection held fast. Connection. *"I went into the engine room and bled it off of the master tank, okay?"*

He slipped the Krilian wrench over the bolt and pulled. The bolt held. Hold, he thought. Jents must have meant the cargo hold. He probably forgot the Restcure was in the cargo hold.

Duke looked up at Bear and nodded. Bear jumped to the roof of the armored car, landing with a thud. He slipped a tube over the ventilation duct and threw a switch on the pumper. There was a purring sound.

"Now!"

Duke yanked on the wrench. The bolt gave, a little at first, then loosened. It needed one more try.

"Why can't we just wait and gas them in the cargo bay?"
Three turns, right? One.

". . . I haven't had any Restcure tanks since my last visit to the Vegas system."

And Jents had a brass coupler that he put in his pocket. Two.

"It's worthless without Vasac. And since it's optional equipment, I could even take it out and sell it . . ."

Midway through the third twist it came to him.

"Rough on the ship, too. We've lost some of our clearing agent."

"NO!"

He feverishly closed the bolt.

There was a muffled protest from the top of the armored car. Duke screamed a third time, snapped the coupler loose from the canister, and heaved it away. It bounced from the pavement and rolled into the trees.

"Duke!"

He ran past the rock, past Li, past the bullet-scarred body of the car and the vents with the gun barrels sticking out of them. He grabbed the doors to the vault and yanked on them. There was a click from inside, and one door opened.

A man in a brown uniform shoved the barrel of a revolver against the Plexiglas faceplate of Duke's gas mask.

"Duke!" Bear was yelling, drawing back the bolt of his weapon.

Duke waved frantically at the approaching mercenary, signaling for him to stop. Bear stopped and peeked around the corner to assess the situation.

"Oh, no," he said under his breath.

The man's gaze rose out over Duke's head. The revolver fell to the ground, and the man followed, falling on top of his intended victim and knocking him to the ground. A yellow-green fog rolled out from behind him, staying low to the ground and dissipating in the breeze.

"What the hell's going on?" Bear asked.

Panicking, Duke tossed the man off and scrambled to his feet, screaming. He kicked and pounded the side of the car.

Anders, gas mask on, emerged from the woods and took Duke by the shoulders. "What's wrong, kid?"

"It was chlorine gas! Jents bled it off of the clearing agent tank in the engine room."

Anders shook his head. "But the nozzles don't match."

"He had an adapter! I saw it! A little brass coupler! He stuffed it in his pocket and thought I didn't see it!"

Anders led him to Winters, who removed his mask. "I'm sorry it was bad for you, Mr. Duke," the big man said solemnly.

Duke pulled off his mask and looked at Winters. The look he was getting was one of genuine concern. "Thanks."

"That's why Jents died," Winters explained. "Because he did things wrong. That's the way it goes."

Battlefield justice, Duke thought. It was distilled down to the bare essence and had a liberal dose of mysticism, but Winters was right. "I guess it is," he answered.

"Duke!" Anders called. "The gas has cleared, and Vonn's going into the truck. Want to come?"

Duke started toward the truck. Along the way he studied Jents's body, Li, and Anders's arm. "Where's Dawn and Sullivan?"

Anders shrugged.

Duke sighed. "Well, let's get what we paid for."

They walked back, stepping around the bodies that Anders and Bear had piled up. Duke climbed into the vault, and Vonn pushed a large chest toward him.

"The good news," Vonn said, "is that this is it. Here's the bad news."

He turned the chest around and showed Duke a small hole in its side. He stuck his little finger in the opening and drew it out. He rubbed his thumb across the fresh film of liquid. "Some of our shots got in. What do you suppose this was? Some person's lifework? A mathematical computation? A new propulsion system? Maybe it's more than one person mixed together."

Duke studied the hole and the trickle of liquid seeping from it. "Let's get it open. It couldn't have ruined all of them."

Vonn drew his pistol and held it to the lock.

"Wait." Anders handed up the laser carbine. "No sense in risking another bullet."

They moved the chest to the edge of the vault and climbed out. Vonn took the laser.

"Half a second?" he asked.

"More than enough," Anders assured him.

Vonn clicked the trigger. The lock blistered and fell off. Duke fanned away smoke and threw open the lid. Set inside small foam-lined compartments were the phials, each with a name etched on the cap. He lifted out the first tray and checked it.

"This one's okay." He handed it to Vonn, who looked at them in wonder.

"I recognize some of these names," Duke said.

"Answers on test questions?"

Duke nodded. "This one's okay," he said, picking out the second tray.

"History," Anders said.

"Trouble," Duke said. "This layer was hit."

"Who got it?" Vonn asked.

Duke picked out shards of broken glass and labeled caps. "T. Victor."

"Political philosopher, I think."

"T'Chacku."

"She was a mathematician."

The list went on. Sixteen phials had been shattered when the bullet had entered the case.

Duke drew out an intact phial and held it up to the light. The cap was the size of his thumbnail, and the container itself was as long as his hand. Inside was a cloudy liquid that slowly oozed from one end to the other when the bottle was tipped.

"Who's Dickson?"

The words fell on deaf ears. Vonn and Anders were arguing over whether someone was a judge or a philosopher. Duke shouted, and they looked at him.

"Either of you ever hear of someone named Eric Dickson?"

"Reckless Eric Dickson?" Anders asked.

"The pilot?" Vonn asked.

"Why not? He was deserving," Anders said.

"Who's Reckless Eric Dickson?" Duke asked.

"He was a pilot," Vonn explained. "A big hero during the Arcolian War."

"He rewrote the book on ship-to-ship combat," Anders

said. "He was a hotshot and a show-off, but could that boy fly."

Duke closed his hand around the phial.

"Dickson's not in there, is he?" Vonn asked.

Duke shook his head. "He was. Phial's broken."

Anders lowered his head. "What a loss."

Duke slipped the phial into his jacket pocket. "Let's get this stuff put away. We need to get going."

They had started packing the phials back into the crate, when they heard a shout. They turned from their work and looked down the road.

"You can help me anytime," Dawn said.

She had Sullivan in a backpack carry. His arms were draped around her neck, and she carried the burden of his weight on her upper back. Both were soaked with blood.

Winters and Vonn ran to her, took Sullivan's arms, and lifted. Dawn dropped to her knees.

"He's still alive," she said. "We've got to get him down."

They carried him to the armored car and laid him on the pavement. Duke found a blanket in the vault and covered him with it, propping his legs up with the chest.

"Did you get the stuff?" Dawn asked.

Anders nodded.

She looked at the carnage: the dead guards, Li's head encased in shattered glass, Jents lying chewed up in the road, Winters's singes and soot.

"I thought we were supposed to give the *Yueh-sheng* a bloody nose."

"We did," Vonn said. "And in return they broke both of our legs."

"Sullivan won't make it back to the ship if we have to carry him," Duke said, "so I'm going to go back for the van."

"Sounds reasonable," Anders said.

"Here's something else. We know that Li was supposed to return the phials to the Essence Corporation, but we don't know any of the details. You might check his body to see if he's carrying any notes. We're going to need all the help we can get."

"Speaking of help," Bear said quietly, "mind if I escort you?"

Duke smiled. "Let's go."

Bear told Winters to mind Vonn and Anders and jammed a fresh clip into his weapon. Duke nodded, and they set off.

"Where do we start?" Anders asked, looking at the wrecked car.

"How about the door?" Vonn suggested.

It opened a few centimeters and refused to go farther. Investigation showed that the hinges had been mangled in the accident.

"Lase it off?"

"Sure. Why not?"

Vonn picked up the laser and had Winters hold the door open. He gave a half-second burst, and metal bubbled.

"Try it."

The door gave slightly.

"You'll have to lase the whole hinge," Anders said.

"One of you reach in and hold Li. If this door comes off, he'll fall on me."

Anders reached in and grabbed a handful of black hair.

"Got him?" Vonn asked.

"Yeah. Hurry it up. I think I'm going to be sick."

"Don't move. I might lase off one of your fingers."

"Not funny, brother."

Two half seconds later Winters tore the door from the side of the vehicle. Anders slipped in and took Li under the arms, trying gently to lift him out.

"His legs are stuck."

Vonn took the body around the waist. "Let's try a good yank."

Anders went pale. "Let's try getting him out in one piece, okay?"

Vonn surveyed the situation. "The steering column's got him pinned in."

They told Winters to lift up on the steering column while

they pulled. Anders held Li, and Vonn worked his way in with the laser. After several minutes of lifting, shifting, and bursts from the weapon, Li was pulled free. Anders dragged him from the vehicle and laid him on the ground.

"Not something I'd want to do every day," he complained.

A hand grabbed him by the throat and squeezed until he could no longer breathe. He braced himself against the asphalt but slipped. His head was pulled down to Li's face.

Li's eyes jumped open. *"What the hell are you doing?"*

Anders strained back in panic. The hand stopped its grip, and Anders fell back onto the road.

"It's you," Li said, gasping for breath.

Anders was on his feet, quivering. "You're alive!"

Li coughed and winced. "And in pain. What was this business with the boulder?"

"Technical difficulties," Vonn said.

Li held his hands over his chest. "You get the merchandise?"

"Most of it. A few phials were broken."

Li noticed Anders's shoulder. "You're hurt."

"Nobody said it would be easy."

"How'd we come out of it?"

"Jents is dead, Sullivan's wounded, you're screwed up, and Winters got burned. The others are okay."

"Any trouble with the guards?"

"They're dead," Vonn said. "Jents put chlorine in the gas canister."

Li shook his head. "Dammit."

"Duke was pretty upset. He feels responsible for them."

There was a honk from the bend, and the van appeared. It stopped, and Duke jumped out, asking if everything was ready.

"Come here," Vonn said. "Got something to show you."

Duke walked over, slowing when he saw Li lying in the road. Li winked, and Duke fell to his knees, asking a stream of questions.

Vonn grabbed Jents's body by the collar and dragged it to the van. "Let's clear the area. May'll be waiting."

They all jumped to life, loading Sullivan, Li, the phials, and what remained of their weapons. Anders jumped into the front with Duke while the others piled into the back, and they were off.

"We did it, kid," Anders said, voice light and happy.

"At what cost?" Duke asked sullenly.

"What do you mean, at what cost? Casualties are a necessary evil. When you work for someone as corrupt as the *Yueh-sheng*, you've got to be ready to pay the price."

"I'm talking about us," Duke snapped. "I'm talking about Jents and Sullivan and Li."

"Jents was a bastard," Anders said. "If he'd lived through this, I'd have personally killed him for what he did. He had no right to jeopardize the mission like that."

Duke pulled the van off the main road and onto a small dirt track that led to the meadow. "Mission," he spat. "The mission? Is that all you care about? What about the human side of it?"

"I don't expect you to understand," Anders said, "but each of us going in knew the odds. We all knew that this might be our last run. We're used to that fact."

"Well, I'm not!" Duke shouted. He looked at Anders, eyes tearing. "You guys might be killers, but I'm not."

"But you saved Vonn and me," Anders said quietly. "And you would've saved Jents if he hadn't been so stubborn." He leaned back in his seat and closed his eyes. "Try not to think about it. It's all over with."

"No, it's not." Duke's foot stomped the brake, drawing protests from those in the back.

Anders caught himself on the dash. "What's wrong?"

Duke pointed out the window. Parked across the meadow from the *Angel's Luck* were three vans and a helicopter. He cautiously pulled the van forward until he saw a familiar logo stamped on the sides of the vehicles.

"It's Transgalactic Affairs," Duke said in relief. "No

problem. We tell them what we've done for the good of the galaxy and scoot.''

"Don't bet on it," Anders said. "You forget where we are. This branch will be as corrupt as you're likely to see."

Vonn leaned up between them. "Talk nice to them, Duke. We'll have to try and bluff our way out."

Duke stopped ten meters short of the open cargo bay. A uniformed man with a pistol waved.

"Two of them," Anders said. "Side arm and machine pistol."

The uniform came to the driver's door and asked Duke to roll down the window.

"The window's stuck," Duke said loudly.

"I said roll down the window."

"I'm telling you it's stuck."

The officer turned to the man with the machine pistol. "Aim it at the window."

Duke rolled the window down. "I'll never get it back up," he complained.

"What are you doing here?"

Duke pointed to the ship. "Getting ready to go home."

"Then you belong to this craft. What is it doing here?"

"Parking."

"Don't you know vehicular landings on Cosen 3 are prohibited?"

"We had engine trouble."

The officer sighed. "What kind of engine trouble?"

"I don't know," Duke told him. "I barely passed Comprehensive Vasac."

Anders winced. The officer shook his head.

"I think I'd better see some papers."

"Papers?"

"ID papers. Cargo manifests. Ship's reg."

"Oh. Yeah." Duke stuck his hand down in his pocket. He touched the phial and froze.

"Something wrong?"

"Me? Oh, no. Nothing's wrong." He handed the man a set of fake papers that Li had prepared.

The officer examined them, face blank. "What have you got inside the van?"

"Parts," Duke said.

"What kind of parts?"

Duke's stomach sank. "Spaceship parts."

Anders winced again.

"What kind of 'spaceship parts'?" the officer asked sarcastically. "Maybe parts for 'the thing that makes it go'?"

Anders slipped his revolver from under the seat and rested it between himself and Duke. "If you're so smart about spaceships, then why don't you take a peek and tell us what we've got?"

"Perhaps I will," the guard said with a sneer. He slowly walked away.

"Get ready to run this mother into the cargo bay," Anders said.

The officer waved, and two more guards appeared.

"Two more," Anders told Vonn. "Shotgun and another machine pistol." He was answered by metallic clicking.

The guards moved to the back of the van as the officer returned to the window. "I hope you don't mind. We've decided to take a look."

Anders smiled. "Not at all."

There was a shout from behind the van.

"It might help," the officer said, "if you unlocked the rear doors."

"Tell your muscle-bound friends to pull. This van wasn't built yesterday."

The officer turned to shout the directions. As he did, Anders brought up the revolver and shot him in the face. The man went down fast, and there was gunfire from the back of the van.

"Drive!"

Duke jammed the accelerator down, and the van lurched toward the *Angel's Luck*. He took a quick look in the rearview mirror and saw three uniformed bodies hit the ground. The van bumped into the cargo bay, jolting Anders out of his seat and bringing protests from those in back. The rear wheels made the bump, and the van was in, fishtailing toward the *Insh'allah*. Duke slammed on the brakes and twisted the wheel. The van screeched to a halt, the noise of the tires reverberating inside the hold.

Anders was out in a split second, with Duke right behind.

"Everyone okay?"

Vonn rolled out of the back. "Everyone's fine. The guards didn't suspect a thing. I think they believed you."

The three of them ran to the open door. Anders and Vonn stood watch while Duke closed and sealed it.

"How the hell did they find the ship?" Anders asked.

"Maybe," Duke offered, "one of them was from Tetros 9."

"In the long run I'd say it did him more harm than good."

They returned to the van. Bear and Winters had taken Li out, and Dawn was tending to Sullivan. Jents was in the corner, wrapped in a tarpaulin.

"Give your arm a rest," Duke told Anders. "Vonn and I will get Sullivan."

"What about *your* arm?"

Duke tapped the white shell. "I've got a cast. You've got an open wound. Go open the hatch for Winters and Bear."

Anders walked to the hatch and punched in the unlatch code. Nothing happened. He tried it a second time, then a third. He asked Duke what the code was, thinking he had forgotten it. Duke rattled off the numbers, and he tried putting them in. After three more failures he gave up and waited for Duke.

"Problems?"

"I don't have the sequence right or something."

Duke keyed in the numbers. Nothing. He tried again. The code failed, and he slammed his hand against the console. A red light near the top flickered.

"The bulb was loose," he said.

"What does it mean?"

"It means this panel was locked out by someone at one of the control centers."

"Who'd do that?"

"May might have if he knew that Transgalactic Affairs was coming. Or . . ."

"Or what?"

"I don't want to think about it." He turned to Vonn. "How much charge is left on the laser?"

"Not enough to breach the door."

"Not the door. The security panel."

"Why not call May and have him do it?"

"Because I've got one of my feelings."

Anders looked at Vonn, then back at Duke. "You're the boss."

Duke looked at the lot of them, battered and bloody. He ran his hand through his hair. "Lase it."

Vonn walked to the van and produced the weapon. He instructed everyone to stand back and took aim.

"I wouldn't do that if I were you."

They turned to see a man coming out of the *Insh'allah*, clad in the colors of Transgalactic Affairs. He rubbed his hands together.

"If you do," he continued, "you'll be putting yourself in more trouble than you're already in."

"It's our ship," Anders said. "We can lase it if we want."

The man shook his head. "Since my colleague didn't live long enough to do it, I suppose I should give you the news. This vehicle has been seized by the Cosen branch of Transgalactic Affairs."

"What for?" Duke shouted.

"Where do you want me to start, young man? First, it made an illegal landing. Second, if you had been making an emergency landing, you would've called in."

"We tried to call in," Vonn said. "We couldn't raise anybody."

"Which brings me to the third point. One of our substations had a bit of trouble with a woman this morning. She cut their radar for about half an hour. I couldn't help noticing that you have a woman matching her description in your company. And the blatant lack of conscience with which you dispatched our scouting party makes me wonder what you're up to. You wouldn't want to tell me that, would you?"

Bear pulled back the bolt of his weapon and pointed it at the man.

"I wouldn't do that, either."

"What's to stop me?" Bear snarled.

"My surviving colleagues are in the bridge. They might suck out all of the air or turn on the freezing coils. You can do all sorts of clever things with a cargo bay." He looked back at the pleasure craft. "I'm sure you can attest to that."

Duke rubbed his face. "What do you want?"

"The truth."

Duke looked at the others. "Fine. On one condition."

"You're not in much of a position to ask for favors."

"Neither are you. Your friends may freeze us, but you won't live to see it."

"Suppose I call your bluff."

"Then we'll call yours. We can do a lot of damage to you and this ship before the air gets pumped out."

"I don't have to deal with you."

"Do you want the truth or not?"

"I can take it or leave it."

"Fine." Duke turned to Vonn. "Go to the back of the van. When I give the word, take the laser and destroy the merchandise."

Vonn stared in disbelief.

"Do it!"

Vonn slowly took his position.

"Brinksmanship?" The man laughed.

"I'll tell you a truth now. If my man pulls the trigger, we won't have to lay a hand on you. Your fate will be sealed."

"You may have nothing of value in there."

"Oh, but there is. That's a truth, too."

"How do I know you'll give the word?"

"Because I have nothing left to lose."

The man looked at the collection of faces. They were solemn.

"I'm going to count to three," Duke said.

"If you make too big of a request, I'll have to say no."

"I want to see the owner of this ship. He had better still be alive or your life will be as worthless as ours is now."

"He's alive. I'll have him brought—"

"I go to him."

The man licked his lips. "Clear everyone away from that door."

Duke waved his hand. The others moved to the back of the van. The man produced a handset from his pocket and keyed in a string of numbers. The door opened one meter.

"After you," he said.

Duke looked at the others. "If I'm not back in half an hour," he said, "do it."

He got down on his hands and knees and crawled through the opening. He heard the door slide shut, followed by a familiar click. He looked up and, for the second time that day, found himself looking into the barrel of a gun.

23

The guards laughed as they threw Duke on the floor of May's cabin. He got up and dusted himself off as the door slid shut, then wandered through the cabin looking for May. He called his name but got no reply. Despondent, he turned to try and leave when the door to the sleeping cubicle jerked open. He gasped and jumped back.

"You scared me to . . ." He trailed off. Both of May's eyes were black, his lips were split and swollen, and there was a cut over one eye. Duke took him by the shoulders. "What happened to you?"

"I fell down the stairs," May burbled through cyanotic lips. He looked at the rips and bloodstains on Duke's clothes. "You look like you've had a fun morning. Did you make the pickup?"

"Yeah, but there's a problem."

"Go ahead. I have all day. Really."

"I had to use them as a trump card." Duke checked his watch. "If I'm not back in twenty minutes, Vonn's going to destroy them."

May threw his head back. "Son of a bitch! Did you have to do that, Duke?"

"It was the only thing I could think of."

May paled. "Did you tell them what we had?"

"Of course not. All they know is that it might be something valuable."

"Nice to see you're learning. Did you smuggle in a weapon?"

Duke shook his head. "They took my body armor, my knife, everything."

"How many guards on the ship?"

"I don't know."

"Let's make things simpler. How many are outside the door?"

"Two."

"What kind of shape are they in?"

"Better than you and I."

"We'll have to take them from behind, I guess. Are you up to the trick we pulled on the *Saint Vrain*?"

"Can I strangle you this time?"

"I've got my old baton from the Merchant's Academy. It's been in the bottom of my closet for years." He returned to the sleeping cubicle. After a moment he returned with a battered black stick.

"I've got a better idea," Duke said. He cleared his throat. He had to make the coming lie convincing. "Before the firefight, Jents gave me a bottle of stuff to hold for him. When the guards searched me, they took it, even though I told them it was medication for a nervous disorder. I could fake some symptoms."

May shook his head. "I don't like it."

Duke looked at his watch. "Think fast, then. We've seventeen minutes left."

May rubbed his forehead. "When this whole thing is over,

I'm going back to being a scummy little merchant and I'm never going to cross anybody again."

Duke got down on the floor and stared at the ceiling.

"Something wrong?"

"I'm thinking of symptoms. When I start, shout my name and slap me a couple of times."

"Details," May sighed.

Duke began to writhe and shake, curling his arms in and letting them quiver. May shouted and slapped him.

Duke stopped. "Not so hard," he whispered.

"Sorry." May slapped him again and shouted. The door hissed open, and one of the guards lumbered in.

"What's the problem?"

"He's dying," May said, rifling Duke's pockets. "Where the hell's his medication? Did you take his medication?"

The guard turned to the door. "Hey, get in here. The kid's sick."

The second guard trotted in and handed his weapon to the first. "Don't worry," he told May. "I'm a Medtech One." He knelt beside Duke and took his pulse.

"He's got to have his medication, or he'll die."

"He'll be fine," the medtech said. "Keep him from hurting himself and make sure his airway stays open."

"He won't be fine," May shouted. "He needs medication."

The medtech cursed softly. "I told you this was going to happen," he told the other guard. "You shouldn't have taken that stuff from him." He unshouldered a soft bag and opened it. He removed the phial and loaded it into a pressure injector, then pressed it against Duke's neck and pulled the trigger. Duke yelped in pain and stopped shaking.

"What did you do that for?" he said, rubbing his neck.

May swallowed. "Amazing how fast that stuff works, isn't it?" He raised the baton and brought it across the first guard's neck with a two-handed swing. It connected with a loud crack. The guard went down hard.

The medtech looked at May. Duke grabbed him with his good arm and tried to choke him. The medtech gagged and effortlessly tore Duke's hand away, punching him in the side of the head. May jumped him, and they both collapsed on top of Duke. Duke kicked out at something soft, and May grunted.

The medtech and May rolled off, tightly clenched to each other. Duke crawled to May's baton only to find that it was in two pieces. He grabbed the fallen guard's shotgun by the barrel, pulled himself to his feet, and swung it down hard.

There was an explosion.

Duke found himself spinning. There was a heavy smell in his nostrils, and white dust filled the air. His eyes watered, and he was choking. The floor found his head and struck it, and his right arm cried out to his brain in distress. He opened his eyes and saw the room twisting impossibly. May was turning over and over, folding himself in half. Duke closed his eyes against the madness, and then darkness came and swallowed him up.

FOUR

He knew he could make them go away. Not just get away from them but destroy them, blow them all to hell and gone.

It was hot, and when he put his hand out, he felt metal. He moved his head back. It touched metal. His feet kicked out at metal. He looked up and saw metal. A metal box. A small metal box. He was hanging inside a coffin. He wanted to pound and scream and kick his way out but held back.

Outside, he knew, was cold vacuum.

2

Duke was hanging in midair with no physical restraints. He stirred slightly and found that he had a great deal of movement but was kept in place by some sort of silken cocoon. He tried to paw with his right hand but could not move it. Each time he tried, his chest ached. He reached out with his left hand and touched something soft and slick. As far as he could reach, he was surrounded.

He listened for a moment, but there was not much to hear. There was a bass rumble that he did not hear so much as feel against his eardrums. There was a hollow rushing sound that was strangely comforting, and when he stirred, he could hear his cocoon rustle.

He opened his eyes. In the subdued light he could see a blank wall across from him. Off to his right was a hatchway. To his left were two other cocoons, glistening dark blue, attached to floor and ceiling with swivel hooks.

Duke began to feel claustrophobic. He scratched at the inside of the bag, trying to grab and tear with his fingernails, but the fabric was impervious to the abuse. He looked down again and saw a gleaming metal rail running down the side of the bag. He struggled to work his hand out of the facial opening—to no avail. His head and neck were separated from the rest of his body by another layer of silk.

He opened his mouth and forced out air, but all that emerged was a dismal croak. The inside of his throat felt dry and cracked. He started to cough.

The bag next to him stirred and swiveled to face him. A chubby face peered out from an elastic-bound opening. Duke tried another word and coughed.

The bag began to wobble and undo itself, and a small figure emerged, drifting in the air next to the bag. It slowly floated over and peered at his face.

"Duke?"

His answer was a croak.

"Are you awake?"

He opened his mouth, but the figure put a finger over his lips.

"Nod twice if you understand what I'm saying."

Duke gave two vigorous nods.

"Do you know who I am?"

He squinted. The face was blurry, and it was dark in the room, but he could make out features in the shadows: close-cropped jet-black hair, matching mustache, and a battered face.

"Li."

"Just nod."

Duke nodded again.

"Your throat dry? You want some water?"

Nod, nod, nod.

Li moved away, and Duke explored the inside of the bag

with his free hand, discovering another layer of material that
kept his hand above his waist. He sighed and watched as Li
returned with a water bottle.

"I'll bet you're thirsty."

Nod, nod, nod, nod, nod.

Li placed the nozzle in Duke's mouth and squeezed the
bottle. Duke sucked and gulped.

"Take it easy. There's plenty."

Duke slowed down and enjoyed it. It was cool and sweet,
and it smoothed over the cracks and splinters that he had felt
in his throat. He took a mouthful and sloshed it around, then
swallowed.

"More?"

Duke nodded, then proceeded to drink the rest. When it
was gone, he licked his lips. "That's the best meal I've ever
had," he said, testing his voice. "Where are we?"

"The medical section of the *Angel's Luck*. The CHARLES
has been looking after us. You had us worried, kid. You're
the last of the wounded to wake up."

"We got away, then?"

"We had to shoot our way off of Cosen, but we did it."

"Radar station blow?"

"More or less."

"And the phials?"

"Saved them."

Duke yawned. "Everyone made it okay?"

Li looked down. "Get some sleep. You're still exhausted.
It's about 0300, ship time, so you can afford it. We'll unhook
you from the catheters in the morning."

Duke yawned again. "Sounds good to me."

In a moment he was asleep.

3

*He chose to remain in the coffin as long as he could bear
it. He stayed for days, the air becoming so thick and fluid
that he had to fight to breathe. Finally he could endure it no
longer. The vacuum would thin the air, and it would feel nice*

*to have his skin temperature plunge to absolute zero. He put
his hand on the latch to open it but stopped.*

Something was out there.

4

When he woke again, they had removed the tubes and
were waiting for him to wake up. They eased him out of the
bag to let him get used to moving in zero gravity, and then
the conversations began.

"We were worried about you," May said. "You were out
for a long time. We thought it might have something to do
with the drug you were injected with. How much do you
remember about the day of the robbery?"

"How long have I been out?"

"Six days."

Duke rubbed the back of his neck. "I remember Jents
getting killed. I remember the chlorine gas in the Restcure
canister and getting the chest out of the armored car and
going for the van. I remember coming back to find that Li
was still alive."

"What about the trip back to the ship?"

Duke took a water bottle and squeezed liquid into his
mouth. "Oh, yeah. I came back to the ship, and there were
T.A. people all over the place. We got into the cargo bay,
and they locked us in. They took me to May's cabin, and it
goes blank from there."

"Do you remember what they injected into you?"

"Injected?" He thought for a moment, and then his mind
fell upon the phial. *Eric Dickson.* Since they were safe, he
might as well come clean and get the trouble over with.
"Well—"

"Do you remember what Jents gave you before the hit?"

"Jents gave me . . ."

"You said Jents gave you something to hold for him, some
kind of drug. Did he say what it was?"

Jents gave him something? The brass coupler, perhaps?
Something he got injected with?

"If you don't remember, that's understandable," Li said. "You've been through a lot."

"We're trying to corroborate what happened to you with some things we found out about Jents," Vonn said.

"I don't understand."

"We checked his cabin after he died. He had a satchel full of drugs, all kinds of stuff. We couldn't figure out if he was selling or using or both. From the looks of things, it was both."

May nodded. "It fits together. He made you his carrier in case he needed a fix. It would have been safer with you in the rear than with him on the front line."

Duke shook his head. "I don't . . ."

"Don't worry about it," the CHARLES said. "With the injuries you've sustained, your memory will be hazy for a while. Then there's what you were injected with."

Duke took another squirt of water. "Why didn't you check the bottle in the injector?"

May shook his head. "Couldn't. It got smashed during our fight. Then you shot yourself. By the time we got the mess cleared up, we'd thrown the fragments out and couldn't check."

"We did run a blood check," the CHARLES said. "It came out negative. He was probably using some substance that broke down rather easily. Do you remember any dreams or sensations?"

"Nothing," Duke said uneasily.

"Then you were lucky," Li said.

"I guess." He looked down at his right arm. It was encased in a fresh cast and held against his chest with tape and cloth straps. The right side of his chest was also bandaged. "I shot myself?"

"Sort of," May said. "You hit a T.A. man in the head with the butt end of a shotgun. The impact set it off, and you took a few pellets."

"Forty-one to be exact," the CHARLES said. "Your old cast was blown off, and you took some in the arm and chest.

Most of the blast went right under your arm and made a nice scar on the wall of May's cabin.''

"Your Tetran luck rides again," Vonn said.

Tetran luck. Duke looked around. "Where's Anders?"

May lowered his head. "I'm sorry, Duke. Anders didn't make it. Neither did Bear."

"What happened?" Duke cried, outraged. "He was okay. He was up and walking around.''

"After you shot yourself," May said, "I dragged you into my sleeping pod and locked the door. Then I took the med-tech's pouch and machine pistol and headed for the cargo bay.

"It wasn't long before the ship was crawling with troops from Transgalactic Affairs. I played hide and seek and took out two pairs of guards on the way to the cargo bay. I got there two minutes after your deadline.''

Duke paled. "I thought you said the phials were okay."

"They are," Li said. "After you left, they pumped the air out so slowly that nobody realized what was happening. Everyone got confused and passed out.''

"And that's when Bear and Anders . . .''

"Nope," May said. "I caught two guards at the cargo bay doors just as they were going in. As I took them out, the ship's engines kicked on. I guess the guys in the bridge had decided they'd taken enough and were taking the ship to the nearest Port Authority.

"I got a couple of the guys who could still fight—Vonn, Winters, and Bear—and started for the bridge. Anders came around, got his gun, and came with us. We got up to C deck and were headed for an emergency standby when we stepped over a couple of guards that I'd nailed earlier. We took about ten steps, there was this loud noise, and I got something all over my back.'' May took a breath and swallowed hard. "I turned to see what had happened. I looked at Bear, and he's falling right into me.'' He choked. "He didn't have a face left.''

He stopped to regain his composure. "I caught what was left of him, and we fell. Winters was yelling like crazy, push-

ing Vonn to the floor with one hand and tossing grenades
with the other. Luckily, he was forgetting to pull the pins.''

"What about Anders?"

"He turned and greased the guy to the floor," May said.
"Emptied a whole clip on him. We stood around trying to
get Winters to stop blubbering. Then we noticed that Anders
was holding his stomach, looking pale. Vonn asked if he was
going to be all right. Anders said he felt sick, threw up a
whole bunch of blood, and fell dead.''

Duke blinked, letting tears run down his face. "Didn't his
body armor stop the bullets?''

"He didn't have it on," Vonn said. "He took it off so
Dawn could work on his arm.''

"After that," May continued, "an alarm sounded. Winters got scared, and I told him it was the bell for the security
system and that our troubles would be over if I hadn't been
so greedy.''

"I told him our worries were over," Vonn said, "because
the security system was programmed to flood the bridge with
Restcure and put the ship in a holding pattern until control
could be taken by other means. Then he reminded me that
he'd taken out the antipiracy system to open up more space
in the cargo hold. In turn, that made me think of someone
else who was greedy—Jents, with his little brass coupler.

"So I grabbed May, and we ran back to the cargo bay. I
found the portable Restcure canister with the chlorine in it,
and May showed me where the hookups were. I fumbled
with the thing for a minute, and finally May got the idea and
made the hookup. There was more than enough gas left to
do a number on the people in the bridge.''

"Then we had another problem," May said. "The ship
started to crash. There's a direct interface between the security system and the Vasac. Since we had no Vasac, there
was nothing for it to base a holding pattern on. So Vonn and
I got to emergency standby and took control. Then Winters
started yelling about pushing the button. We couldn't figure
out what he was talking about until he pulled this transmitter
out of his pocket. We had him push his little button, the radar

substation blew, and we left. We've been on a mad dash ever since.''

"The ship's running okay?''

"After a few repairs. Transgalactic Affairs left a few surprises for us, and Vonn and I yanked the Vasac out of the *Insh'allah* and installed it in the *Angel's Luck*. It's too small to do everything required by a ship this size, but it does make life easier by helping with navigational plotting. It'll hold out until we can cash in on the phials.''

"When is that?''

"Soon. We're going to stop for fuel at *Garland Outpost*, and Li's going to start the wheels in motion for delivering the goods to the Essence Corporation.''

"Will we be safe there?''

"Hopefully,'' Li said. "The whole purpose in blowing the Jaxx substation was to keep them from getting a tracking vector on us. The *Yueh-sheng* shouldn't even have a guess as to where we are right now.''

"Are we going to bury Anders and Bear there?''

May shook his head. "It's a station like the *Saint Vrain*. We gave them a deep-space burial three days ago. We put them and Jents into the van and blew it out of the cargo bay.''

"Sullivan pulled through, then?''

"He's right over there,'' May said, pointing to the third cocoon. "He's taking to healing in zero gravity rather well. He's obviously done it before.''

"Listen, Duke,'' Vonn said. "Bear and Anders left their belongings behind in their oral wills. There were some things that Anders wanted you to have. I'll bring them to you later if that's all right.''

"Fine,'' Duke said softly. The others left, and the room became silent and dark. Sleep welled up behind his eyes, but he resisted it. The thought that kept pushing it away was one of Anders and what had happened to him because Duke had not been there to protect him.

5

Duke had his hand on the latch and was about to blast himself out into the cool of space when he heard the buzzing. There was something comforting to it, and he took his hand from the latch to find that his coffin now had more size to it. He walked through a spiraling corridor, ears tuned to the noise.

Soon the buzzing became a drone and possessed a warmth that made him want to follow it. Farther down the corridor he became aware that the drone ran in spurts, running on for seconds or minutes, then stopping and starting again. He reached the end of the corridor and looked up to see a tunnel and ladder running up so far that the end was a pinprick of light. The source of the noise was definitely up there. He climbed.

Up the ladder he realized that there were two parts to the drone, two characteristically different sounds that alternated. Farther up, he was able to discern modulation, so the sounds were no longer drones. By the top of the ladder, the sounds were quite human. He had been listening to a muted conversation. When he climbed out of the tunnel, he found that he was wrapped in some kind of fabric, and though he had seen light, all about him was dark.

He was in the medical section. He smiled over finding his way out of the dream and stretched inside the bag. The conversation stopped.

"We'll continue this elsewhere," Dawn whispered. "He's waking up."

"He's dreaming," Sullivan said. "He's had strange dreams ever since the day of the robbery. It has something to do with the drug Jents gave him."

"You're sure he's asleep?" she questioned.

"I promise."

"He'd better be."

"What's wrong with you lately? You're acting like everyone's out to get you."

"It's getting close, that's all," she said, tension in her voice. "I don't want him or anyone else in the way."

Sullivan laughed hoarsely. "Listen to this. Cold-blooded Dawn, not wanting anyone to get in her way."

"And what's wrong with you?" she snapped.

"I've been learning how you really work. How you have to placate your own ego at any cost, even if it means jeopardizing the mission. That's backstabbing the organization, Dawn."

Duke swallowed.

"Yeah?" she challenged. "What about what Li's doing? Isn't he doing the same thing?"

"He's still giving one hundred percent, Dawn. I've got a hell of a lot of respect for every one of these people involved. They're either professional, or they're like Duke and try to act that way. I've got a lot of respect for that kid. I'd like to take him with us."

"He wouldn't leave May."

"I know that. That's why I've got to act in a professional manner when the time comes." Sullivan stirred in his bag. "And that includes taking care of you if you get in the way."

"Who carried you when you'd been shot all to hell, Par?"

"You did, out of some sense of duty, I suppose. It was your job. Had it been any other time, you would have left me to rot. I want you to know that when this job is over, we're splitting up. I've drawn up my request for a new partner."

Dawn was silent. Duke shivered.

"We might have had something," Sullivan said, "but whatever was growing got crushed at the Jaxx substation."

"I had to take both guards."

"Sure you did. You had to do it to satisfy your own ego."

"But I had to!" Dawn sobbed. "You don't understand!"

"I understand. There's a part of you that likes to watch me turn a little green when you do things like that. You like to make sure I'm still hooked. This time your playing screwed up the whole mission. By forgetting to reengage the radar, you got Anders and Bear killed. You nearly got the phials taken away from us. And you almost got me killed. Don't worry your precious little head about things. I'll finish this job and pull you out of the fire, but that'll be it. After we get the payoff, I never want to see you again.''

Dawn sobbed. Duke felt his stomach roll.

"When we dock tomorrow, I'm supposed to meet Bell and discuss the final details. I don't want you along. In fact, you're going to stay on the ship. I'm handling the rest of this on my own. Understand?''

If Dawn answered, it was too soft for Duke to hear.

"Good. Now, get out of here.''

There was rustling as Dawn floated out of the doorway. There was a breeze as the hatch opened and closed, gently rocking Duke's bed.

The motion should have put him to sleep but did not.

6

Duke ran down the corridor after Li and stumbled in the restored gravity. He grabbed a handhold to keep from falling and continued after the short man.

"Li!''

The little man stopped and looked back. "What do you want? You should be getting ready for shore leave.''

"I've got to talk to you.''

"I'm sorry, Duke. I haven't time. I've got a million things to do.''

"But this is important.''

Li stopped and looked at Duke. "You think what I've got to do isn't?''

"No, but . . .''

"Okay, then, let me be. I'll talk to you later.''

Duke stood helplessly as Li walked away.

"But you don't understand . . .''

7

The door to Vonn's cabin opened just as Duke arrived. Vonn stepped out and greeted him as the door slid shut.

"How's it going? Ready for leave?"

"I need to talk to you," Duke said urgently.

Vonn looked at his watch. "I'd love to chat, but I need to go over the I & S manual for the *Insh'allah*. We're going to put in a cheap Vasac and unload it on *Garland*."

Duke tugged at him. "It isn't a chat, Vonn, it's—"

"Sorry, Duke." Vonn shrugged. "I promised I'd do this yesterday. May'll kill me if he finds out I've let it go this long."

"But Vonn . . ."

"We'll have plenty of time to talk on *Garland*. I'll take you around and show you the ropes." He disappeared down the hall.

"By then it'll be too late," Duke muttered.

8

Duke walked down the corridors to the bridge. May would listen. Duke could make him listen.

He walked until he was certain that he was being followed, not by someone but by some*thing*. It was dark and crept like a thick fog that was slowly gaining on him. It was a fear, a fear of the dark, a fear of the unknown, a fear of what lay on the other side of the latched door. A fear of what would happen on *Garland Outpost*.

He suddenly felt its breath on his neck. His skin went prickly, and he screamed and bolted down the hall. He turned the corner to the bridge and collided with Dawn, sending both of them to the floor.

Dawn was up first, cursing and helping him to his feet.

"Sorry," he said sheepishly.

"Sorry I was so short with you," Dawn said. "Is your arm all right?"

"Fine."

"I heard you shout," she said, slowly looking him over. "Are you okay? You look like you've seen a ghost."

Duke swallowed hard. "I'm just . . . just . . ." Make it good, he told himself. "I'm getting restless, that's all. The ship seems to be getting smaller every day. I swear the walls are closing in on me."

Dawn put her hand to his forehead. "No fever. It's probably being in space for so long. May said this was your first year out. It'll happen."

Duke tried to swallow again. He had nothing to do it with. "So I've heard."

"You'll be okay once you do some running around on *Garland*."

Duke nodded.

"You want me to walk you back to the medical section?"

"Well, I wanted to talk to May."

"Sure. If you want. You'd be lucky to get a word in edgewise, though."

Duke looked at her.

"He and Par are talking component specs. May's thinking about upgrading some of the stuff in the bridge, and Par used to work for a brokerage that dealt in ship components, so he knows a lot about it. I was trying to follow what they were saying but was totally lost."

Finding out what May's put in so you'll know when the time comes . . .

She gazed at him with concern. "You're sure you don't want me to walk you back to medical? How about your cabin?"

Duke felt light-headed and queasy. It was all too much. The arm and the dreams and Reckless Eric Dickson sloshing around inside his brain and the prospect of having a knife stuck between his shoulder blades were making him come unhinged. He felt the air escaping from his lungs, and the floor seemed to slide. Dawn caught him before he hit the wall.

"Can you walk?"

Duke twitched his feet. "Yeah."

"I'm taking you to medical."

"Cabin," he said.

"You want to go to your cabin?"

He nodded. "I want to lie down in a bed for a change."

She gave him a smile that he could see straight through. "Of course. You're probably gravity sick. Your cabin it is."

When they arrived, she laid him out on the bed and propped pillows under his legs. She said, "Sleep well," which seemed terribly sardonic to him.

He waited until she was gone and the dizziness had passed, then slowly rose. He listened at the door on the chance that she might be waiting. When he was satisfied she was not, he went to his closet and dug out a metal ammunition canister.

Anders had wanted him to have it. He ran his fingers over the initials painted on the side, then opened the case. He removed the custom-fit body armor and set it aside, going for what was in the bottom of the box. He found what he was after and picked it up, weighing it in his hand. It was heavy and cold. He held it in his left hand, pointing at his image in the mirror, bracing it against the cast on his other arm. He pointed at the mirror until he could hold it still. He practiced squeezing his hand around it the way Anders had shown him. He practiced his breathing. Lungs full. Release half. Squeeze. Breathe.

Tomorrow, when he squeezed, it would not be so easy. The clip would be in, so there would be a catch, a point of resistance. He would have to squeeze past it.

And whomever he pointed it at would burst.

9

"Remember," Li was saying. "We're leaving forty-eight hours from now regardless of where any of you are, so if you plan on being paid when the time comes, be here. Otherwise you'll be broke, vagrant, and stranded at this edge of the galaxy."

The others murmured.

"Are there any questions?" May asked.

"Can we have any fun at all?" Vonn asked. "After the rules you gave us, I'm wondering if it's going to be worth getting off the ship."

Li patted May on the back. "I'm sure that James was a bit

overzealous in making restrictions. I'm certain you all know your limits and will do your best to remain well within them. We're not out of the woods yet."

"If there are no other questions, then your leave has officially started," May said.

The group in the boarding hatch disbanded. Vonn went galloping off to the left, with Winters trailing. Sullivan went to the right.

"Time to do it," May said.

They stepped outside and were closing the hatch when there was a shout from within. May thumbed the hold switch and watched Duke approach the door.

"You almost got locked in," Li said.

"We thought you were going to stay aboard," May put in. "Vonn said you weren't feeling well."

"A little gravity sickness, that's all. I'm over it now." He climbed through the half-open hatch. "You didn't happen to notice which way Sullivan went, did you? I owe him money from poker and thought he might want to spend it here."

May motioned to the right. "*You* played poker with Sullivan?"

Duke nodded. "Lost my shirt, too. He cheats." He started off, vanishing down the length of the hall.

"You know, Li, when this whole thing is over, I'm going to have to take that kid out for a beer and tell him how fine he is."

"Paternal instinct?"

"Fraternal instinct. I used to have to watch his every move, always thought he was going to get in trouble. He's changed so much since this all started."

"For better or worse?"

"A little of both," May said.

Li clapped him on the back. "Do it soon," he said, moving into the corridor. "I'll see you later."

May waved and turned back to the panel. His thumb was over the switch when there was another shout from inside. He cursed under his breath. "I'm never going to get out of here."

"Sorry about that." Dawn smiled at him and stepped off the ship.

10

Away from May and Li, Duke paced the corridor until he caught sight of Sullivan. He slowed to observe him from a distance.

At one point Sullivan stopped and turned, paying careful attention to a video screen in a store window. As he followed, Duke stopped to glance at what had caught Sullivan's eye. It was a display for the day's issue of the station's daily news diskette, *The Garland Garland*. The front page slowly scrolled up the screen. Duke watched numbly until a corner item on page one caught his eye. PHIALS RESCUED? the headline read. Duke froze to the spot.

FROM AN *AIIAAGA HERALD* EXCLUSIVE. INSIDE SOURCES ON COSEN 3 HAVE REPORTED THE OCCURRENCE OF A MAJOR UPHEAVAL WITHIN THE RANKS OF THE *YUEH-SHENG*, APPARENTLY CAUSED BY WHAT RUMOR SAYS TO BE THE DARING DAYLIGHT RAID TO RESCUE THE FAMED SERIES ONE ESSENCE CORPORATION PHIALS.

WHILE DETAILS AT THIS POINT ARE SKETCHY, SPECULATION HAS IT THAT THE RESCUE WAS MADE BY INSIDE SOURCES, PERHAPS INFILTRATED AGENTS OF TRANSGALACTIC AFFAIRS OR MEMBERS OF THE *EBITSUKA*. WHILE THE T.A. HAS ADMITTED THAT AN ATTEMPT TO RESCUE THE PHIALS WAS IN THE WORKS, THEY ARE DENYING ANY CONNECTION WITH (CONTINUED ON SLATE SIX) . . .

Duke fumbled through his pockets for his account plate. He jammed it unceremoniously into the dispenser and was rewarded with a silver pocket-sized disk.

"Who do you think got them phials?" came a voice from behind. Duke jerked his head around to see an elderly man with bright blue eyes staring right back at him.

"Phials?" Duke asked.

"Them Essence phials. I'll bet the *Yueh-sheng* is plenty upset about them little suckers gettin' snatched from right under their noses." He popped a small brown marble into his mouth and sucked on it. "If you ask me, I'll bet you it was the *Ebitsuka*. Be a nice political move on their part, and it'd keep Transgalactic Affairs off their back. Even the T.A. is a little afraid of the *Yueh-sheng*."

Duke swallowed. That was the last thing he wanted to hear at that point. He frowned. "What are you talking about?"

"You know. The Essence phials. The little tubes of brains that the *Yueh-sheng* swiped a while back ago."

Duke shook his head.

"Where you been? Sol? Everybody knows about them." The man motioned to the disk in Duke's hand. "Don't you do any readin'?"

Duke flipped the disk like a coin and snatched it out of the air. "Who reads the news?" he said snidely. "All I read is the sports and the holofunnies."

He turned and walked down the hall, watching for Sullivan. He caught him going into the Hilton. Keeping a close eye on his prey, Duke cautiously strolled into the lobby and sat down at a disk scanner. He slipped in the diskette and began to read the latest news.

It was uneventful for a long time. Eventually Sullivan appeared from one of the elevators and walked to the front desk. He talked with the clerk, tipped her with a credit chip, and stepped into a telecom booth.

Duke stood and crossed the lobby to look at some package vacation posters. He circled around and ended up looking over Sullivan's shoulder as he sat in the booth. He could not make out the number that had been called, but there was a face on the green cathode tube that he committed to memory.

The face blinked out, and Sullivan was out of the booth. Duke spun and retreated to the tour posters, submerging himself in the copy about the wonders of the Disney system. He turned back in time to see Sullivan walk out the main door.

He tailed Sullivan to a small bar squeezed between a delicatessen and a sexual aids shop along one of the seedier corridors of the outpost. Sullivan tipped the bartender and was given a table at the rear. Duke wandered through the bar until he found a table with a good view of his target, then sat and ordered a beer. He drank it slowly, not wanting to get too relaxed.

As he drained his glass, a stocky blond man walked in. Duke squinted and tried to imagine him with a green tint. It was the man whom Sullivan had called. He met with the bartender, tipped him, and was directed to Sullivan's table.

One-third of the way into his second beer, Duke realized that he had been slouching in the traditional drinker's pose, staring into his beer instead of watching his prey. He looked back at the table to see Sullivan sitting alone, sipping a drink. He went pale and shook, quickly scanning the bar. He saw the blond wobble out the door. Duke threw a couple of credit chips on the table and left.

At a T intersection, the man made an unsteady turn to a dead end cluttered with rest rooms and telecom booths. He stopped and stared at the choice of doors, then pulled an account plate from his pocket and slid into a telecom booth.

Duke looked carefully at the men's room door. That was the place.

He went inside and took the first stall. Sitting down, he pulled his pants leg up and removed the pistol from the ankle holster. The silencer appeared from a jacket pocket and was screwed onto the barrel. A clip appeared from the other jacket pocket and slid into place, and a round was pumped into the chamber.

All he had to do was wait. He hoped the blond would be carrying evidence with which he could confront Sullivan. He needed something to show the others when he told them what he had had to do.

Duke sighed. His target was taking his time with the call. Finally the main door squeaked, and he heard footsteps. He got up from the seat, braced the barrel of the pistol across his cast, and inched the stall door open, starting to aim.

A hand grabbed the gun by the barrel and jerked it away. Another caught his upper arm and pulled him out of the stall, slamming him into the opposite wall. A body hit his chest, pinning him.

"What the hell do you think you're doing?"

It was Li.

"You wouldn't listen to me."

Li pushed Duke back into the stall, closing the door behind them. "Make it quick. We haven't much time."

"You know when I spent all that time in the medical section?"

"Get to the point, Duke."

"Dawn and Sullivan have sold us out. They're working for somebody else, maybe Transgalactic Affairs. They're going to kill us and take the phials."

"They're not from T.A., I can promise you that."

"What?"

"They're working for the *Ebitsuka*. Heard of them?"

"Only recently."

"They're dedicated to fighting organized crime, especially the *Yueh-sheng*. The problem is, centuries of fighting crime has made their own methods criminal. Dawn and Sullivan both work for them."

"When did you find this out?"

"I knew it when I hired them."

"You *what*?"

"Listen, Duke, I'm doing all I can to take the heat away from us. Some of that entails putting it onto someone else. Being so close to Cosen, Aiaaga has a lot of people from the *Ebitsuka* hanging around, trying to infiltrate and move in on *Yueh-sheng* operations."

"You son of a bitch," Duke said, astonished. "You set them up. You're going to make it look like the *Ebitsuka* hit the *Yueh-sheng*."

"Wonderful plan, no?" Li smiled wickedly. "Now, would you mind telling me what you're doing with this gun?"

"Sullivan met this blond guy—"

"I know. He's with the *Ebitsuka* here on *Garland*."

"You knew all this?"

"I've been watching them. I've been watching you, too. You have a thing or two to learn about surveillance." He waved the weapon. "Were you going to use this?"

"I had planned to."

Li shook his head. "Wrong. We need to do a little disruption first." He handed the pistol back to Duke. "We're going back in the bar. I'll sit across from Sullivan, then you come and sit beside him when the blond comes in here. You jam your gun in Sullivan's ribs and we'll take a quick little walk."

"Where to?"

"There's a vacuum disposal chute right down the hall. He's going to take a little ride."

Duke swallowed and nodded.

"If he makes one wrong move at any time, you pull the trigger on him. There's a lot of noise in the bar, and with that nice toy you've got, nobody'll hear a thing. We'll carry him out on our shoulders like he's drunk. You think you can do that?"

"I've been ready to kill him for days, Li."

"Excellent. After Sullivan's been taken care of, we go back to the bar. When the blond comes back and sees Sullivan isn't there, he's going to go straight to the man in charge." Li pulled his coat open to reveal his revolver. "That's when we dance. We waste the blond and whoever he's the mouthpiece for and do a quick ransack of wherever he's staying. Then we get out. I'll make it look like a *Yueh-sheng* job."

"What about Dawn?"

"She's ruined. When the *Ebitsuka* finds out that their main man here is dead, it's got to fall on somebody. Chances are, Sullivan's already made noise to his superiors about her."

"How do you know all of this?"

"Sullivan and Dawn have been at each other's throats since the day of the hit. Sullivan even complained to me about her unprofessional conduct. He didn't give me the entire story, but I supplemented it with a couple of good guesses. You ready?"

"As I'll ever be."

Li walked out of the men's room. Duke tried to slip the pistol into his jacket pocket. With the added length of the silencer, it did not fit. He unscrewed it and put it in his other pocket. He could always reattach it under the table in the bar.

He sat on the stool and waited, drumming his fingers on the wall. He noticed the heavy smell of disinfectant and the sound of leaky plumbing echoing in the tiled room. The door squeaked open. Duke froze and listened. There was a belch, and the door closed. A slow, uncoordinated shuffling went past the stall in which Duke sat. Through a crack in the door, he saw the blond stagger by. The end stall opened, and the sound of retching graced the air. Duke flushed the toilet and walked out.

Hand on his gun, he walked back into the bar. Li was sitting across from Sullivan, weeding through the debris on the table. Sullivan was staring into the tall glass before him. Duke pasted a smile on his face and slid in next to him.

"Sullivan, old boy. You look down."

Sullivan did not move.

"You really should be more careful about what you say around your roommate. Some of us aren't always asleep."

Li shook his head. "Save it. He's not hearing you."

Duke smirked. "Dead drunk."

"Just dead."

Duke looked up. "The blond?"

Li shook his head. *"Yueh-sheng."*

Duke felt a knot form in his stomach. "A routine assassination between rivals?"

Li looked pale. "Afraid not. If you'll look at the base of his skull where it attaches to the neck, you'll find a small hole. He was shot there with one of the *Yueh-sheng*'s special bullets. The skull is intact, but inside the brain is like uncooked scrambled eggs. That's a special kind of hit called a Warning Sign."

"I don't think I like the sound of that."

"It's saved for the ranks of the *Yueh-sheng* who have fallen from grace. You leave a couple of friends lying around with

Warning Signs, and a guy knows his turn is coming. And his turn is unpleasant, indeed.''

Duke swallowed. "The future doesn't look too bright, does it?''

"It might be a good idea if we left this place. The sooner the better.'' Li stuffed ink-laden napkins in his pocket.

"We need to find Vonn and Winters," Duke said.

Li swore. "They could be anywhere.''

"We can't leave without them," Duke protested.

"You're right. We don't dare leave them. They could lead the *Yueh-sheng* right to us. Let's give it our best.''

11

It seemed futile.

They ran as much as they could, covering bars, checking hotels, going by name and description. At times the information came slowly and mild threats had to be made in order to find out where Winters and Vonn were not.

Li kept looking at his watch. "I don't want to be here much longer.''

"We can't leave them," Duke insisted.

"We both know Vonn is capable of fending for himself.''

"But he's got Winters in tow. That's going to be a burden.''

"Providing they're still alive." Li sighed. "All right. Let's give it another few minutes. Then we have got to leave.''

"Agreed.''

They checked every hotel they could find and made their way through *Garland Outpost* until they found themselves in one of the most elegant sections of the station.

"Hold it," Li said. "Look where we are.''

Duke looked in both directions at the hotels, restaurants, and gift shops.

"This is the expensive part of town. Vonn's not going to be here," Li explained.

Duke sighed. "Why do I have the feeling you're right?''

They turned to leave, when Duke stopped and cocked his head.

"What's wrong?" Li asked.

"I hear something."

Li tried to listen but heard nothing. Duke turned back, listening as he walked. Li followed, not sure what to listen for. Finally something pricked his ears.

"Somebody's crying," he said.

They followed the sobbing until they found Winters wandering aimlessly down the corridor. Duke ran to him. "What's the matter?"

"Mr. Vonn locked me out of our room."

"He what?"

"He gave me money to go and play games and said that he was going to go to a bar. I got tired and walked back to the room. I tried the key, but he's fixed it so it don't work."

Li cursed. "Did you talk to him?"

"Yeah. He gave me money to play games with and—"

"No, no. I mean when he locked you out of the room."

"No."

"Did you hear any noise at all?"

Winters shook his head.

Li looked at Duke. "Not him, too."

"Take us there, Winters. We'll get you in."

Winters turned to go. "It's this way."

They only half ran behind Winters's slow trot. They passed several posh establishments, going deeper into expensive territory. They kept asking Winters where it was. He merely kept up the slow pace. Finally they approached the Galaxy House.

"That's the one," Winters said. "They wanted money from me to get in until I showed them the key."

"Which room?"

Winters stopped and fished out his key. He squinted. "One nine one nine."

"Meet us inside." Duke and Li made a mad dash for the door.

Winters dangled the key at them. "They'll charge you money!"

The uniformed man at the door smiled and held out his hand. "That'll be twenty-five credits, please."

Duke rammed him with his shoulder and bolted through the door.

Li paused. "Winters, go back to the ship. *Right now.*" He vanished into the hotel. Winters screwed up his face and started to cry.

Duke and Li ran across the lobby and were intercepted by a large burly guard. Li broke to the right, and Duke to the left. The guard weaved and lunged for Duke, who side-stepped him. The guard made a fist and swung.

Duke dodged again, and the guard went off balance. He gritted his teeth and swung the casted arm down on the falling man's head. There was a thump. The guard hit the floor and stayed down. Pain ripped through Duke's arm. He was very surprised to see the cast intact.

Now in the lead, Li was met by a smaller man. He tucked his head and barreled into the man's stomach. Both went down. Duke caught up and pulled Li to his feet. They made for the elevator, where Duke stopped and rang for it.

"We don't have time for that!" Li yelped.

"I know." The door slid open, and Duke reached inside, pushing buttons at random. "Now they'll have trouble finding us. We'll have time to find the room."

"I already know where it is. This floor, ninth wing, nine-teenth room. That's the nice thing about Galaxy Houses—they're easy to find your way around."

They located the room, stopped, and rang the buzzer. They waited for a moment and then rang again. Li cursed a blue streak, pounding on the door and shouting for Vonn.

"Maybe he's got the soundproofing on," Duke said. "We should have gotten Winters's key."

"It wouldn't have done us any good. He said he was locked out. Find a security guard."

"That should be easy. The place is probably crawling with them by now." Duke drew his pistol. "Back in a second."

He ran the maze of hallways until he found a guard, back turned to him, occupied with talking into a portable radio. Duke waited until he finished talking, then pushed the barrel of his gun into the man's ear.

"Drop it."

The radio bounced off the plush carpet. Duke kicked it down the hall.

"Now the weapon."

The dart gun went the way of the radio.

"Do you have the override key to the rooms on this level?"

The guard shook his head.

"Don't give me that. Where is it?" He cocked the gun. The guard produced a ring of keys. Duke grabbed the guard's hand and pinned it up between his shoulders. "This way, please."

He guided the guard back to 1919. Li was nowhere to be seen. Duke called for him, and he appeared from down the hall.

"Sorry. All I saw was the guard."

Duke shoved the guard into the door. "Open it."

"I need an authorization."

Duke banged him against the wall. "You want authorization? I'll give it to you." He pressed the pistol under the guard's chin. "We've got a friend in there whose life is in danger. He may already be dead. If you don't open this door, you'll know where he is before we will."

The guard swallowed. "I can't do it this way."

Duke took him by the collar and turned him to face the door. "Thirty seconds."

The guard dutifully bent over the lock and worked it with the key.

Duke handed the pistol to Li. "Cover me."

He grabbed the guard by the neck. There was a click, and the door opened. Duke shoved the guard, who stumbled wildly into the room and slammed into a bureau. Duke dived to the foot of the bed, and Li, a weapon in each hand, darted in and hit the door seal with his elbow.

A woman screamed.

Vonn was up in a split second, machine pistol cocked and waving around the room. The woman sharing his bed shrieked and slid under the covers. Li rolled into a corner and aimed at her,

"What the hell is this?" Vonn demanded.

Duke was on his feet. "You're alive!"

"I'm fine," Vonn said sourly. "I'd be a lot better if you guys hadn't come in here like gangbusters. Can't a man have a little time to himself?"

Li waved Duke's gun. "Who's the woman?"

Vonn lowered his weapon and laughed. "Roz? You came to save me from Roz? I'm afraid you're too late."

"Where's she from?" Duke asked.

"She lives here on *Garland*. I met her at a club."

"Did she pick you up?"

Roz peeked out from under the covers. "What's going on?"

"A very unfunny practical joke," Vonn told her.

"Unfunny is right," Duke said. "Sullivan's dead. The rest of us will follow suit if we stay here."

Li held his aim on the woman. "Did she pick you up, Vonn?"

"This isn't funny anymore. Come on, guys."

"Answer the question."

"I picked her up."

Li sighed and lowered the guns. "That's all we needed to know."

"Would you mind telling me what's going on?"

"The *Yueh-sheng* has found us. The place is probably crawling with their operatives by now. One of them put a bullet into Sullivan's head."

Vonn stared at them in disbelief. "How did they find us here?"

"Good question," Duke said. "We're safe as long as we keep moving."

Li gathered Vonn's clothes from the floor and tossed them into his lap. "I really hate to break this up, but we're leaving as soon as you're dressed."

Vonn complacently began to pull on his shirt. Roz pulled the sheet loose from the bed and wrapped herself up in it.

"What about me?"

"I'm sorry. We've got to go. You heard what my friends said."

"Yeah, I did. What is this about being found by the *Yueh-sheng*? You guys pull something? How come you have all these guns?"

"We're special agents," Duke said. "We've got some information on drug-smuggling operations here on *Garland*, and the *Yueh-sheng* would do anything to keep us from turning it over to Port Authority."

"So you run away?"

"The information has to be turned over to Transgalactic Affairs before Port Authority gets it. They like to lend a hand to local agencies in matters like this."

Roz paced the room, gathering her clothing. "Does this have something to do with those little bottles of stuff?"

"No," Li said emphatically.

Roz pointed at Vonn. "I have to hear it from him."

Vonn stared at her.

"Well?"

"Yes," Vonn said. "It does."

Li threw his revolver on the bed. "Son of a bitch!"

Roz pointed at him. "Watch your language. I don't like it."

Li sullenly held the pistol out for Duke. "Take it," he said, "before I use it."

"You guys have some guts, you know that?" Roz said. "I wish I'd been there to see you do it. I'll bet that was something." She slipped her pants on under the sheet. Duke sat on the bed and held his head in his hands.

"Thanks, Vonn," he said sourly.

"Sorry, guys. She's got a right to know."

"Like hell she does," Li said.

Roz turned away from them and slipped her shirt on. When she turned back, she had a worried look. "You said the *Yueh-sheng* knows you're here?"

"Looks that way," Duke said.

"Then I've got the right to go with you."

Duke moaned.

"No," Li said.

She put her hands on her hips. "Why not?"

"It's dangerous," Vonn said. "We've lost half the people we started with."

"You think it's going to be fun and games here? What happens when the *Yueh-sheng* finds out that I shared a bed with you?"

"You can't come," Li said.

She walked over to him and glared in his face. "Look, mister, you can't write me off like that. Understand?"

"Nobody will know if you keep your mouth shut."

"You think it's that easy? You really think so? If the *Yueh-sheng* really is swarming to this place and knows all about you guys, all they'll have to do is ask questions, and scared people who don't like pain will tell them everything they want to know. You don't think for a moment that they'll kill me, do you? Of course not. And let me tell you something. I'm one of those people who doesn't like pain."

"You wouldn't dare."

"Ask him how I feel about pain," she said, pointing.

Vonn blushed.

"I'll tell them everything I know, *right down to anatomic details*. I'll even come with them to find you."

"We have room," Vonn offered. "She could stay with me."

"Okay," Li said. "Let's get out of here."

"Can we go by my place and pick up a few things?"

"No."

"Have a heart."

"You have a heart. We're taking you with us so you won't get your—your head shot off. That's our favor. Your favor is coming with us, *right now*."

She did not move.

"For heaven's sake, Vonn will buy you a new wardrobe."

"He will?"

"You bet he will. He's going to be a rich man when this is over."

"It didn't take long for them to find us," Vonn said.

"I knew it might happen eventually," Li said, "but frankly I'm amazed that it happened this fast. Very efficient of them."

"Well," Vonn said, "your body wasn't at the site of the hit, which may have made your involvement obvious. But you could have gone anywhere. How did they trace you here?"

"Resourceful, aren't they?" Li said, voice cracking.

"I'd give anything to know how they did it," Duke said.

"So would I," Li said.

He rubbed behind his ear.

12

James Theodore May was whistling a happy tune. He bounced through the bridge of the *Angel's Luck*, the I & S manual for the *Insh'allah* under his arm. He plopped down in the pilot's chair, worked the gears to tilt it back, and propped his feet up on a console. Then he turned on the manual and forwarded it to the section on Vasac installation.

He had finished the introduction when the bridge door hissed open and five people burst in, waving weapons and swarming through the cabin. The manual flew out of May's lap, and he rolled behind the chair, pulling the back around for cover.

"What are you doing here?" he barked at them. "You're supposed to be on shore leave."

Vonn buckled himself into the copilot's seat and looked over the console. "We're leaving."

"Like hell we are. I've got a buyer for the *Insh'allah*. He's going to pay in cash equivalents so there won't be any grief—"

"Sorry, May," Li told him. "You'll have to find a buyer elsewhere."

May looked around the bridge in disbelief. Everyone was

finding a seat and getting ready for departure, and there was a strange woman wandering the bridge.

"Who's the girl?" he snapped.

"Roz, this is James May," Vonn said. "May, Roz." He started energizing the magnetics.

"Will someone please tell me what's going on?"

"The *Yueh-sheng* has found us," Duke said. "They've killed Sullivan. Any one of us could be next if we stay around here. We've got to leave right now."

May threw his hands in the air. "Let me get in touch with my buyer. We were going to close the deal tomorrow, but if I tell him we're leaving—"

"You're not telling anyone," Li snapped.

"Then what's she doing here?" May demanded, pointing at Roz.

"She knows," Duke said.

"This is getting out of hand," May said. "If everyone would keep their mouths shut, this would be a sure thing."

"There's no such animal," Vonn said.

"What about Dawn?" May asked.

Li smirked. "She's our insurance policy against the *Ebit-suka*."

"The *Ebitsuka*? What do they have to do with this?"

"Dawn and Sullivan are both members," Duke explained. "They were going to set us up and take the phials, but Li set them up instead. As long as we hang on to her, the *Ebitsuka*'s going to be hesitant about moving on us."

"I wouldn't put money on that," May said. "Dawn's not here."

"Where is she?" Li asked.

"She got off the ship right after you left."

"Why didn't you stop her?" Li hissed.

"I didn't know I was supposed to."

"It's not your fault," Duke said. "She was under orders from Sullivan to stay on board."

"We've got to get her," Li said, color leaving his face.

"After what you put me through?" Vonn snapped. "You mean we've got to go back?"

"We'll never find her," Duke said. "Remember how hard it was to find Vonn?"

"We've got to."

"Good," Roz said. "Then I'm going to go pick up a few things."

"No. Don't you dare."

"Why not?" Vonn said. "It's only fair."

"They've got a point," Duke said. "Besides, you said yourself that her life was over. The *Ebitsuka* may not care if they burn her with us. It's not worth the risk."

"Forget her," Vonn said. "She's damned. We don't need her."

"All right," Li whispered.

Vonn put the headset on and opened the frequency. "*Garland Outpost* Port Authority, this is dock pod five-eight B, merchant vessel *Angel's Luck* three seven four nine one requesting departure clearance frequency two one."

"Absolute, *Angel's Luck*. Standby manifest."

There was a moment of silence.

"*Angel's Luck* three seven four nine one, *Garland Outpost* Port Authority, state manifest."

"Manifest eight zero nine eight zero," Vonn said. "Passenger transport."

"Absolute, *Angel's Luck*. Clearance in three zero."

They watched out the bridge window as the ship rotated toward the pod bay doors. It stopped, and the doors opened.

"Clearance time."

May nodded at Vonn. The ship rumbled. Duke's feet left the floor.

"Gravity down."

The *Angel's Luck* wobbled and stabilized, then slowly made its way out of the pod.

"We're clear," Vonn said.

"Activate magnetics," May said. "Get ready for the push."

A low hum came through the walls of the ship.

"Polarity matched with station hull," Vonn said.

Duke drifted toward the back of the cabin.

"Disembark speed. Ready engines."

Duke craned for a view of the monitor console. He squinted his eyes, thinking that perhaps he was absorbing something from Reckless Eric Dickson. But the console still looked foreign and confusing. He cursed and looked around the cabin. He was sure it was his imagination; the place was getting smaller all the time.

13

They came for him again.

He was in the coffin, the big coffin with the doors and the hallways and the access hatches and the tunnel with the way out of the dream. He knew there was a way, but this time he became hopelessly lost while looking for it. There were no voices to lead him gently home.

He remembered that the voices had come with his intent to open the latch. He made his way back to the little room and waited for it to heat up. It did not take long. He waited until the feeling became suffocating, unbearable. He put his hand on the latch, and he knew that they were out there, waiting. And when he opened the latch, they would force their way in. They would rip his flesh apart and feed on his bowels, then put a spike through his head and nail his carcass to the wall and let it hang. He knew. He had seen that done to the others.

So he waited as long as he dared. He kept his hand on the latch with the knowledge that when it got so far, the voices of Dawn and Sullivan would come to save him.

But Sullivan was dead, and Dawn was back on Garland Outpost. *Their voices would not come, not ever again.*

He gasped. The latch had caught, and the door had cracked open, letting in blasts of cold. There were choruses of glee from outside, and a cold, clammy hand with eight fingers reached in and grabbed him by the throat. Its skin burned his. The fingers around the neck choked, and others snaked around his head and threatened to crack his skull like an egg.

*"Warning Sign," they sang. "Warning Sign, Warning
Sign . . ."*
  Things began to grow dark.

14

"Duke! Duke!"
  Vonn shook him until he took a big gulp of air. It strained
in with a loud sucking sound and felt cool in his lungs. Each
breath that followed was that much easier.
  "Are you okay?"
  "Yeah," Duke croaked. "Thanks."
  "You scared me to death. I was passing down the hall and
heard you making strange noises, so I came in. Hope you
don't mind. You were turning blue, no kidding."
  "I must've been dreaming."
  "About what? The hit?"
  "I don't know what the hell it was."

15

He wandered down to the lower decks. He drank a paper
cup filled with coffee.
  He played chess with the CHARLES.
  He talked with Vonn about mercenaries. About weapons.
About past capers.
  About being afraid of the dark.
  He taught Roz how to run the communications board.
  He used the star maps to find a little pinprick of light that
might have been the star Tetros.
  He did not sleep unless he could not help it.

16

*The door slipped open. The hand slid in and embraced his
head and neck. The flesh burned, his head ached, the breathing stopped, the darkness came. There was no Vonn to bail
him out this time. He realized that and fought against the*

*dark. Making his way back to light, he heard the gleeful wails
and saw other hands joining the first, wrapping their fingers
around the door and pushing. He remembered what would
become of him. He had seen the others.*

*Fear coursed through him, and with it came adrenaline.
He cried out and shoved the door. It slammed shut, severing
fingers and hands. Thick yellow liquid seeped from the limbs
and burdened the air with a pungent smell, sharp like am-
monia. The hand around his throat tightened, then went limp.
He pulled it from his face, tossed it to the floor. The arm
twitched.*

*The coffin had grown cold, and with the cold his mind
cleared. At last he knew where he was. He looked over at
one wall of the room and saw the controls. He had them
now. He had the inspiration. He knew he could make them
go away. Not just get away from them but destroy them, blow
them all to hell and gone.*

*He laughed. For how long he was not sure. He shivered in
the cold. He ran to the wall and looked at the controls.*

He had no idea where to start.

*He searched, frustrated by the maze of lights and dials. It
was there, he knew. He had to find it. It was there.*

They were still outside, shouting and pounding on the hull.

*Fear and cold crept up behind him. He shivered, and his
teeth chattered. He reached out a finger to press a button and
balked. He began to shake uncontrollably.*

*Getting his bearings, he reached out for the panel again.
It dissolved.*

17

He was still shaking.

But he realized that it was not so much shaking as it was
being shaken.

He opened his eyes. A woman's face was hovering over
him.

"Mother," Duke said. "Mother." He sat straight up.

"It's Roz," she said.

He fell into her arms and hugged her. "I had them." He shook. "I had the bastards right where I wanted them, and I couldn't find it. I just couldn't find it." He trembled with rage.

Roz rocked him until he calmed down. She spoke soothing words.

"I'm never going to sleep again," Duke said.

"You'll get them next time."

Duke closed his eyes and filled his nostrils with her scent. He tensed up and pulled away from her.

"What am I doing here?"

"Nothing is wrong, Duke," Roz said firmly. "You're dreaming. We're in your cabin."

"What are you doing here?"

"I came to get you. May wants you in the bridge."

Duke swallowed. His throat was dry. "What for?"

"I think he'd rather be the one to tell you." There was a look of uncertainty in her eyes.

He took a deep breath. "Okay. Let's go."

When they got to the bridge, the others were all waiting, their faces long.

"Well," Duke said cheerfully. "The last supper."

"Quiet," May barked, checking the bridge clock.

"What's with the gloom around here? We snatch the wrong phials?"

"It has to do," Vonn said, "with having a pleasure-craft-rated Vasac in a merchant-sized vessel."

The radio crackled, and May repeated, "Quiet."

There was the snapping of static, and a voice cracked.

"Attention, crew of the merchant vessel *Angel's Luck*," the voice said gruffly. "This is Ryuichi Hiro, acting commander of the *Roko Marie*, battle dreadnought of the planet Cosen number three. I chose to speak to you directly because of the irresponsible attitude of your captain, James May, with whom I had a conversation ten minutes ago.

"Your vessel is well within range of our main armament and magnetics. It would be no problem for us to snuff you out without so much as a second thought. However, I have decided to offer you a choice. We will let you go free on the condition that you turn over to us the Essence Corporation phials, James May, and Myron Li. You have thirty minutes after this transmission to decide the course of your action and act accordingly. If we have not heard from you by then, you will be brought onto this vessel and tortured in the most brutal manner that my crew and I can devise. Any attempt to flee will result in the immediate vaporization of your craft.''

The speaker went dead. Duke felt the blood rushing from his head.

"We're caught," he said.

"Before you make any snap decisions," May said, "I want you to be aware of a few considerations. First, I have already tried to negotiate with Mr. Hiro. I made one mistake. I told him who I was.

"Second, as you heard, we are well within range of the *Roko Marie*'s magnetics. They could have as easily have captured us as not, but I think Hiro wants to twist the knife by getting my crew to betray me. If you decide to turn us in, I wouldn't blame any of you.''

"I'm sticking with you," Duke said. "I'm not selling you out.''

"We're unanimous on that," Vonn said.

"May offered the phials in return for safe passage out," Li said. "Hiro wouldn't have it. He wanted exactly what you heard him demand. Hence, we have reached this impasse.''

"How did they find us?" Duke asked.

"How they tracked us to this particular sector of space, I don't know," Vonn said. "But I can guess how they snuck up on us.''

"I know," Duke said. "Vasac works off of ship diameters, and we're using a pleasure-craft-sized unit in a merchant-class ship. Since yachts are roughly one-tenth the size of a merchant, we might as well have been looking out the windows as using the *Insh'allah*'s Vasac.''

"Something like that.''

"Other considerations," May continued. "Roz has been

monitoring low-end communications from the *Roko Marie*
and found out that there is an *Ebitsuka* destroyer in the area."

"What are they doing here?" Duke demanded.

"Good question," Li said. "My guess is that we made a
mistake leaving Dawn back at *Garland Outpost*. She probably led her people to our dock, and when they saw we weren't
around, they came after us."

"I'll bet they didn't count on the *Roko Marie* showing
up," Vonn said.

"Obviously not," Li said, scratching his ear. He stopped,
and his eyes narrowed. "Wait a minute. Maybe there's a way
we can get out of this."

"Play both ends against the middle," Roz said.

Li flexed his hands. "Exactly. We've got two starving dogs
looking for a handout. What happens when we toss out one
piece of meat?"

"A fight." Vonn chuckled.

"What do you have in mind?" May asked.

"A smoke screen that'll allow us to slip out the back door
while the two ogres fight between themselves. How well will
a pleasure craft do without Vasac?"

"Considerably better than a merchant ship without one."

"We could open the cargo bay doors and magnet it out
like we did with the van," Vonn said. "The flight computer
would kick in and take it from there."

"Excellent. All we have to do is bait it."

"With the phials?" Duke asked.

"That's what we tell them. We program the *Insh'allah*'s
computer to kick into full speed once it's free of us, on a
course that sends it right between the *Roko Marie* and the
Ebitsuka ship. Each will think that we're making a break for
the other."

"But that won't be fair," Winters said. "A little ship
against a great big one."

"He's right," May said. "That fight won't last more than
two minutes."

"Two minutes is all we'll need," Li said.

"Exactly," Vonn said. "The *Yueh-sheng* will have to drop

their magnetics in order to fire at the *Ebitsuka* ship. The destroyer may even get a couple of good shots off."

"And when they do," Li said, "we make a jump and are on the other side of the galaxy before they know what happened." He clapped his hands together. "Okay, we haven't much time. Roz, you go down to medical and transfer all of the phials into storage. We'll put the chest on the yacht in case there's a transmitter hidden in it. May, you and Vonn get things ready on the *Insh'allah*. Program the flight computer and set up to dump it. Winters, you go and carry the chest for Roz."

"What about me?" Duke asked.

Li put his arm around him. "My boy, you're going to help me come up with a big lie."

18

With minutes to spare, they reassembled in the bridge. Vonn was poised over the communications board, drumming his fingers on the console. "You think this is going to work?"

"It had better," Duke said. "It's our only chance."

"Call them," Li said.

Vonn tuned up the radio. "*Roko Marie*, this is merchant ship *Angel's Luck*, acknowledge." He licked his lips and looked at the others. "*Roko Marie*, this is merchant ship *Angel's Luck*, acknowledge."

"Course is locked in," May said. "Heading for Jubilo 3. Tell me when."

Roz looked up from her headset. "The *Ebitsuka* ship is monitoring. They know we're trying to reach the *Marie*, and they're trying to get a make on her."

The speaker crackled. "Merchant ship *Angel's Luck*, this is the *Roko Marie*. Have you reached your decision?"

Vonn silenced the others. "We have. James May and Myron Li have been sedated and secured in a pleasure craft in our cargo hold. Also inside are the phials you requested. It will take us approximately ten minutes to unload, after which we go our way and you go yours."

"Not quite," Hiro said. "There's one more detail. You will wait until we have recovered the pleasure craft and made certain that the goods promised have been delivered. Our satisfaction must be assured before you can leave."

"And if we try?"

"We'll burn you to ash."

"You're the boss," Vonn said. "But at least let us get out of the way. I don't want to get in a tug-of-war with your magnetics."

"You may move up to twenty ship diameters from your current position."

"Thank you," May whispered. "I knew they'd pull this. The minute they get the *Insh'allah*, they'll torch us, satisfied or not."

"So they think," Li said. "Let's dump it and run."

"*Roko Marie*, this is the *Angel's Luck*," Vonn continued. "We're opening the cargo bay doors. The *Insh'allah*'s hull polarity will be locked onto positive mode, and we'll be locking the same to push it out of the hold. When we reach fifteen ship diameters, we'll lock into neutral so you don't suck us in while retrieving the *Insh'allah*."

"Absolute, *Angel's Luck*. At fifteen ship diameters we'll lock in negative hull polarity."

"They bought it," May said. "Duke, the minute you get their negative hull polarity reading, tell me, and I'll lock ours in the same. They're going to give us one hell of a push."

"I'm showing the cargo doors open," Duke answered.

"Thank you," May answered. He activated the magnetic charger in the cargo bay. "Polarizing now."

"*Roko Marie, Angel's Luck*. We're polarizing the cargo bay. The *Insh'allah* should be heading your way in a moment."

"Absolute," the *Marie* crackled.

Duke stared at the video monitor, watching the pleasure craft rise from the deck floor. "Clearance."

"Locking," May said. "Here's the push."

While Duke watched, the *Insh'allah* glided out of the cargo bay as the doors started to close. "Clear," he said.

"The event clock should be running," May said. "The engines should kick in in thirty seconds. Duke, watch the polarity on the *Marie*. I'll take us away from here."

"Here she comes, *Marie*," Vonn said.

"I'm seeing action on the grid," Duke said.

"Bastards." May smiled. "I knew they'd do this. Talk to him, Vonn."

"*Marie*, I'm reading a grid charge on your hull. Stand by until we have range."

There was no answer.

"Bastards," May repeated.

Li put on a headset and keyed in to the *Yueh-sheng* frequency. "Action on the *Insh'allah*," he said. "It's starting to move."

"Go," Duke whispered.

"Nothing from the *Ebitsuka*," Roz said.

May bent over the console and worked it frantically. "Polarizing hull. Talk to me, Duke."

"As we expected. Negative charge."

May slapped a switch. "Run!" he cried.

Li pressed the receiver deeper into his ear. "Incoming!" he shouted.

A ball of light traced a path to the front of the *Angel's Luck* and burst.

"They've neutralized their grid!" Duke cried.

"Doing the same," May shouted.

"That was a warning shot," Li said. "We're about to get a message."

Hiro's voice flared from the speaker. "You'd better tell me what's going on before I burn you!"

"It's Duke," Vonn shouted into the headset. "He's gotten onto the *Insh'allah* and has taken control. He's making a break for it."

"And what about the rest?"

"The rest?" Vonn cried. "What rest?"

"I'm showing that the chest is on the pleasure ship, but that Li is not."

"What?" He put his hand over the microphone and looked at Duke. "What do I tell him?"

"Fake it," Duke hissed.

"I don't know what's going on," Vonn stammered, "unless it's Duke. We'll have a search party cover the ship."

"You do that," Hiro shouted. "And if you move one meter before we get that boat pulled in, you're old news."

"Trust me," Vonn said. He looked at May.

"Wait until they return fire from the destroyer," May told him. "Their magnetics will be shut down, and we'll be able to slip right through."

Static gushed from the speaker.

"The *Ebitsuka* ship has a fix on the *Insh'allah*," Roz said. "They're turning for intercept and have fired on the *Marie*." She listened for a moment and blushed. "Such language. They've figured out how big the *Marie* is and are trying to cut and run." A burst of static filled the bridge. "Now they're hitting the *Marie* with all they've got. They're trying to buy time enough to jump."

"The *Marie*'s taking it hard," Li said. "They weren't ready for incoming fire. They've closed magnetics and are aiming."

Static made everything else in the room inaudible. Duke reached over and cut the volume.

Li cheered. "They missed!"

"Jump!" May shouted. He and Vonn engaged the drive, and the *Angel's Luck* convulsed wildly. The others on the bridge scrambled for seats and belted in.

Looking out the window, Duke watched as the stars began to move. There was a rumble that made his teeth hurt, and the stars vanished.

"Jubilo 3," May announced, "is seventeen hours away."

Everyone applauded. May pivoted in his seat and waved triumphantly. As he did, the trouble beacon sounded and made him look at the protection board.

"Oh, no!" He jumped in his seat. "Take it out of short space," he shouted at Vonn. "The Vasac—"

There was a loud report from the Vasac, and sparks hissed

out of a newly formed hole in its face. Extinguisher jets pumped cold smoke, and they all came out of their seats. Vonn grabbed the control yoke and fought to steer the craft. May went for the interrupter switch, but another report from the console knocked him across the room. Duke jumped into May's chair, hit the interrupter, and shut down the gyros and the artificial gravity. There was a grinding that rattled the ship down to its rivets, and the stars reappeared in the front window.

"What was that?" Li asked.

"Vasac overload," Vonn answered. "It couldn't handle the logistics of keeping a craft this size in short space."

"Which means?"

May pushed himself up from the floor and drifted to the command center. "It means," he said, "that Jubilo 3 is now seven weeks away."

19

The door to Duke's cabin was open, and the lights were on. Curious, Vonn wandered down the corridor and found Duke perched on his bed, absorbed in the *Angel's Luck* I & S manual.

"Doing your homework?" he asked.

Duke looked up, startled. "Me? Oh, I'm just checking a few things."

"How long have you been studying?"

Duke turned off the manual. "Only for the last couple of hours. I thought I'd do something constructive to keep myself entertained."

"That was a nice move you pulled in the bridge this morning. Saved everyone a lot of trouble."

"Someone had to do it. May was on the other side of the bridge, you were tied up, and I was the only other person who knew something about the ship."

"Where'd you learn the trick?"

"What trick?"

"Pulling gyros and grav during an interruption."

"Isn't it common sense?"

"Only in short space. In real space you can interrupt and continue while effecting repairs. But the gyros and gravity system are especially vulnerable in short space. You knew exactly what to do to get them down, and it's not something you learn out of an I & S manual. Where'd you pick it up?"

Duke looked down at the floor.

"Listen, Duke, if you don't want to tell me, fine. As long as you don't lie to me about it. That's the one thing that would upset me. I came by to say that I thought that was a really pro trick for a beginner to think of, and I'm proud of you. Enough said." He turned to leave.

"Vonn, I've got to level with you. I owe you an apology."

"For what?"

"I've done a lot of growing up over the past few weeks. That's nothing to be afraid of, I suppose, but you get into a situation like this and then look back at how you've been acting, and you want to kick yourself."

Vonn wandered back in and took a chair. "I don't think you've acted rashly. You've got to expect it from someone who's . . . well . . ."

"Green?"

"Pardon the expression, but I think it applies."

"I still owe you an apology, though." Duke got up and paced. "When you turned out to be a pilot, I thought it was great. I wasn't much help to May, and you took a lot off of his mind. Later, when I saw how good things were, I felt cut out of the picture. I became hateful. I was always a coward at heart, so I was nice to you, but I avoided you and May as often as I could. That's why I agreed to stay on Aiaaga with Li.

"I thought of all sorts of nasty things that I was too scared to pull. I wanted to show you up in some way but couldn't think of how. So when we got the Essence phials and I found Eric Dickson, it all came together. I had to check with somebody to make sure who he was, but I had a pretty good idea to begin with."

"You've *got* Reckless Eric Dickson?"

"Sort of. I lied about the phial being broken and took it with me. I wanted to take it as soon as I could, but the idea of mixing someone else's chemicals with mine was kind of scary, even with the sugar coating. I'd talked myself out of it, but when I got caught by Transgalactic Affairs, I told them the phial was my medication."

"You weren't injected with drugs at all."

Duke shook his head.

Vonn stared. "Have you picked up anything else?"

"Nope. I thought it had been wasted. Its been weeks since they shot it into me, and nothing has happened. That trick today was the first I've seen of it, and even then I didn't realize what had happened until after I'd thought about it for a while. So I pulled the I & S manual from the library to see if anything else came to me. Nothing has." He looked at Vonn forlornly. "To tell you the truth, I don't think the Essence people have a very good product."

Vonn clapped Duke on the back. "It helped us out of a jam, and that's good enough for me. As far as your apology, I'll accept it only if you'll accept mine for being such a pompous ass when we first met."

"That's not necessary."

"I think it is. Absolutely." They shook hands. "By the way, don't worry about your secret," Vonn said. "My lips are sealed."

20

There was thunder, and Duke thought he was back on Tetros, home in time for the rainy season. He smiled and sniffed the air for the sweet scent of rain in the fields, but it was different from how he remembered it. The scent he caught was thick and heavy. It was sharp with heat and plastics. He shook his head in dismay and watched the boiling clouds.

There was another thunderclap. It jarred him and tossed him to the ground. The grass was smooth, cold tile. He shook his head again and coughed from the smell of the rain.

When he looked up, he was on the floor of his cabin. Smoke was stinging his eyes. Coughing, he stood and hit the light switch. The bulb started to glow but flickered out in the haze. He tried to open the door. Nothing happened. He found a small panel and cranked it open.

Panic was crawling up his spine. He was back in the dream, a part he had never seen before. It was all there—the heat, the choking, the smell. All he had to do was keep his head. He threw his closet door open and jerked out the search beam, its light making a gray finger in the smoke.

Thunder roared, and he stumbled into the hall. He braced himself until it was over and then started for the bridge. Then there was a voice shouting from behind. He turned and pointed the light. It was Roz.

"What's going on?" she cried.

"What are you doing here?"

"Trying to find out what's happening. Are you all right?"

Duke blinked against the smoke. "I'm awake."

"What's wrong, Duke?"

He shivered. "This is like the dreams."

The *Angel's Luck* shuddered.

"Let's get to the bridge." He aimed the light down the hall.

Another few meters and they found Winters sitting against the wall. Handing the light to Roz, Duke grabbed him and laid him on his back. The big man opened his eyes and whimpered.

"You're alive," Duke said. "Are you hurt?"

"I'm scared," Winters said. "All the noises. The lights and doors don't work. And it smells funny."

Roz offered her hand to the frightened man. "Come with us."

They continued to the bridge. Duke cranked the door, and light poured from inside. Vonn and May were in position, and Li was at a far console, headset microphone in his hand.

"What are you doing," Duke asked.

"Negotiating," Li said.

Out the front window, a ball of light passed the ship and burst. The lights flickered, and the radio crackled.

"Once again the *Roko Marie* is right on our tail," May said. "They're trying to take us out the hard way."

Duke felt the blood drain from his face.

"They can't seem to catch us," Vonn said. "They should be able to overtake us, or fry us with one shot. Their ship must have taken a lot of damage from the *Ebitsuka* destroyer." There was another burst of light from outside, followed by thunder in the ship. "They're trying to break us down with proximity hits, but most of them have been way off. Their targeting computer must be out."

Duke turned to Li. "What have you offered them?"

"Myself and the phials for safe passage. Hiro wouldn't even talk to me."

"And you're going to give it up just like that? You bastard!"

"Duke, you don't understand. It's not like we still have a choice. There aren't any more ways out of this."

"All right, then." Duke looked around the bridge. "Let's blow ourselves up."

Nobody moved.

"We can't let them get the phials, can we? All we've fought for isn't going to be worth a damn if they march in here and take them back. We're heroes now. Didn't any of you hear the gossip back on *Garland*? We're going to let everybody in the galaxy down if the stuff gets taken back."

"We could load it into the escape boat and shoot it off for Jubilo," Li said. "They'd take us, and the phials would get through fine."

"Wrong. They'd laugh and pick them right up. And they'd torture us just for the hell of it."

"But they'd be there for the next rescue operation. I'd rather see them safe."

"No, Li," Duke said. "There will be no next time. If the *Yueh-sheng* gets the phials back, they're going to have them for good. They've got to be destroyed, and we've got to go with them."

Vonn looked into Roz's eyes. "I'm sorry I got you into all of this," he said, "but I think Duke's right."

Roz blinked, holding back tears. "That's okay, soldier boy."

Winters licked his lips. "You aren't going to do it, are you? You aren't going to blow us up, are you?"

"It won't hurt," Duke said. "You won't even know what happened. It'll be like going to sleep, only you won't have any bad dreams, not ever."

A guttural cry broke from Winters's throat. Duke moved to comfort him. Winters grabbed Duke by the lapels and tossed him to the floor, then bolted out the door. Duke jumped to his feet and started to follow.

"Leave him," Li said.

"I don't want him scared," Duke said. "I owe him." He started down the hall.

Winters was easy enough to follow. The clunking of his large feet and his sobbing led Duke to the same air lock that he had once, in his ignorance, tried to step out of. The inner hatch was wide open, and Winters was inside, hysterically tugging at the outer hatch. When he saw Duke, he stopped and whimpered.

"It's okay," Duke said. "You're not going to get hurt."

"You want to kill me," Winters sobbed.

Duke watched him pull the latch and shivered. There was no way the door could be opened without the proper sequence being followed. In his blind panic, Winters had not realized that.

Sweat stung Duke's eyes. The heat in the ship was becoming unbearable. May and Vonn had probably cut life support to a minimum in order to keep moving. The *Angel's Luck* rumbled.

"If you go out there," Duke said, "you'll die."

"I'll die here, too. I'll die the way I want to. I don't like your way."

"If you go out there, they'll get you," Duke said.

They'll get you.

"They're waiting on the other side of the door. They're waiting to get you."

They are waiting on the other side of the door.

"And when they catch you, you'll wish you were dead."

"How do you know?" Winters's jaw trembled.

"I know. I saw what happened to the others."

"Was it bad, Mr. Duke?"

"It was horrible," Duke said. *They had been disemboweled and nailed to the walls of the ship with large metal spikes.* "And they'll do things to you after you're dead to warn others."

Winters gave one final tug on the latch and then fell into Duke's arms, sobbing.

"Don't let them get me, Mr. Duke. Don't let them get me."

"I won't. I promise."

"But don't kill me. Please don't kill me. I don't want to die like Bear and Anders did. Please, Duke."

"I won't kill you," Duke lied.

"Promise. You have to promise."

"I promise."

That consoled Winters. Duke wiped the tears from the big man's face. "Good. Now we have to go back to the bridge and fight them."

"Yeah." Winters moved out of the air lock. Duke looked back and noticed that the latch had been taken out of the safety position. He put his hand on the latch and locked it back into place.

Hand on the latch.

He stared at it in disbelief. He sniffed the heated air.

Heat.

"Come on, Duke," Winters called.

There is a way.

"I can do it," Duke said.

"I know you can," Winters said confidently.

Suddenly it was there. Duke knew he could make them go away. Not just get away from them but destroy them, blow them all to hell and gone.

It felt very cold in the ship. Duke shivered. He looked at Winters, who was waving him on.

He ran to the bridge and planted himself between May and Vonn at the console, studying the maze of lights and knobs. They were beginning to make sense.

"I can do it," he said.

"So could Winters," May said weakly. "All you have to do is push enough buttons and you'll eventually blow us up. Doing it efficiently is the problem."

"I can get us out of here," Duke said. "Alive and well and with the phials and without the *Roko Marie* or Hiro behind us ever again."

May stared at him. His face was white. "That's not funny."

Duke leaned over the console. It looked sweetly familiar. His hand moved hesitantly over a knob and then turned it. Cool air filled the bridge.

May grabbed his hand and pulled it away. "I said you're not funny. I wouldn't worry about comfort. We'll be dead soon enough, anyway."

"That's just it!" Duke cried. "We don't have to die!"

"We're not surrendering. We voted. It was unanimous."

Duke threw another switch. The *Angel's Luck*'s exterior lights began to shimmer. A ball of light exploded nearby.

May grabbed Duke and shoved him away. "Of course. You turn on all of the lights and let the *Yueh-sheng* do it for us." He rose from his chair. "It's my ship. I've died slowly for twelve years to get this thing paid off. I'll blow it up my way."

Duke turned to Vonn in desperation. "Eric Dickson."

Vonn looked blank for a moment. Another ball of light detonated nearby, and the ship rattled mercilessly.

"Let him go, May," Vonn said. "He knows what he's doing."

May's face fell in disbelief. "No."

Fire erupted on Li's panel. He bounced away, yelping. There was another thunderclap.

"Winters!" Vonn shouted. "Get May away from Duke!"

Winters moved. May threw Duke into him. He sat back in his seat and began to arm the destruct. Vonn grabbed him under the arms and yanked him away.

"He can do it, May! Let the kid do it!"

Winters slid in next to Vonn and threw May over his shoulder.

"You big, dumb son of a *bitch*!" May swore.

"Put him in a corner and sit on him," Vonn ordered, sliding back into his seat. "You're the boss, Duke. What do we do?"

Duke carefully buckled himself in and rubbed his eyes. "Turn everything on."

"No!" May shouted.

"Environmental, exterior supports, the freezer in the cargo bay, turn on everything."

"You'll strain the power plant!" May screamed. "Let me do it!"

"You want to blow the ship up," Li said, slipping to the floor as the ship shuddered. "They have something else in mind."

"What next?" Vonn asked.

Duke stared blankly at the controls. The air was beginning to cool off. It was easier to think. "Is everything on?"

"Every unnecessary gadget on the ship," Vonn said. He watched the sweat roll from Duke's face. "Don't push it. Let it come."

Duke wiped his forehead with the back of his hand. "Put all of the transmitters and receivers on the EMP protection circuit. It'll be rough on them."

Vonn leaned to his right. "Done."

Duke held his head in his hands and shivered. There was a flood of light from the window.

"Relax," Vonn said.

From the back of the bridge, Li watched. His lips slowly parted into a grin. He looked at May.

"Short space," Duke said. "We've got to jump."

May kicked Winters from his chest and leapt to his feet.

He bolted across the bridge, grabbed Duke by the neck, and pulled.

"You can't!" he screamed. "With no Vasac it'll kill us all!"

Winters and Li pulled May away. A wave passed through the ship, and the three of them fell.

"What acceleration level?" Vonn asked.

"It doesn't matter. Anything over plus one. What's the max?" He laughed. "I read it in the I & S, but I don't seem to remember."

"Plus five."

"That's fine. We don't have to be there for very long." He began to make preparations. "I still don't know why I'm doing this."

"We'll find out soon enough."

Duke's teeth hurt, and the stars vanished.

21

The small red dot on the holoscreen blinked out. Hiro rubbed his eyes and looked at the board.

"They're gone!" he shouted. "They've gotten away!"

"Calm down," the uniformed man said. The screen flickered, and the red dot returned. "They've jumped into short space."

"Colonel, we can't use the weapons in short space," Hiro hissed.

"But our short space navigational system has sustained minimal damage. We can outmaneuver them. They've played right into our hands."

A chuckle rose from deep in Hiro's belly. "Excellent. Make the jump."

22

The noise was loud. Roz pulled the headphone from her ear. "They've followed us!" she cried.

Duke blinked.

"What now?" Vonn asked.

"They're gaining," Roz said. "They estimate capture range in forty-five seconds."

Duke knuckled his eyes and looked at the console. "It's there. It won't come."

"Range in thirty seconds," Roz said.

"Relax," Vonn urged. "Give it a chance."

Duke looked at the board. Everything looked foreign to him. He pulled his hair. *Where are you, Eric?*

"I don't mean to keep bringing this up," Roz said, "but you have fifteen seconds until—"

"Shut it down!" Duke shouted. "All of it! Engines, coolant, life support, everything!"

"No!" May screamed. He bolted for the panel and was shoved to the floor. "You'll overload the engines! You'll ruin them!"

"We'll buy you some new ones," Li said.

Vonn looked at Duke. "It may come to that, you know."

"Dead stop," Duke said.

Vonn gritted his teeth.

There were sparks.

23

"Where are they?" Hiro screamed. "Where did they go?"

The colonel said nothing. The pit of his stomach fell. This isn't possible, he thought.

"What's going on?" Hiro screeched.

"I've seen this done," the colonel said. "On Arcolia."

"Dammit, man, you haven't answered my question. Where are they?"

"They've returned to real space." His mouth went dry.

Hiro slammed his fist on the holoscreen. "Well, shut down," he said slowly. "Have a volley of shots ready. I want them."

His hand shaking, the colonel opened the mike to give the order. He had to clear his throat twice before it would come out.

"Back up to jump threshold!"

Duke had to shout before Vonn heard him. The overload alarm had filled the bridge with its insistent ringing.

"Everything back on! Set up for another jump!"

May screamed hysterically, pinned to the floor by Winters and Li. Roz shut down the receiver and huddled with them.

"You can't screw with hydrogen fusion!" May shouted. "You said you weren't going to kill us. Oh, you bastard, Duke!"

Duke kept his eyes pinned to a liquid crystal display of the engine overload. The thick black line crawled into the red.

"What's next?" Vonn shouted. "The engines won't stand for much more."

Duke stared at the display.

"They're about to blow! Duke!"

Duke looked at Vonn, tears running down his face. "I'm sorry, Vonn. It's gone. I can't remember any more."

"Try, dammit! There has to be something!"

"I can't!" Duke wailed above the din. He beat his head with his fists. "It's not coming anymore! It's not there!"

"Duke, you've got to! The engines—" Vonn looked at the board. There were red flickering lights at every junction. The engines were creating a demand on the power supply that it could not fill. With the coming jump, it was going to get unruly very quickly.

And then it struck him. He bolted from his chair and ran to a corner of the bridge. "I've got it, Duke!"

Vonn opened a metal door and looked at an array of slots. He grabbed a mechanical key and began to twist it into each slot in sequence. A metal wall parted to reveal a handle with a trigger set into it. He jerked a cotter pin out of the base of the handle and pulled it away from the wall.

May saw what was happening. He sobbed hysterically.

"We'll buy you some new ones," Vonn shouted.

The handle would pull back no farther. It clicked into place. Yellow words flashed. JETTISON READY.

He turned the handle 180 degrees, and it locked again. The yellow words were replaced by red.

JETTISON ARMED.

He licked his lips. Shaking, he took hold of the cotter pin that locked the trigger into the handle. On the third yank it popped free.

BACKFIRE ARMED.

He slowly wrapped his hand around the handle and put his thumb on the trigger. He looked back at Duke, who was bent over the engine overload display helplessly watching it climb. He turned his head toward Vonn.

"Last chance, Duke!"

Duke's eyes flickered with recognition. "Yes! That's it! That's it!" He looked back at the display. "Now, Vonn! Do it now!"

Vonn bit his lip. His thumb pushed on the trigger until it clicked. The ship shuddered.

ENGINES JETTISONED.

25

The red dot split in two. One continued to move ahead at its normal rate. The other moved slowly toward the light that was the *Roko Marie*.

"What does that mean?" Hiro asked. "Is that an escape boat, or what?" He looked angrily at the colonel.

But the colonel was gray-faced. His lips parted, and in a thin voice he began to sing a song that was centuries old.

It was a death chant.

26

The alarm went dead. Duke leaned over the board and powered down. Except for his clicking, the bridge was strangely quiet.

Vonn dangled the cotter pin from his finger and looked around.

Roz cleared her throat. "Is that it?" she asked. "Nothing happened."

Duke swiveled in his chair to face them.

"Hang on."

The *Angel's Luck* boomed and rattled. There were reports from all over the bridge. The extinguishers filled the cabin with fog. The walls rattled, and the main hatch burst from its housing and clanged to the floor. The gravity monitor exploded, and weightlessness overcame them.

Li began to scream and swim through the air. He clawed behind his right ear, shredding his skin with his fingernails. Vonn sailed over and caught him. As he did, Li's skull exploded, spraying blood, brain, and bone across the cabin.

All at once there was a rush of air and a deafening electrical hum. Saint Elmo's fire bled into the bridge from the equipment, leaping from console to chair to Duke to Roz to Vonn to May to wall to ceiling to floor. Dry static was in the air, and their hair came to life, moving with a will of its own.

Winters panicked at the electricity that was flowing in and out of him. He kicked from the wall and flew out into the hallway. He screamed. The fire was leaping and circling the walls in reds and blues and golds, flowing like a whirlpool down the corridor.

The buzzing grew louder, and they tingled with a sharp prickly sensation that covered their bodies. The air grew thick. Breathing was slow and labored. The scent of ozone filled their nostrils, stung their eyes, and choked them.

May's head was throbbing. He pushed his hands against his head to keep his brain intact. Roz choked and went limp. Winters threw up. Vonn was sucked against a wall and held there, growing numb. Duke cupped his hands to his nose, trying to stop the sudden flow of blood.

The point came when the air was too liquid to breathe, and so they stopped.

27

May's head had a familiar throb to it. He pushed in on his temples to ease the pain. He was back on Tetros, in the Nurturing Care Hospital of Callenda. This was the big hangover. Dexter was sleeping his off in the next bed. May groaned. He would have to tell Dex just where he could stick that silly smuggling idea of his.

When he finally realized that he was on the bridge of the *Angel's Luck*, he became dizzy. The air had a sharp scent, and clouds of smoke drifted by. The cabin was filled with drifting bodies and droplets of blood.

Seized with fear, May scrambled from person to person, checking for pulses. With the exception of Li, all were alive and appeared to be in good shape. He floated back to the status board. The engines were gone; the movement the ship now had was momentum. The artificial gravity was burned out, with only emergency systems left for medical areas. Life support had been cut back to a minimum. All power lines to the cargo bay were ruptured. The three emergency standbys were dead, as was the CHARLES. All doors were frozen and would have to be cranked by hand. Power was cut everywhere but the bridge, the medical section, and food processing. The ship had been left powered down except for minimal supports to essentials. The work of a professional. May looked at Duke and shook his head.

He strapped himself into his chair to take readings, but it was too depressing. A lot of the indicators had burned up. He sat for a long time, staring out into space, his mind a blank.

Then something caught his eye. Something outside, something drifting past the window. His stomach sank as he thought for a moment that it might be a cow.

It was not. It was a twisted piece of metal, one end sheared and the other end a melted stub. It was followed minutes later by a charred coolant tank, the letters OKO ARI still visible on the side.

For the better part of an hour he watched. There were

pieces as small as rivets and others as big as sections of bulkheads. He saw a ladder, a medicouch, a computer desk, and several vacuum-damaged bodies.

It took a while to sink in, and when it did, he cried.

They were safe.

And Duke had done it.

28

A day or two later, when everyone had recovered and cleaned up, they assembled at one of the disposal bays. They gathered around the reinforced glass and looked through at a large, tarpaulin-wrapped package.

"Does anybody want to say anything?" May asked.

There was a moment of silence.

"No," Winters said.

"What the hell for?" Vonn said.

"I'd like to know what happened to him," Duke said. "Everyone else came out of it. His head didn't just spontaneously blow, did it?"

"It was probably the same way they tracked us here," Roz said. "The same way they knew he wasn't on the *Insh-'allah*."

"How's that?"

She sighed. "I've heard that people with Transgalactic Affairs have little transmitters surgically implanted before they go into the field so they can be tracked—or located if they 'disappear.' If they were sitting on that technology, I'm sure the *Yueh-sheng* could have gotten their hands on it."

"It would explain why he thought the heat would all fall on him," May said. "Do you think he knew?"

"I doubt it," Vonn said. "Why should they tell him?"

"He was always scratching at one ear," Duke said. "Like it bothered him. He couldn't have known, then. If he had, he never would have put us through all of this."

"None of us expected to go through all of this," May said.

"At least it's over," Roz said.

"But how did they kill him?" Duke asked.

"Maybe they didn't," May suggested. "Maybe it was an electromagnetic pulse from when the engines blew."

"That wouldn't have taken the top of his head off," Vonn said. "Fried the transmitter, yes, but that would have been it."

"If the technology exists for transmitters," Roz said, "why not put in a receiver as well?"

"The *Yueh-sheng* set it off?" Duke asked. "With what?"

"Danteum Gel," Vonn suggested.

"How much would it take to do that kind of damage?"

"A lot less than you'd think."

"We'll never really know, will we?"

Roz looked at the others. "And I hope we never find out." They stood in silence, staring at the parcel.

"Is that it?" May asked.

There was no answer.

"Duke," he said.

Duke squeezed the grip on a lever and pulled it back. A gate on the exterior collapsed, and the body of Myron Li shot out of the disposal bay. Duke muscled the lever back into place, and the gate closed.

"That's it, then," May said.

The group dispersed and started down the hallway.

"Tell me, Captain," Roz said. "How much longer until we come to the Jubilo system?"

"Five and a half weeks," May replied. "Give or take."

"It'll be close," Vonn said.

"But comfortable, I think. We can run most of the essential systems using the *Reconnez Cherie*'s power plant."

"Time to make plans," Roz said, squeezing Vonn's hand. They turned the corner and disappeared.

"If you'll excuse me," Winters said, "I gotta go get busy, too." He turned and went toward the front of the ship.

"Where's he going?" Duke asked.

"I've got him dry-scrubbing the bridge."

"May . . ."

"I'm paying him."

"Not that. Aren't you afraid he's going to hurt something?"

May laughed. "What's left to hurt, Duke?"

"I guess you're right."

"And how do you plan on passing the time, my good man?"

Duke shrugged. "I thought I'd study the I & S manual and see if I get anything out of it."

"Oh, no, you're not. You're going to come down to food processing with me. I'm going to buy you a drink."

"What for?"

May punched Duke in his good shoulder. They drifted away from each other. "I have something I want to tell you."

About the Author

Once upon a time there was a young advertising major named Joe Clifford Faust. While sitting in class one day, he decided that writing novels would be infinitely more fun than writing toilet paper commercials. Rather foolishly, he left college and started to write.

Along the way he got married, started a family, and was confronted with handfuls of bills that arrived on a monthly basis. He paid them by working as a disc jockey, a newsletter editor, a salesman of wire and cable, and a film critic. He also worked as a sheriff's dispatcher and was certified to teach law enforcement officers in the state of Wyoming.

Mr. Faust currently makes a precarious living by writing the novels he dropped out of college to write. Against the advice of his lawyer, he now resides in the state of Ohio.